MURDER BY FALSE PROMISE

MURDER BY FALSE PROMISE

By

J. M. Dixen

ISBN 978-1-300-00284-0

Acknowledgement

This book is dedicated to Riley, to my brother-in-law Gary, and to Mark, whose words remain with me, "Never take the easy way out."

Thank you to my family and friends for their unwavering support and encouragement, and a special thank you to Tasha and Stephan, the two readers of the first draft of this book, for their valuable critiques.

CHAPTER ONE

The line of sweat made its way through the mutton chop sideburns, splitting into small tributaries around the remnants of adolescent acne until it fell drop by drop on Billy Sanders' gun hand. His nodding head jerked upward as he startled fully awake, forcing his eyes to focus through the splintered glass that remained in the front window after the last warning shot from his 12 gauge.

"Daddy?"

"Quiet, Sara." Billy tightened his grasp on his three year old, adjusting the barrel of the gun as she sat on his lap. In his peripheral vision he saw his wife Karen, holding their six month old son, take a small careful step toward him.

"Billy, honey, you haven't hurt anyone yet, let the police help you."

"Great idea. You mean like those TWF Healthcare whores helped me by doping me up and brainwashing me?"

"You're a good person. You're a good father. We need you."

"Did they tell you to say that?"

"They, who, honey?"

"You know. Dr. Anderson, Dr. Matthews, managed care money grubbing whores all of them, and Dr. Burke the head pimp. Yeah, that's a good one." He giggled, then shook his head.

Karen watched as his face went slack and his eyes emptied in a way that she had seen more and more often in the past few months. "Isn't there someone you trust? That Lieutenant said he could get a therapist for you to talk to. What about that psychologist you liked? Remember? You said she helped you. Something with a P. Dr. Paulsen?"

"Pearson" Billy's face softened. "Mikelena Pearson. I haven't seen her for over a year."

"But you saw her for months. She could help you." Karen's face looked hopeful as she forced herself to appear confident in a way that she no longer felt. It was unlikely Dr. Pearson or anyone else could make a difference now, but something was better than nothing, or they all could be dead.

The kitchen phone rang. The only phone that Billy had not yet ripped out of the wall.

"It's them again, Billy. Won't you talk to the Lieutenant?"

"Pick it up."

"What?"

"You heard me. Pick it up. I'll tell you what to say."

"Hello."

"This is Lieutenant Mills. Is this Karen?"

"Yes."

"Can you put your husband on the phone?"

"He won't talk to you."

"Don't answer their questions, Karen. Tell the Lieutenant to get Dr. Pearson down here. I will talk to her and only her."

"Lieutenant, he says to get Dr. Pearson here and he will talk to her."

"Who is Dr. Pearson?"

"She's a TWF Healthcare psychologist he saw a year or two ago."

"Tell your husband -"

"Don't answer any of their questions, Karen."

"But Billy-"

"They will try to get inside your head. Tell them to get the doctor down here. I'll give them two hours. That means by, he glanced at the clock on the wall next to him, four o'clock."

"Billy says to get the doctor here by four o'clock."

"Karen, can you-"

"Hang up!" Billy shrieked, awakening the baby who immediately started squalling at the top of his lungs.

Karen quickly replaced the receiver and began rocking her son, knowing the consequences of not obeying Billy when he used that tone, aware that her jaw was finally healing from his raging last week. She looked at her husband, the once gentle man who had never even yelled at her before the past nine months. Maybe having a second child was too much for him. Billy Junior was always crying, not at all like their good girl Sara. Or maybe they were both too weak to hold up under all the pressure. She exhaled quietly and began to sing softly to soothe the baby. Billy turned toward her for the first time with a slight smile, "Now we see what happens."

CHAPTER TWO

I grabbed the phone on its third ring.

"Dr. Pearson." The clear bass voice at the end of the phone receiver announced my name.

"Yes?" I reached for the clock on the little table next to my bed, and turned its face towards me. 2:15 am. I wasn't on call for the hospital. Which meant this could not be good.

"This is Lieutenant Mills of the San Cortez police force SWAT team services. Are you Mikelena Pearson who works for TWF Healthcare?"

"Yes. What's going on?"

"We have a situation in San Cortez in which one of your patients, Billy Sanders, is holding his family hostage. He has an arsenal of guns and has shot into the floor and out the window. He has said he will only speak to you, and only if you come out here. Dr. Burke, the on call psychiatrist from the San Cortez TWF medical center, is on site standing by and he gave us your phone number. Sanders wouldn't talk to him. How soon can you be ready?"

"You said Billy Sanders?"

"Yes."

I remembered him. Out of the hundreds of new patients I saw each year in the TWF clinic. He was a young guy, not educated but smart, with a vulnerability that was right under the surface of his tough guy veneer. Treatment started out a little rocky, but he was motivated. We connected and he made progress.

"Why does he want to talk to me? He's not my patient. I haven't even seen him in over a year. He's supposed to be in treatment in the Chemical Dependency program."

"You're right. That's what Sanders and Dr. Burke told us. However, Sanders is saying he will only talk to you. And he's given us a window of time until 4am so I need your cooperation."

"What do you want me to do? And do you have any other information about why he is doing this? I'm not certain what I can do but…" I stopped myself, not clear on what I was thinking, what I wanted to know, or what to say. "What's the address?"

"One of the officers will pick you up. He should be there within the next 5 to 10 minutes. And the only information we have is that there was a domestic violence incident with gunshots. We know that the wife and two children are in there with him. The neighbors are the ones who called 911. They also said Sanders may be on drugs, but they weren't sure."

"I don't know why he would ask for me but I'll do what I can. This is my cell phone number, just in case."

"Fine. Our hostage negotiator will continue to try to connect with him until you arrive, although he has not been successful at getting him to talk. We will let Sanders know you are on your way."

I moved into crisis management mode. Trying not to panic as I rinsed my face, pulled back my hair, dressed as quickly as I could. I waited on the outside steps. The officer madegood time. I got into his squad car, and he used siren and lights to clear the little traffic there was at this time of night. Billy's part of town was used to the sounds of sirens and gun shots. There were only a few people outside their houses watching. Two local news vans were present. We parked behind the police cars. The officer handed me a Kevlar vest. "Precaution only," he said, "we won't let you close to the house."

We walked over to where the detectives, the hostage negotiator, and Dr. Burke, the Chief of the TWF Psychiatry Department, were assembled. Introductions were made but I wasn't paying attention to names.

"We have the phone set up and we'll start by trying to get him to talk. The goal is to get him to come out or to have him send his family out," said the Lieutenant.

Dr. Burke took my arm and directed me to the phone. "Talk to him. Tell him what he needs to hear."

The phone was placed on speaker. It started ringing, and kept ringing. I turned to Burke and the Lieutenant just as I heard a female voice "Hello?"

"Hello. This is Dr. Pearson. Your husband asked for me."

"Thank God. Billy. Billy. It's Dr. Pearson." There was a pause, then "He's coming to the phone."

"Dr. Pearson?"

"Yes, Billy it's Dr. Pearson. I want to help you."

"Hello doc. Glad you made it. I can't trust the others, especially that Burke."

"You can trust me. I know you. You wouldn't hurt anybody. What happened?" I could see Burke to my right motioning me to speed it up and get him out. I ignored him.

"I wanted to talk to you, Dr. Pearson, because you need to know that I always knew you were never one of them." His speech was becoming more pressured. "Will you pray with me?"

"Pray with you?"

"Yes, can you do that with me?"

"Of course, Billy, go ahead." I reflexively closed my eyes.

"Dear Lord, protect my family and help me find peace. God, my sponsor told me you said in the Bible that vengeance is your job, so now that part's up to you. Keep your promise, God. In Jesus name, Amen."

"Amen. Will you let me help you now Billy? I will do whatever I can. Will you come out and talk to me so I can see you and know you are all right?"

There was silence.

"Billy?"

"Yeah, I'm ready now. My family is all okay. I'm coming out. But stand so I can see you."

"I will, Billy. You will be able to see me."

"He's coming out. Thank you." We could hear his wife on the phone.

SWAT and the officers were all focused on the door, ready to act if needed. I was positioned so that my upper body and face would be visible to Billy when he came out. The door opened and he took a step out. With one hand he shielded his eyes from the bright spot lights focused on him but his other hand was in his jacket pocket.

The Lieutenant was using the bull horn, "Sanders, get both your hands up and get down on the ground."

Billy was looking around until he saw me, nodded, but kept walking.

"Stop. Hands up. Get your hand out of your pocket. Now. And get on the ground."

Billy stopped for a moment and then began walking again as he pulled his hand from his pocket clutching something. There was a glint of metal. I heard the gun blasts from both sides of me and

I watched Billy fall. There was screaming in the house, and officers ran to Billy's body. He was dead. A metal cylinder was next to his hand and there was no gun.

CHAPTER THREE

The Psychiatry Department meeting was only on agenda item two and I was already restless. Most of the staff had shown up today. Rows of chairs lined up one behind the other, all filled, as if it was final exam day in high school.

"Mik, I heard the Billy Sanders lawsuit settled this week, and Tara took the hit for Burke. Is that true?" William had leaned back from his chair right in front of me to whisper his question.

"Who told you?"

"I assume that means it's true. I can't believe they named almost every therapist he had contact with. Except you, of course. They claimed TWF made some medication error? It was one of those suicide by cop situations if you ask me. I'm surprised that ball buster attorney Bevers settled after only six months."

"Seven. Seven months, and Tara wasn't at fault. But I don't want to talk about it. And face forward. Tara's going to notice we're not paying attention."

William shrugged his shoulders and turned toward the front of the room. Disappointed that I was not willing to provide him with more diversion from the tediousness of our 90 minute monthly mandatory staff meeting. My heart started pounding, as it did any time someone brought up Billy Sanders. None of us who knew Billy or had any connection to the lawsuit surrounding his death ever talked about it anymore. It had been an unspoken agreement among us. Even though he still appeared in my thoughts almost every day. But in the past month I could finally sleep without awakening in panic every couple hours at the sound of gunshots in my dreams.

There had been no answers. But plenty of accusations and speculation. It still didn't make sense to me, and that included from a therapist perspective. I had one deposition subpoenaed by Bevers, the attorney for Billy's family, but that was my only involvement. The metal cylinder that Billy had pulled out of his jacket pocket and that the police thought was a gun had papers in it. No one allowed me to see what they were. They might have helped me understand what he was thinking. Billy had talked about vengeance. For what? William was right about one thing. It was suicide by cop, but why?

TWF legal did its best to keep me out of the information loop because I was not named in the lawsuit and my testimony did not help them. In my mind, there was no adequate explanation for his apparent paranoid decompensation. There was, however, a monetary settlement for the family before it could go to trial with a signed no disclosure agreement for TWF. The agreement of "We'll pay you to go away and not say anything about TWF and what happened."

The strident, high-pitched voice of Tara interrupted my thoughts "I am quite excited to report this is an increase that is consistent with moving toward our goal of 15 groups to improve accessibility. You will recall that this number was determined by our group task force that examined diagnoses from all patients seen last year, data collected by our IT specialist in the Data Operations Delivery Offset department located within the Controller's office."

Dr. Tara Anderson, psychiatrist, Assistant Chief, and the principal defendant in the Sanders law suit was presenting the most recent patient statistics provided by the TWF Healthcare Administration. TWF. Many patients and even staff didn't know what the initials stood for. Trenton, Williams, and Friechus – the three original founders of the health care corporation. Three medical doctors who had been early adopters of the managed health care trend. But those doctors were long gone and the organization was now known as TWF Healthcare.

Tara was continuing, "Amanda, our administrative assistant, who has been invaluable in setting up the presentation today, will hand out coupons, one for each staff, to be redeemed at the TWF Health store that will be opening next week, right off the lobby. This is a token of our gratitude for all the work you do in providing outstanding care to our members. It also supports our focus on ways our members can readily access products that will help them be proactive in their total health. Remember each of us is both a valuable member and an employee or medical doctor of TWF Healthcare."

"Thank you, Dr. Anderson!" I looked to find the owner of the enthusiastic, adolescent sounding and unfamiliar voice. It was the new social work intern, holding up his two dollar coupon. The interns were transient unlicensed TWF therapists who were at the bottom of the hierarchy. However, this one would likely do well here. Public exhibitions of adoration of TWF upper management, although not listed on the internship position posting, were still required for the intern's successful completion of the supervised clinical work needed for licensure in this state.

"No. Thank you. Each of you. Every single one" Tara smiled as she punctuated each phrase with a finger jab at different parts of her audience. "It is the least we could do to acknowledge your contribution."

William began writing on his notepad, and then held it up at an angle so I could see what he wrote."She's right. It is the VERY VERY LEAST TWF could do." I maintained my silence, but I agreed with William. My two dollars would have been better invested in a lottery ticket.

Tara was continuing with a detailed description of more statistics from the other medical centers that were all part of the TWF network.

"Pardon me." The side door to the hall slammed against the back of Tara's chair as Dr. Bruce Jackman attempted to slide through the 45 degree angle opening. As always, his pelvis made its way into the room first. Accessorized by an ox blood red cover on his PDA that hung prominently below his hand-tooled black and silver belt. "For better balance," the TWF orthopedic surgeon informed new staff members during their orientation.

He forced himself through the opening, readjusted his PDA left of center, nodded to Tara, and proceeded to pull up two chairs as close as possible to our Chief, Edward Burke. Just short of creating the airport chair chain where there is only one armrest for two people. His stocky, muscular frame filled one chair and the other he used to place the materials he had brought for his presentation later in the meeting. He leaned toward Burke, smiling and whispering to him, then turned his attention back to Tara; he centered each hand on each hip just below his waist, elbows bent. A movie gunfighter stance. Jackman's favorite position for meetings where he was not in charge. Anyone who worked at TWF Healthcare for more than a month knew Jackman liked to think of himself as some sort of cowboy and the six months he spent working on a cattle ranch when he was 17 had produced story after story, as though that had been his real life. We also knew that every eight months – the time security designated that had to elapse before a password was reused – his password was Paladin. Paladin, the Wild West hired gun antihero from the 1960's television series, who could always take out the problem when no one else could. None of us ever thought it worth it to discuss the obvious psychological interpretations of that.

To her credit, Tara had nodded acknowledgement of Jackman's entry but did not stop. The room had rapidly resumed its previous catatonic state. Everyone was used to interruptions by sudden needs, real or perceived. Sometimes it was the demand of a disturbed patient. In recent months, it was the urgent need of one more newly appointed administrator.

"As you know, one of our initiatives for this year is entitled Partners in Care that focuses not only on us as therapists and doctors partnering with our patients, but also the psychiatry department partnering with other departments in areas of interface for greater coordination and quality of care for our patients," Tara turned in Jackman's direction. "Today I would like to introduce our new pain program director, Dr. Bruce Jackman. Although he has been a valuable part of TWF for over 10 years in his position as Chief of Orthopedic Surgery and many of you are likely familiar with his research papers co-authored with our own Dr. Burke, in his additional new role he will be working much more closely with us in the Psychiatry Department. We anticipate a productive cooperation."

Jackman nodded. "Thank you for the kind words, Dr. Anderson. I hope everyone here is as excited as I am to begin this journey together. The start of the marriage of medical and psychological spheres in the treatment of the complex conditions of chronic pain and their sequelae. However, unfortunately today I have only a few minutes." And as if prearranged, his cell sounded. He glanced at the number, looked up and shrugged. "I will need to respond to that, and I will leave these for you." He shoved the stack of papers at Tara who deftly handed them off to her assistant Amanda. "I look forward to working with all of you." As he walked toward the door, he patted Burke's shoulder in a moment of public demonstration of the fraternity.

Tara took over again, "Dr. Jackman is conducting a research project in the sports medicine clinic geared toward evaluating different treatments for young athletes with chronic pain. He had planned to discuss more of the particulars with us because it includes psychiatric patients. His study is a clinical treatment study and it will include psychiatric comorbidities that are usually excluded in purely academic experimental designs. For us, that means that one of our patients may be participating in the study at the same time they are in treatment with us. The general outline of treatment options is in the handout that is being passed around. There may be different combinations of treatments, including physical therapy using Dr. Jackman's patented traction devices, trigger point injections, and at times medications such as muscle relaxants. Amanda will be working as an administrative assistant for the program 25% of her time; she already has been helping out in setting up the program."

Amanda, who had finished handing out Jackman's outline and had resumed taking notes for the meeting now beamed, shifted in her seat and gave a little wave to the group as if she was newly crowned royalty. Everyone knew she adored Dr. Jackman.

"How will we know if one of our patients is in Dr. Jackman's experiments?" James as one of our new psychiatrists asked the question many of us were thinking.

"Good question. You won't. Dr. Jackman does not want to introduce unnecessary bias into the treatment. However, the usual clinical note will be in the chart because these are all patients with some type of pain condition who are in treatment with Dr. Jackman. His study will be a small group at first, most of the patients you see who also are treated by Dr. Jackman will not be patients in the experiment."

"So we won't know but will the patients be aware they are in an experiment?" James asked.

"All patients screened for the study will be informed that they may be part of the study but not told if they are in an actual experimental condition. Dr. Jackman will elaborate further at future meetings or you can always e-mail him. As most of you know he prefers e-mail correspondence to phone. A reminder to everyone. Out staff education meeting next month will be a presentation by our community liaison Detective Sustern from the San Cortez Police Department. It is part of our overall TWF Healthcare community initiative: 'TWF cares for its members and its community.' Now, I will turn the meeting over to Dr. Burke."

"Thank you, Dr. Anderson. First I want to underscore your support for Dr. Jackman's pain research. Particularly, since I taught him everything he knows. Some of you newer staff may be interested in the fact that I have worked with Dr. Jackman since our medical school days and I became his Chief Resident."

William held up his notepad again so I could see what he had been scribbling: "No, no one is interested, and Yes, Dr. Burke, we know YOU are the King of the World not Jackman." I coughed and cleared my throat to cover the start of a laugh. The competitiveness between Burke and Jackman was relentless and never subtle.

"Next, I would like to thank Tara for the great amount of effort evident in these reports." Burke pointed to the statistics she had handed out. "My job today is to fill in the blanks about the meaning for each of us in Psychiatry."

William looked over his shoulder at me and moved his paper to the right so I could again see what he was writing. "Did he say he's shooting blanks??????" was written in a loopy penmanship. I shook my head and sat back in my chair. William was a combination of the old school psychoanalytic therapist and a third grader. He was always using psychoanalytic theory as an entrée into some food, sex or other body function joke. Anytime someone objected to his humor, he would interpret it as a psychological deficit. He was also close to retirement and no one thought it worth the effort to rehabilitate him. He was funny enough, benign in intent and at the hub of gossip so that he was one of my work buddies. His office was also right next door to mine. His humor made these meetings tolerable.

Tara had moved her chair off to the side several feet away from Burke and was taking notes as he talked. She always gave him the full range of the front of the room as he required so he could give his monthly report to the staff. In the past year, Tara had been promoted by Burke to Assistant Chief in the Department of Psychiatry. Over more senior psychiatrists. But the latest rumor was that Burke was becoming disenchanted with Tara. "Not a team player" was the stated problem. However, it was the widely publicized Billy Sanders' lawsuit naming her as one of the psychiatrists at fault that had made the one with ultimate responsibility – Burke - appear less Godlike. He blamed Tara for tarnishing his image. And since that was not cause for firing, his retaliation took the form of politically hobbling Tara.

"This cannot continue." Burke's voice pierced through the dissociative thinking process I was using to cope with this month's general flogging of the Department and its staff members. He now had my attention and everyone else's. His placed his hands in the pockets of his waist length dark grey jacket and slowly scanned the room. At over six feet, slender with narrow shoulders and narrower hips, he presented as casual and athletic, yet stiff. A department store mannequin, the clothes draped well on him but the flesh underneath was hard, unforgiving. Burke's face was filled with something. Emotion that only showed in the tight line of his compressed, almost colorless lips that usually were undistinguished from the pallor of his skin. Grey blue cat eye marbles set widely spaced above his long nose. Hard edges to his cheekbones and a jaw that would have been the envy of 1940's movie actors. When you looked at him, you kept looking. As you would a piece of art that required study for true appreciation. He took a couple steps closer to the group. "I repeat. This cannot continue."

Two of the therapists, David and Lizzie, both in the front row, were leaning back in their chairs, trying to increase the space between them and Burke's rage. As the last two to arrive for the meeting they were forced to sit where they and the rest of us who had been here more than a year knew never to sit. Within spitting range of Burke.

He turned back to his computer and moved to the next slide. "Our department is failing. Let me say it again. We are failing at TWF's primary goals of accessibility, accessibility, accessibility. Look at this graph. Of the eight TWF Healthcare psychiatry departments, we are second to the bottom. I repeat, second to the bottom. Our target for new patients seen per week is 10. Since we anticipate a no show and late cancellation rate of 30%, you need to be overbooking new patients, scheduling a minimum of 12 per week to compensate for this loss."

Overbooking? I thought. Was TWF Healthcare becoming the Southern Airways of managed care? At least Southern Airways didn't force four or five passengers into three seats when they overbooked. This was in contrast to TWF Healthcare that was known internally for frequently "squeezing" patients into therapists' full schedules when that 30% predicted loss did not occur, but patients needed to be seen.

Edward was using his laser pointer to highlight the clinic's transgressions on each slide generated from his laptop.

"But Edward, I mean Dr. Burke, isn't it expected that a good portion of psychiatric patients will no show? It's consistent with the chaotic nature of many diagnoses. We aren't the same as the medical departments in TWF where practitioners are interchangeable." Only David, handsome, charming, Prom King of the Department, and a classic narcissist would have thought it smart to interrupt Burke at this point. We all had seen him in his upward mobility mode for the past couple months as he bonded with the good old boys by socializing, joking around with Burke and Jackman at every opportunity.

"You are absolutely correct, David." Burke seemed pleased. "We are not like the Medical Departments. In fact let me show you more clearly how we are different." As he pressed the remote, another slide emerged with a listing of departments and percentage of "LT" which stood for Lost Time otherwise known as unbooked or open appointment time, but made most of us think of an amnestic state.

Psychiatry was 4th from the bottom of 17 departments in the medical center – right above the LT no show rate for the GI's sigmoidoscopy center. We were ranked only slightly better than the place that sends a camera up people's butts. Not good.

"See David, this is how we different." Burke continued. "We are below average. We are less than other departments. And your contribution to that position is…" He looked through the stack of papers he had on the table "Congratulations. You have significantly contributed to that bottom position; 54% of your schedule in the last month for you was lost time. Do you really work here? Well at this point it appears you still do. This is yours."

David took the paper he was handed. He was silent, looking down at the statistics and rapidly blinking.

"Any other thoughts, David? Good. Happy to see we are all joining together to solve this crisis. From this point on all staff with open hours in their schedules are available for any patient to be booked. Our administrative assistants led by the experienced Amanda, since she will still be working with Psychiatry 75% of her time, will book into your schedules. If you have a complaint bring it to me or your manager. Not Amanda. This new way of decreasing LT will not only be a service to the patients, which we all know is TWF's primary concern, but also will help balance the recent financial hemorrhaging of legal fees due to – well missteps – by some of you may be too strong a word and I am unable to give you specifics, but let's say it is imperative my department, we, do not become a liability for TWF Healthcare."

"I know I don't have to remind you that one of our health care competitors decided last week to lay off 25% of its mental health workers and outsource to community therapists," he paused for effect, "who are willing to work for their money. We also don't know what new mandates from the state or federal level we may have to respond to in these times of health care reform and how we will have to adjust to survive in the future. If that scares you, it should. Fear can be a turned into motivation."

"Dr. Burke?" Anthony, standing by the door, had raised his hand. Burke nodded to him. "I don't understand how can we see so many new crisis patients and still treat our regular patients? And the electronic charting takes so much time."

You could tell that Anthony had been hired only three months ago. He genuinely wanted to know. I was concerned that he would become one of the occasional "scout ants" that entered the system. They were the therapists who sought unentered clinical and ethical territory outside the bottom line economic fenced perimeter of TWF. One had to admire them. Even with the awareness that as in the insect kingdom, they would most likely not survive their venture. That they would have to be terminated to maintain the system.

"Anthony, you are new to this service, and I can see how anxious you are. Let me say that as Chief for over 10 years I have seen how the energy in that anxiety can be focused to increase productivity and I am certain you will be able to do that. Today I am handing you your individual scores and I want you to take a good look at them to see where you can improve. If you need help, come to Tara or to me. You have a reprieve today. Next month I will be publicly posting all therapists' scores in ranking order. Good luck everyone. I am optimistic that our department ranking will be much higher next month."

We were dismissed. I glanced at my statistics. Thank God. They were all in the excellent range. I tended to be at the top of these types of statistics because of my workaholic nature and a little compulsiveness – perhaps more than a little compulsiveness. But being a "star" in this department meant you could be seen with suspicion by your peers As if it made you management's bitch. Still, I was thankful that I was genetically engineered to be high energy, although my colleagues at times used the less flattering term "hypomanic" to describe me. They were not completely inaccurate. But that energy level combined with several years training on a crisis unit with severely mentally ill patients had saved me a number of times in this corporation.

When we started TWF Healthcare we were all ambitious. Driven to succeed, to be at the top. For most of us, the motivation that drove us to be high achievers had been worn down to some extent by the intrusive management, the bombardment of the high volume of patients, and the sniper fire style statistics. But it was not totally dead. The notion of public ranking produced an initial demoralizing enervation followed by a surge of competition.

I walked with William down the hall to Rachel's office. We had 15 minutes before patients arrived, which was the amount of time needed for our monthly meeting postop recovery time. Rachel's office was the farthest from Burke's and one of the largest, making it the best suited place for our discussions.

"I'll show you mine if you show me yours," William leered.

"I am not interested in yours, William."

"You always say that." He grabbed the paper from my hand. "You must be at the top of class again Mik. I, on the other hand, am in the coveted position of being average. Right in the middle. Above harassment from management and below their top of the list notice. Where for most people, excluding you of course Mik, when the person is at the top of the list one month, they have nowhere to go but down, which is then inevitably followed by management's concerned 'You were doing so well. What made your scores drop to the middle?' type of scrutiny. I have the ideal position." We reached Rachel's office. Rachel and Tara had cut through the other hall and were there already.

"What were you two whispering about?" Tara looked from William to me.

"What were they whispering about?" Lizzie arrived right behind us, "What do they usually whisper about in meetings. Here's my guess. You," looking at William "made some Freudian interpretation about Burke's and Jackman's need for electronic penis extenders, or even better what it means that Amanda who promotes herself as super mom wears her two sizes too small short skirt when she knows Jackman will be in the meeting. Then," Lizzie pointed at me, "then Mik counters with some comment about William's obsession with coke addicted psychiatrist's theories that involve sex, sex and sex. The result is that we all wonder if William's interpretations are projections because he is overcompensating for some deficit?" Lizzie sat down and crossed her legs, looking smug.

"That's right, Lizzie, I am compensating for being one of the few to continue the path of Freudian enlightenment amongst you self psychology, psychodynamic, and cognitive behavioral theory types." William was never affected by her comments. "And don't be paranoid Tara."

"I'm not being paranoid."

"Of course not." Lizzie moved over to Tara and put her arm around her. "None of us is safe from Burke's rage, even the MDs. He's a complete prick."

"I think Edward's stressed. I don't want this repeated but I know a couple of weeks ago, he had to fly his stepmother to the Mayo Clinic for medical tests," Rachel interjected. Rachel was one of my best friends, but her frequent excuses for others' bad behavior was irritating at times.

"Rach, that's an overly generous interpretation. His psychopathology is part of his character, not situational." I said. "Remember 10 years ago when Edward was first appointed as Chief? The sweep he did of the Department as if he was eliminating a seedy criminal element. Twelve people resigned or were fired within two months. He told us that it was his job to clear out the dead wood."

Rachel was slowly nodding as if she was starting to retrieve this painful piece of suppressed history, "I think his stress makes him act that way, but you're right Mik, it was awful when my good friend Bob came in that Friday and Edward told him he was fired. Security walked him out to the parking lot without allowing him to terminate with his patients. He was devastated."

"Bob and several other staff exited TWF within the first month." I added.

"I don't think Edward would do that again," Tara said. "He and I are seeing more eye to eye lately on clinic matters. Although I have to warn you that the content of the last few partners meetings about TWF finances has been grim. I can tell you more tonight. Are we still getting together at Zack's Bar?"

There was a knock on the door. "Yes, Tara we're getting together. The door's open." Rachel said.

Anthony's round face shiny with perspiration face emerged as he opened the door a bit and looked in,

"Rachel, I need you to co-sign this form for my patient's disability."

"Come in." Rachel motioned for him to sit down. "You can stay. We'll be finished in a moment."

We all felt for Anthony. He was struggling in adjusting to TWF, but only Rachel was willing to extend herself to keep him afloat. He sat down, not taking his eyes off her. His general demeanor that of a nervous but devoted Jack Russell terrier.

"Did you see David's face? Edward seems to be back into his Red Queen stance of off with their heads." William and I laughed at Lizzie's comment, although it was not the first time that description had been used for Burke.

"I heard he and Jackman have been working out regularly in the MDs only TWF gym. Maybe he has "roid rage." William chimed in. "Let's check with one of the insiders." William moved his overgrown black eyebrows up and down in a Groucho Marx move and leaned over to Tara.

Tara took a step away from William. "Don't be ridiculous. Edward and Bruce have been work-out partners since medical school. Plus Edward doesn't believe in contaminating the purity of his body. It is a temple you know."

"You're right." William admitted, while Rachel and even Anthony nodded. Edward did not make it a secret that he was opposed to any non-essential medications or supplements. He even included vitamins in that category. "Signs of weakness of character" he had said to me once. The irony of that statement was that he was always ready to prescribe for patients, fitting his "they are weak I am not" life philosophy.

"Does Dr. Burke have a private practice? One of my patients lost her job and her TWF insurance. She needs a psychiatrist in private practice." Anthony entered the conversation speaking in a barely audible tone.

"The Chiefs of Service aren't allowed to have private practices because TWF wants their full loyalty to the corporation." Rachel answered Anthony's question. A question every new therapist ultimately asked since it wasn't something that the leadership of TWF volunteered in an a new hire orientation. That loyalty to TWF created a conflict of interest at times when there was a question of approval for a patient to receive more than the average amount of care or a particularly expensive type of treatment, because expensive care meant a decrease in the Chief's annual bonus. Although TWF management made a point of denying that money had anything to do with the care decisions, most of us knew the truth.

"Really, Anthony, it's like a chastity belt, with TWF owning the key," William added.

"Although Rachel's right," Tara turned to look directly at Anthony, "the Chiefs are allowed to collaborate with pharmaceutical companies in research studies, as well as work with the Universities in research protocols, so they are connected to other organizations in addition to TWF Healthcare. In fact, William here has worked with Dr. Burke on a number of his medication outcome studies. Right, William?"

William paused for a moment, and then nodded. "She's right. I hate to admit it, but in spite of his megalomania or maybe because of it, Burke has done some very good work trying to determine the psychotropic medications that work best with a particular diagnosis, especially acute stress disorder and PTSD."

"I'm bored." Lizzie was known for her emotional shifts, being outraged, predicting Armageddon, then as quickly disengaging and wondering with disdain why everyone else remained upset. "This is same old, same old. How many times are we going to obsessively process these meetings and Burke's motivations. I am more interested in the types of pain management Jackman will be providing Amanda in the after-hours chronic pain program." Smiling, Lizzie got up from her perch on the arm of William's chair, stretched her five foot, size two frame, and started applying raspberry frosted lipstick from the little black tube she always carried in her pocket, the only color on her flawless, young for 61 skin.

"What?" Rachel and Anthony asked in concert.

"Grow up Lizzie." Tara said, "Jackman only goes after the big hair, big breasted, no ass, long leg types. And of course he never consorts with individuals outside his social class."

"We all know that's his MO now, Tara. All you have to do is look at his current wife, and every female assistant he hires. But there was a rumor, from a reliable source I might add, that many years ago he and Amanda had a hot and heavy, screwing at every opportunity in the patient rooms kind of affair when they worked together at St. Matthew's Hospital. Right, Mik?" William said.

I nodded. It was not a secret. Everyone at that hospital had known about it, including an old friend of mine. I hadn't seen the point of spreading that around, not because of some moral high ground but because it wasn't worth risking the ire of either Amanda or Jackman.

"Stay tuned folks" Lizzie was enjoying watching the little drama she had started. "But on a more immediate matter, I need the usual contribution. It's my turn to buy the lottery tickets this week and I have a feeling that our freedom is just around the corner."

CHAPTER FOUR

"Hey Johnny Depp!" Charles had appeared at the top of the stairs, outlined by the blinking light of the stylized neon sign "Zack's Bar," and he turned at the sound of Lizzie's voice, searching the dimly lit bar for our group, and smiled. Even Charles' perfect teeth were sexy, and he looked especially delicious in the black leather jacket that draped his body, with the added inches of height from his black boots. Lizzie was right; he did have that Johnny Depp bad boy look. Quite a contrast from his TWF Healthcare persona. Too bad he was short. Short men didn't quite do it for me. My therapist friends interpreted my over 6 feet height requirement for the men I date as an unresolved father issue, given that my father has a 6 foot 5 inch frame. Occasionally, I would be shamed into dating a short man, and it never worked, and unfortunately it also didn't with Charles. We enjoyed flirting even after he was married. It was all harmless. He was always the last to arrive for our weekly happy hour retreat. Tara, Rachel, William, Lizzie and I had started without him.

"Nice threads, Charles. Grab a seat" William moved over to make room for Charles at the table.

"Why thank you very much," Charles settled in next to Lizzie squeezing her shoulder as he sat down. Our server was immediately at his side. "What would you like, sir?"

"I would like a Rob Roy."

"How retro of you, and yet it sounds yummy. I'll have one too," Lizzie spoke to the server, including her as if she would be interested in Lizzie's choice of a drink subtext: "I'm always looking for the perfect dinner in a drink. Yes, I am still aspiring to be an alcoholic but haven't quite managed it yet. I guess I'm too much of a control freak."

"Yes, you are, but we love you anyway" Tara reassured her before taking another sip from her martini. Charles took off his jacket, rolled back the cuffs of his sleeves, and hit the side of the glass closest to him with a stir stick. His version of pounding a gavel for order. "Time for the best story of the week. And because," he lowered his voice half an octave, "I expect results from you slackers, not excuses, particularly those of you with 140% net loss" Charles did a surprisingly accurate Edward impersonation, "who thinks they have a contender?"

Tara started "Well, I'm not certain this qualifies, but last Thursday night on call, I finally saw a man who had an adverse reaction to trazodone. The ER doc had to inject him 5 times to disengorge him."William gave an exaggerated yawn and started to snore.

Lizzie spoke up "I'm with William on the snooze meter. First of all disengorge is not a real word, and second, I know you aren't too inhibited to use the word penis. You could use a romance novel phrase, like his manhood was permanently erect. But you are right. That's definitely not a contender. Painful, but not a contender."

Rachel giggled a bit at this. She never played the game, our version of a reality show where the therapist with the most pathetic story for the week received a prize. The winner in our little game had drinks for that night paid by the rest of us. Rachel never said anything bad about anybody. She adhered to the "if you don't have anything nice to say, don't say anything at all." A trait like that was good as gold to TWF management. It also made her a great audience for the rest of us attention seekers.

"I already said it wasn't. How about this?" Undaunted, Tara started again. She first looked around to make certain the other customers could not hear her or worse that one of them might be a patient. Reassured, she leaned forward, but kept her voice as low as possible. "Last weekend that new psychologist Kristina Babcock was on call and the ER doc paged her to evaluate a 22 year old male thought to have severe anxiety and had been brought into the ER by his father. When Kristina arrived she introduced herself to the patient and his father, and started her assessment. The young man started to speak in a pressured agitated way, clearly not anxiety but the beginning of a psychotic manic episode, and with averted eyes, said to Kristina, 'I can't talk to you.' In her best soothing therapist manner Kristina coaxed, 'Yes you can. Start by telling me how you have been feeling the past few days.' Apparently the patient abruptly stood up, turned to his father and yelled angrily 'I can't talk to a woman with a cock in her name', and fled the ER, leaving the stunned father and Dr. Bab…cock. It took four police officers to bring him back."

There was silence at the table then laughter and groans. Lizzie even gave Tara a congratulatory pat on the back. "We have a contender." The competition had begun.

CHAPTER FIVE

"Well you seem happy today, Dr. Pearson." I looked over at the Patient Information Booth to see our 88 year old volunteer smiling at me as he finished directing one of the members to the Radiology Department. When I met him three years ago, and addressed him as Mr. Billings, he said, "Always call me Artie. Never Mr. Billings." But when I encouraged him to call me by my first name he responded "It's not professional." Everyone loved him.

"Good morning, Artie. Beautiful out today."

He nodded and turned back to assist the next person in line. It was true that it was sunny and warm out but my smiling was in response to internal stimulation. I had been thinking about the stories from the night before. My friends and the patients were the best parts of this job.

The day was relatively uneventful, several garden variety depressives, a few anxiety patients, a bulimic, and another eating disorder patient who ruminated her food and spit it out—in some ways more obsessive compulsive than eating disordered. With the nine patient visits done for the day I began charting. It took me longer to complete my charting than most of the other therapists who charted during the visit while the patient talked. For me, that interfered with the connection with the patient.

I heard the faint bell tone of a new TWF Healthcare e-mail's arrival in my inbox. I stopped for a moment to switch computer screens and read it. A High Priority Message with its little fire icon next to it. What William called the TWF burning bush. From the Office of the President of TWF Healthcare: Congratulations to Dr. Bruce Jackman and Dr. Edward Burke for receipt of the prestigious "Excellence in Clinical Research" award presented to them last week by the National Psychiatric Council. Burke did have an impressive resume. Harvard undergrad, Harvard medical school, and published research from his work with veterans. At first I couldn't figure out why he decided to work at TWF Healthcare. He made it clear that his passion was research and he could have been an academic type. But he also had difficulty playing well with others and the freedom allowed to Chiefs at TWF far outweighed the prestige of a major University. The fact that the one million members of TWF Healthcare were a readily accessible, with no recruitment necessary, research population was another plus for Burke. It was also one of the reasons he recruited Jackman to join TWF after he did. They continued their projects together without the pain in the ass, rigorously ethical University Human Subjects committee to prevent their more ambitious projects from being implemented. Members signed on to TWF as their healthcare organization not only for medical or psychiatric care, but also that signature gave TWF permission for their participation in clinical research studies. Most patients never knew that's what they agreed to.

I resumed documenting patients' visits, entering diagnoses, and calling back patients. There were no short cuts. It was all time consuming. Hours later I had progressed to the point of searching for two patients' old paper charts in the small stuffy room adjacent to our reception area. Although we were electronic now in charting, patient visits from years past were in the old paper charts. Charts that eventually would be archived in a central location for all TWF medical centers at some undetermined point in the future. Finding the charts should have been a simple task, but was not. The charts were not filed by name. To add a little challenge to the search, they were first filed by a letter that was not connected to the letter of the patient's last name. Then by the last three numbers, then the other eight. I could find only one of the two. The other chart could be in another therapist's office. We were supposed to place a bright yellow space saver file in the place where the chart had been and sign our name on it when we checked the chart out. This rarely happened. Charts seemed to disappear. As a result, we had dubbed the room the Stephen Hawking room for its black holes and appearing and disappearing charts that defied the usual laws and properties of physics.

I decide to take a break, savor the quiet, and sat cross-legged on the floor in the back file row. I had always loved the quiet of library type surroundings, first when I was a child reading classic science fiction books by H.G. Wells and Frank Herbert in the public library on weekends, and then later in college, sitting on the floor in the stacks at the library reading the psychological and medical journals until my legs would go to sleep.

I found the chart I needed and as I started to read it, I heard the door to the reception area open and someone walk in. I didn't expect anyone to still be working. Most therapists and all reception staff left the evening clinic before 8:00pm. Drawers were unlocked and opened, other sounds that I couldn't decipher, then footsteps coming closer as the person stopped and must have glanced into the chartroom. I was blocked from view by the bottom row of charts, and I was not in the mood for conversation so I kept still. A chair creaked and I wondered if it was Jimmy, the night custodian. I had seen him at other times in the late evening. Sometimes he would sit in the receptionist's chair and have a snack before his as he watched the television in the waiting room through the glass wall.

I loved to play spy, even had a small telescope as a child. My patents had bought the telescope for me with the intent of identifying birds or star constellations. But when I climbed my favorite gnarly oak tree the telescope was used mostly to allow me to watch what was happening in the neighborhood from a distance without being observed. Now I decided to wait a few more minutes before I let the person know I was there. If it was Jimmy, this could be an opportunity for a little detective work since there was an ongoing question of who was periodically changing all the settings on Amanda's expensive, bought by TWF, ergonomically correct chair. I always suspected Jimmy. He resented his job and had a passive-aggressive streak more commonly evident in his forgetting to clean certain offices or areas. Amanda was infuriated each time she came in and found her chair defiled as she dramatically described it, even though it only took a minute to reset it. It would be interesting to catch Jimmy in the act. Not that I would report him. Amanda was not all that likable, but she considered herself a friend of mine. I was often supportive to her because it made my life easier. She was notorious for making therapists' lives miserable if you crossed her. Surprising how many patient messages got lost when you were not in her good graces.

Amanda was smart, quick witted and 10 years ago, when she was first promoted to lead receptionist she had been excellent, hard-working and innovative. She had, however, in response to ongoing domestic problems gained about a hundred pounds over that time, as Lizzie had pointed out yesterday, and at 5'3" this was more than

Amanda's slight frame could accommodate without something breaking down. She developed lower back problems and knee problems to the point you could expect that at least once a month she would call in sick because the pain was too bad. With her three daughters attending a high priced private all-girls school and a husband who was regularly out of work, Amanda couldn't afford not to work. State disability payments would hardly be enough to support the family.

I was starting to feel the numbness that indicated my legs were going to sleep. I was still waiting for a clear sign it was Jimmy so I could move from my position, when I heard a voice that was not Jimmy's Georgia drawl but the clear soprano tones of Amanda.

"Hey, it's me. I got your message and no problem doing that for you. But it takes extra time so I need to be paid more. Yes, that's more than fair. How many do you need? Leave the info in the usual place. Of course. Why do you think I'm using this phone? There will be no problem. Thanks for the opportunity. I have to go. You too. Bye."

There were sounds of drawers unlocked and then locked and papers shuffled. I heard Amanda lock the door to the waiting room after leaving the reception area. As I waited to make certain Amanda had left the building, I wondered what kind of scheme she was into now. Apparently, her promotion of assistant to Jackman was not going to be enough of a salary increase. She always had a business on the side; a hopeful "get rich quick" enterprise that ranged from selling the latest weight loss products to sex toy parties, a project that was short lived. She had crafted and painted tiny colorful wooden birds and sold them, mostly to staff who wanted to stay on her good side. She only had problems conducting her businesses once. That was when she was giving facials to patients and staff for a reduced fee on the lunch hour in one of the vacant group rooms. She had been written up by Tara, but since it wasn't on TWF Healthcare time, and she had been a union employee for over 10 years, nothing was done as long as she stopped the practice, and she did. I admired her ambition but worried about her judgment. I had no idea what she was doing and probably better I didn't at this point. My right leg was asleep and I needed to leave. I moved my leg back and forth until it would bear weight, although it was still tingling, and took my one chart back to my office.

I finished charting but it was too late to make routine patient calls. I needed to leave and force myself to my athletic club even if it was late. Working out was the mainstay of my stress management and I had chosen a club that was open late so I had no excuses, or at least fewer excuses for not working out. I logged off the computer, locked my cabinets, grabbed my briefcase and headed out the door. It was 10:30pm. Good. I could work out and be home by midnight.

As I headed for my car, I could hear arguing in the Doctors Only parking structure. I took the sidewalk that wound close to the structure to hear better. The voices belonged to Burke and Jackman, I stood behind one of the concrete pillars and quickly took a look into the lot. Jackman was outlined in the dim light. He was holding the handle of one of his traction device carrying cases and the trunk of his car was open. Burke was standing next to him. I could hear Burke clearly now, "What do you thinkyou're doing? This is my clinic, my experiments. I brought you to TWF."

"You didn't bring me in, you arrogant ass. TWF wanted me. They drooled at the thought of having me in this place so don't pull that shit with me. I'm the star now. No one is going to support you over me. I can do whatever I want." Jackman set the case in the trunk of his car and slammed it shut.

"No, you can't." Burke tried unsuccessfully to grab Jackman's arm.

"Watch me," Jackman got into his car and sped out of the lot. I remained behind the pillar for a few minutes to make certain I remain undetected, then walked to my car. It was not the first disagreement I had witnessed between Jackman and Burke, but I had never seen either of them this angry before. Perhaps the brotherhood was beginning to wear under the strain of TWF politics. I drove out of the lot, even more eager to get to the gym to detox from the day.

CHAPTER SIX

"Dr. Pearson," Amanda's voice cut in from the intercom on the phone speaker. I glanced at my watch. The morning had passed quickly. It was now 12:30 pm. 12:00pm to 1:00pm was designated as the clinical staff's lunch time, which meant I was likely one of only a few therapists on site. Sometimes the only one. I picked up the phone. "What is it, Amanda?"

"I need you out here immediately." Amanda was a veteran in handling patient situations at the front desk, but her voice had panic in it.

"I will be right out." I closed the patient screen on my computer, slipped on my shoes, and checked the mirror to make certain there were no food bits on my face from the salami and jack cheese sandwich I had been eating. The waiting room was partially filled with patients waiting for their appointments that would not be starting for another 30 minutes, after the lunch hour.

"Amanda, how can I help?"

"This is Mrs. Brauer."

"It's Doctor Brauer. And this, this is my daughter." Forced against the protective glass in front of Amanda was an 8" x 10" photo of the body of a young woman, maybe an adolescent, lying on her side with one arm flung awkwardly outward. A dark red vertical cut on her wrist. Thick strands of long white blond hair covered most of her face. Her other arm, equally bloodied, was clutching a doll. I stood in shock, rapidly becoming lightheaded. My usual response to the sight of blood. Any blood, real or virtual. I steadied myself against the desktop behind me for a moment to try to stop the impending syncope that was inevitable if I kept looking at the photo. I moved forward to the window.

"Are you one of them?"

"One of whom, ma'am?"

"Those who killed my daughter. It doesn't matter. You work for or with them and this," she slid the photo across the glass closer to me, "is what you all did to her."

I began my response to her as I would any patient I did not know who was angry and agitated. "I am Dr. Mikelena Pearson, a psychologist in the clinic. Let me help you."

"Help me? Like you helped my daughter?" The volume of her voice was now at a critical stage. I needed to get her out of the waiting room so that she would not cause damage to the patients, but I also did not want to place myself at risk. There was a reason the bullet proof glass separated the reception area from the patient area, and there was no barrier of any kind in my small office. She looked to be in her 40's, thin, expensively dressed, no sign of disorganized or psychotic thinking, an air of someone who was used to others giving in to her wants. More outrage and fear, than rage with direct revenge. I had at least six inches of height on her, and although that did not outweigh a weapon, it made me feel less intimidated. I was certain Amanda had called security, but particularly at lunchtime, our two security guards had never been able to arrive before 10 to 20 minutes had elapsed. I had to make a decision.

"Dr. Brauer, I would like to hear everything you have to say. Let me direct you back into my office."

"Why would I believe you?" The intensity and volume of her voice had decreased. A good sign. She stood for a moment. "Maybe you don't want your next victims in the waiting room to hear." She turned to the three patients waiting for their appointments. I followed her gaze: A thin young man in clean but torn blue jeans quietly and repetitively counting his fingers for whom this drama had no impact; a fashionably dressed woman in her 30's, who had been focused on the small electronic device in her palm, looked up at this point but returned to her schedule planning, aware this was not something she wanted to be witness to; and an older man, long grey hair tied back in a ponytail, eating some type of trail mix from a small brown paper bag and holding a large convenience store container of coffee in his other hand---demeanor, munchies and caffeine said likely addict in recent recovery. He was the only person I was concerned might actively support a self-identified victim of the system but when he stood up, it was to leave the waiting room in the direction of the men's bathroom.

"I know you don't know me. But I want to know what happened, and I will do whatever I can to help." All that was true. She nodded to me and moved toward the door to our offices. I led her back to my office and motioned her to take a seat. She immediately sat in the chair next to the little table and took out more paper and pictures which she handed to me.

"My brother-in-law is a retired police officer. That's how I got these" motioning toward the pictures with the tissue she had clenched in her hand, "and the coroner's initial report. I know you have to keep what I say confidential so I can tell you that."

She said that as if confirming our status under patient - doctor privilege. If it wasn't clear before, it was now. Smart woman, and indication of less histrionic personality structure than at first glance.

"I can't believe she's gone. I called Dr. Burke because Dr. Jackman spoke so highly of him. Bruce is a family friend and had treated Jessica for her pain conditions. I checked Burke's website and his credentials are impeccable and his face intelligent and kind."

I listened as she went on; as she tried to convince herself she was not the one who had made the mistake by referring her daughter to Burke.

"My friend Susan said Dr. Burke had changed her son's life; Dr. Burke had been the only one to diagnose him accurately as having asperger's. But all Dr, Burke did with my Jessica was talk to her, and then another doctor prescribed a generic Prozac and scheduled her for three weeks later. I can't remember the doctor's name, but she told her Jessica that she could call daily for a cancellation, but when she called in she was told Dr. Burke was out of town for two weeks but she could leave a message."

I wanted to support her emotionally but I was also aware of the limited time I had before my afternoon patients. "Dr. Brauer, I know that nothing I can say right now will lessen the pain you are feeling, but I'm wondering if it would be useful to spend a little time together now so I can understand more of what happened. Then perhaps we can schedule a time to talk more at length, and I can see if I can find more information or can provide more answers for you."

"I want to know how they could treat my daughter like they did? The coroner's report shows the highest level of substances in her system was the antidepressant. I know it looked like she died from cutting her wrists but she actually was overdosed."

Was overdosed. Someone did this to daughter. "I know this may be difficult to talk about but you said substances---had she taken other medications?

Dr. Brauer took a moment apparently trying to decide whether I was truly trustworthy or was I one of the TWF Healthcare minions.

"Opioids, a tricyclic, and a benzodiazepine. They were for her chronic nerve pain from all her early athletics. She had been on them for years. I hope you're not missing the point. I would think with all the press on that other TWF medication error tragedy with the Sanders boy, you would be looking for the cause in your own backyard, not questioning my daughter's behavior." She was starting to sound angry again and I realized I probably shouldn't have asked but the damage was already done.

"I am trying to get the full picture, Dr. Brauer. It helps me to know everything I can."

"She had a difficult time when she was benched from the basketball team due to a knee injury. It was her whole world. Even though she was beautiful and intelligent but that didn't matter to her – only sports."

I waited.

"She became very depressed and I kept trying to talk to her and help her. I got her to see a therapist here, Eva Baker, but Jessica told me Mrs. Baker was more interested in talking about her own grandchildren, and suggested Jessica take up crafts or scrap booking. She offered Jessica freshly baked snickerdoodle cookies. Cookies. She offered cookies. But Jessica hung in there and went for a couple visits but then stopped. Someone called to offer her a group but a group wasn't appropriate. She didn't even talk to her friends about her feelings. She stayed on the medications, but the medication follow up appointment was cancelled by the doctor with no rescheduled appointment."

"What happened then?"

Dr. Brauer hesitated, probably weighing the guilt she must be feeling with the need to say the truth.

"She did make a couple of suicide attempts. Once she took extra medication but she told me about it, and it wasn't enough to make her ill. She did cut on herself and was seen in the Emergency Department and she was seen by the Psychiatry therapist on call but no one thought it was serious. They said she was trying to get attention."

Of course she was trying to get attention. No one was treating her and she needed help. She was trying to get attention the same way a drowning person is trying to get attention. She needed a lifeboat or at least a life line. Instead someone dropped a flyer with instructions on how to swim.

"But no one would offer her anything but the day treatment group program, which meant she would miss school, and that would have been more depressing for her, and it would have interfered with her college prospects."

"I can't imagine how frustrated, frightened, and helpless you must have felt. Can you tell me when the suicide attempts were? I would like to try to track her visits on the computer and see if I can figure out what happened. If that's okay?"

She nodded. "Yes. Please. I want to know what happened."

I turned to my computer screen and looked up her patient number. The few appointments described, the letters sent to the patient as outreach from Baker, prescriptions sent to the pharmacy by Jackman for the pain meds, the ER doc and Tara who must have been the Psychiatrist filling in for Burke. But nothing else. "You said she was seen here after the suicide attempts?"

"She was. The last one was about a year ago."

I entered the computer code to obtain all history for the past 10 years---the basic electronic data capture had started then. If you entered the patient number for history without a date you were given the past six months. If something occurred six months and one day it didn't show up unless you took two additional steps. Unfortunately for many patients, including this one, most therapists did not take the time to check. Adding two more steps to the clinical information gathering process for therapists who were overbooked and overwhelmed was not an option many chose. For some it was denial of "if I don't see the problem I'm not responsible for fixing it" and for others it was a survival mechanism if they had any hope of having a life outside of TWF. Whatever the reasons, for Jessica, her therapists not taking the extra time to assess her fully may have been fatal. Jessica's clinical life and death was right there on the computer screen. Visit after visit to several different therapists shifted from crisis team to intakes to repeat intakes with other therapists to evaluate for their groups. Emergency Department visits with diagnoses of depression, suicidal ideation, and suicidal gestures. Unusual for these types of behaviors to become chronic in a girl that young. If what her mother was telling me was true.

"I can see the visits you're describing, Dr. Brauer. You also know I can't release this information to you from my office. I will have someone from our quality oversight department call you and follow up. I do believe you that your daughter really did want help.

And I am very sorry." The tears in my eyes were reflected in hers. I handed her my card with my direct phone number. She took the card, looked at me for a moment and said nothing, then stepped toward me, gave me a quick hug. With a muffled "Thank you" she grabbed the documents off the table and walked out. I stood there for a moment, staring into space, struggling with what just happened. I glanced at the clock and realized I was now 20 minutes late for my next patient, a new patient. I tried to shift my focus from the horror of the photographs and the inevitable legal fallout for TWF that would soon come. That also meant a lengthy note to be written later.

As I reached the door to the waiting room, I realized I knew nothing about the patient except his name. I forgot to read the chart and the reason for his visit. I took my hand off the door handle and sprinted back to my office, entered the patient's number and scanned through the last 10 years of data. Done. I took a deep breath and smoothed back my hair behind my ears, preparing my apology for being late as I flashed my "so happy to meet you and how delighted I am to be the one to help you" smile.

CHAPTER SEVEN

Adversity builds character. How many times had I heard my father say those words as I was growing up? I had thought it meant coping with natural disasters. Flooding, drought, or disease afflicting the cattle or pigs on our 200 acre farm. Not countering the viral outbreaks of economic bottom line greed-seeking behavior that had begun to afflict TWF Healthcare in recent years. The result appeared to be an increasing body count if today's incident was at all representative. Well, I thought, as I slid my parking card into the slot to exit the reserved employee lot, if adversity does build character, then mine might soon start resembling the Winchester mystery house. I turned to the old school rock station and upped the volume on Marvin Gaye's "I heard it through the grapevine" as I maneuvered my 1976 BMW – the 2002 model - into the lanes of rush hour traffic. The BMW was an unexpected gift passed on to me from my grandfather Olaf when I graduated with my PhD right at the point he could no longer drive. When he died a few years later, his will had monetary provisions to care for the car's maintenance and insurance; a long term care policy for the entity he loved most.

My commute home was often a form of therapy for me, particularly today with the young girl's death still on my mind and her photo entering each one of my therapy sessions that had followed her mother's entrance into the clinic. What had her mother done after she left my office? I would have heard if she had contact with anyone else there. Had she left for her attorney's? Or to make funeral arrangements? My cell phone rang.

"How late will you arrive tonight?"

"What?"

"Since you answered your cell at this time of day I assume you are on your way home or sitting in line at the order window of Dairy Queen."

"Hi Erik." It was my younger brother and one of a very few who knew of my drive home Dairy Queen stop coping strategy after those work days when waiting until I got home to open the Haagen-Dazs was out of the question. He was only 10 months younger and born within the same calendar year – causing confusion throughout school – the assumption made that we were twins, and we assumed so too, being inseparable. At least until high school when the interlopers of hormones and opposite interests divided us. "When does this event start again?"

"This event? How enthusiastic, Mik. But being the better person I will ignore that. You need to arrive by 9 at the latest. It starts at 8. Do you need directions?"

"No, no. I will be there. No later than 9, I promise." Erik had already ended the call. He was likely on to the next name on his list to confirm. Even though I attended every event of his I could, I still didn't know exactly what he did. Or more accurately, ever took the time to find out. He was considered a lobbyist for environmental and education legislation and general causes, and did some legal/political consulting. He was an attorney. He had passed the Bar exam, but never practiced law in the traditional sense. Our father never attended Erik's events, and our mom died when we were seven, so when Erik required family be present at one of his functions, it meant me.

Erik was the lucky one. True luck, not hard work or intelligence or particularly good judgment but luck. Not that he didn't have the other qualities. He had invested in a friend's Silicon Valley start-up company and the company struck gold. Erik sold his shares four months before the market crashed after 9/11. He made millions. The timing was luck. Erik could have chosen not to work but he continued on with his life for the most part as if he didn't have the money. With a few exceptions, that included his choice of causes, supporting our father's overseas missionary work, and his ability to repeatedly take the moral high ground in any work or life situation. The moral high ground was an expensive piece of real estate at times. Not everyone could afford it. Erik didn't understand that. He didn't have to.

We were both interested in law school after undergraduate school and we both received our law degrees. Erik thrived in law school. I didn't. I loved the logic and making a case but I disliked the practice. I applied to clinical psychology doctoral programs in my final year of law school and I started right after I received my JD degree. Erik and I chose different paths, yet we each had the same overdeveloped sense of justice and independent yet oddly rule bound characteristics of the Danish culture consistent with our genetics.

When I arrived home, I didn't bother to check messages or even look at my mail. I grabbed a black body skimming tea length dress and black satin peep-toe high heels from the back of my closet– the "Erik's events/evening" reserved section of my wardrobe. Make-up would be quick. I flicked the "blackest night" mascara on my lashes with the curved brush, not blinking so as to prevent spider leg marks above and below my eyes. As I waited a moment for it to dry, I thought about a remark made by five year old Kenny, from one of my first children's psychiatric hospital internships. We were sitting in the back of the little bus that took the kids out for day trips. He stretched his hand up to my face, in an attempt to touch my eyelashes. He asked "Are those real?" When I nodded, he shook his head in disbelief, as if he had been told too many lies to believe what adults said. "They're too long." Kenny was a sweetheart, an "old soul" if you believed such things. I had just smiled at Kenny when he made his eyelash comment. He was only a child, but it was not a comment I hadn't heard before. People seemed compelled to critique my appearance, good or bad, throughout my life. I had gained my height preteen. I tended to move in one direction while looking in another, resulting in falls, broken arms, scrapes, and an awkwardness that provided frequent opportunities for the "dork" type comments. Some of the teasing was common, some was creatively cruel, but none uncharacteristic of the sociology of adolescence.

By the start of my junior year in high school, somehow my body parts all connected properly, and all of that changed. My social ranking rapidly elevated with a resulting tiara and a red velvet pillow with my name stitched into it when the high school Homecoming Royalty were named. Much to my surprise and to the dismay of my brother, who found all this quite repulsive.

But times change. Erik now mandated a certain appearance when I attended his fund raisers. His sister would be seen as an extension of his persona. I rarely objected. The parties always contained a cast of interesting characters. This made them entertaining to me, regardless of the cause he was promoting. A quick application of my favorite lipstick and I was out the door.

I found the Sierra room at the nearby Hilton Hotel with little difficulty. There was some congestion at the door. I could see the room was already filling up; several round tables arranged in such a way to facilitate a sense of community, at the same time everyone would be able to see the speakers who were at the front.

"Mik," Erik's event coordinator, Angie, took my hand in both of hers. "I am happy you made it tonight. Erik wasn't certain you would be able to get out of the clinic in time." Angie was extremely loyal to Erik and had worked with him for years. I assumed that they had an affair, but neither had said so. They had that familiarity with each other that projected it. She was someone who always appeared upbeat and positive. Most people gravitated to her, but to me she seemed a little too good to be true. Everyone has a dark side.

"I'm going to find a seat, Angie. In fact, Alan's waving at me now. Great to see you, though."

"Hi Alan. How are you?"

"I'm quite well but you, Mik, are looking a little cachectic," my cousin Alan, an endocrinologist, announced as he tipped his head in front of mine as if to continue his diagnostic work-up "Yes, I believe you are precariously balanced on the edge of a coma inducing sugar low. Let me get you an infusion. Erik's set up the usual ample supplies of caffeine and sweets for his patrons."

"Thanks Alan. I would love a cup of coffee right now. But I'll get it myself. Be right back." I lingered at the sugar supply table. Madeleine cookies with all sorts of delicious frostings – I decided on the dark chocolate. I reached for the plate just as another hand reached it.

"Excuse me." I made eye contact with the face connected to the hand." Well, this is... unexpected." The fashionably dressed man in the fitted European style suit was Edward. I could never quite figure out his politics and he disclosed only the personal information he wanted people to know. But I never would have guessed he would attend something like this. "You do know my brother is the organizer of the event."

"I didn't. My stepmother knows one of the speakers. In fact, this plate of confections is for her. She invited Bruce as well." He gestured toward the table in the corner. She was sitting next to Jackman, laughing, talking, and patting his hand." Jackman and Burke. I started calculating how soon I could leave with minimal irritation from Erik. At the same time, I maintained my social façade

"I'm glad you could all come to the event. How is your stepmother, Edward? I haven't seen her in some time."

"Mik, are you flirting with strangers again?"

Edward and I both turned, and I stared into the most intense green eyes I had ever seen, with an annoying cat-ate-the-canary look in them. The coffee from my cup sloshed over, spilling onto the toe of Edward's shoe. I set my cup on the table, and grabbed a napkin to wipe off the Italian leather. I knew Burke would see this as an act of deference to him but I didn't care. I needed the time to regain my emotional equilibrium. I also doubted that Burke would have been able to bend down that far in his slimly tailored trousers. I stood up and shifted my stance to face Ryan, my ex, now standing too close to me. At the same time, Ryan recognized Edward, "Sorry Edward, didn't recognize you for a moment."

"I didn't realize you two were together again."

I shook my head. "We're not."

"Oh. Well, I need to deliver these. Good to see you both." Edward nodded to Ryan, and then appearing uncomfortable, quickly turned, almost pirouetted and walked away.

Ryan calmly stood there.

"Where's Ashley?"

"Oh… we're separated."

I stepped back. "Separated as in legally separated on the way to divorce, or separated as in I am so pissed off at Ashley I am single for the night?"

He leaned forward and smiled. "You know me too well."

The smile that while its warmth enveloped you told you "we are the only two people in the room and I want you and only you. There is no other woman in the universe for me." And in that moment I believed it. Even though both of us knew it was a lie. He took my arm. We walked in silence to the table.

Handsome, sexy, unavailable men. It was my only real vice. Maybe vice is too strong a word. Is it a vice if you have the compulsion but can act on it very rarely because the supply is so limited? It had never caused me any problems, or more accurately, no serious problems. Although there have been a few times, not unlike being offered one of the richest darkest melt on your tongue bittersweet truffles, when the better judgment part of my brain was bypassed and I had succumbed to it. As I did at this moment. But yielding to temptation only enough to allow my fingers to linger on the curve and hardness of Ryan's upper arm through the thin silk fabric of his shirt, as I accepted his invitation to escort me to my seat. The spell was broken by a welcome sight. Blue eyes, blonde hair falling over his forehead. Smiling face attached to the lanky 6'3" frame. Erik. In his subtly expensive suit.

"Hi guys. Are you all taken care of? Great." Didn't wait for a reply. On autopilot. "I'm having Angie bring a friend over to your table." He looked from Ryan back to me. "Play nice you two." He was making his rounds of the patrons before the start of the program.

"Hi." Angie had quickly produced the friend. "This is Erik's friend Luke Sustern. He wanted you all to meet so I am seating him at your table. This is Erik's sister Mikelena, but we call her Mik, his friend from Yale law school Ryan, and Erik and Mik's cousin Alan who is an Endocrinologist and practices at the University hospital."

Luke shook hands with each of us. My hand was submerged in the size and warmth of his. Usually I had to be careful with any handshake not to dominate whether man or woman, given the size and strength of my own hands, but not this time. We settled into our seats since there were only a few minutes before the speakers were scheduled to start. Luke sat next to me.

"Luke, Erik has spoken highly of you. Aren't you scheduled to give a staff education presentation to the Psychiatry Department at TWF in a few weeks?" I said.

"Yes, I am"

"But you're a detective, right?"

"That's right."

"So…what is it that you do in the liaison work with Psychiatry and TWF"?

"It is a community law enforcement connection. TWF Healthcare is one of the largest health plans and providers of Psychiatry services in San Cortez."

"I'm still not certain what that means in practical terms. What is a community law enforcement connection? Any particular area of interest? Are you domestic violence, gang violence, elder abuse?" I listed off the usual psychiatry - police interfaces.

"Mik," Ryan interrupted, "don't interrogate the poor man." He turned to Luke, "She would have been a prosecuting attorney if she hadn't chosen psychology. Luke's here for social reasons, not professional. Right, Luke?" Luke did not respond to Ryan, and continued focused on me.

"Am I making you uncomfortable with my questions?"

"No, not at all. Your questions are ones that are often asked. The abbreviated version is that I started out in a combined clinical and social psychology doctoral program. After receiving my PhD I did a fellowship 50% time in treatment with a prison population, particularly death row inmates, and the other half in a Domestic Violence Center – a lot of trauma work in both settings."

"Hard core choices."

"It was what was most interesting to me. I am not someone who can sit in session after session while people of privilege complain about their hangnails, or listen to them free associate to the details of their toilet training." There was intensity in Luke's eyes. He had become lost in the emotion of his decision. Even though he must have told this story many times before. The look in his eyes shifted, softened and a slight grin appeared. "Not that that sort of analysis might not be valuable for some people." He stopped for a moment, and then nodded to me.

"By the look on your face, I will assume you share some of my same beliefs or penchant for action oriented interventions."

"As a matter of fact, to some degree I do. But what happened? You don't practice as a psychologist do you?"

"No. I realized I wasn't certain if I believed that people could change or at least certain people – those who commit violent acts. But I could stop some people from hurting others and protect some of the real victims. I know that sounds somewhat naïve - but that was how I made my decision. I entered the police academy and here I am – 95% law enforcement and 5% psychology. A decision I have never regretted. And the answer to your question is not as short as I intended." There was silence at the table.

"I'm impressed."

"Me, too." Angie had lingered after delivering Luke to our table, and she now shifted her gaze away from Luke. "It's almost time to start. I should make certain everything is set up properly," ambivalence in her voice. But being the professional she was, she gave us all a bright smile and walked away.

Luke stood up. "Great to meet you all. I'll be back in a moment, after I grab a cup of coffee."

"I could use a refill myself." Ryan followed Luke and I could see Ryan attempting to place his hand on Luke's shoulder to direct him. Luke easily shrugged it off and placed space between them. Score one for Luke. Gracious, socially adept and unwilling to allow Ryan to do his usual control mode.

I pushed myself back from the table and stretched out my legs, massaging the side of my foot where the shoe strap tended to chafe. I watched Ryan. He hadn't changed in all these years. I met him at a symphony opening gala. He had been walking in front of me to take his seat in the symphony hall, and I inadvertently stepped on the back of his heel. When he turned in surprise, as I stumbled back a bit, my apology caught in my throat. He was stunning. The handsomest man I had ever seen in real life. He graciously accepted my apology, then sought me out at intermission, and asked for my number. Which I gave to him. Compelling evidence that his charisma overwhelmed my good judgment, a pattern that was destined to repeat itself. Even when his self- absorbed demands depleted me over time, our chemistry never changed. But Ryan could only ever truly be in love with Ryan. As he became more controlling of my time and friends, I began to hate him and still wanted to sleep with him. My women friends just hated him. And I could never tell Erik the full story. When I finally broke it off with Ryan, he concluded it was because of my relationship commitment issues. Although it was true that I had difficulty with commitment, in this case it made it easier for him to blame me and give up the pursuit. If I never saw him again, that would have been fine with me but Ryan's long term friendship with Erik made that impossible. Erik tended to overlook Ryan's faults, including what I considered Ryan's creative ethics in his representation of the pharmaceutical company for which he was chief counsel.

There was also the inevitable awkwardness with those who had known us as a couple. The most complicated was with Edward, as evidenced by that quick exit of Edward's tonight. Ryan and I had socialized with Edward a couple of times. Or more accurately Edward and his stepmother, Edward's most frequent date for the Symphony events. Edward had been a staff psychiatrist then, not the chief, and I had enjoyed his intellect and wit. We had in common our workaholism; we were the only ones who were in the clinic at times on Saturdays, me catching up on the week's work and Edward seeing patients. He didn't even use reception staff. He did everything on his own. Remarkably dedicated to patient care. Empathic and caring. One Saturday I was at the clinic, and I had been upset the week prior because a good friend of mine from graduate school had been killed in an auto accident. Edward, without my asking, seeing how tired I appeared, asked if I was sleeping well. When I said "No" he handed me 10 samples of Ambien, a sleeping pill, and he said "We can't have TWF Healthcare therapists falling asleep on the job." We never discussed it, but that act of kindness had stayed with me. Even though he changed so much after that time. And even after he turned in his soul to become Chief.

Laughter from a nearby table interrupted my trek through relationship history and I turned my attention back to present time.

Ryan and Luke were talking next to the dessert tables. Erik was at the main podium. The assembly of speakers up front was ready to go and Angie was ushering the last few stragglers to their tables. Ryan and Luke returned to their seats. I sat through the first speaker talking on the sociology of the homeless, and the economic impact of joblessness. The second was from the VA on the plight of the veterans when they return from war. The third was a clinical researcher, funded by Ryan's company, examining medication trials for treatment of acute and posttraumatic stress disorder. Three speakers and Erik was the discussant. As much as I would have loved to stay to talk more to Luke, not to hear more depressing statistics or have to talk to Burke and Jackman, I could feel the vein above my eye beginning to throb. A migraine on a "school night" was more than I could bear. I knew Erik would forgive me for sneaking out. He often had. I excused myself from the table and headed for the ladies' room, which was thankfully only a short distance from the delivery entrance. I slipped through the doors to the dark outside, and to the air that was cool and dry Fragments of the day's and evening's events tried unsuccessfully to force their way into my consciousness. Images of Ryan and Luke floated in and out. My only thought was the anticipated smooth feel of 350 thread count sheets and the quiet of my own space. I was far too tired for ruminations of any sort. Although I did not usually find the guiding principles of hysterical Southern belles helpful to me, in my current state I could not agree more with Scarlet. After all, tomorrow is another day.

CHAPTER EIGHT

The clanking sound became louder and more insistent. I sat up realizing the sound was outside my bedroom window. Damn garbage truck. What time was it? I checked my clock. I must have hit the snooze button and fallen back to sleep. I had set the alarm earlier than usual to try to connect with Tara at the clinic before the patient onslaught started.

I made it into the clinic early if not as early as I had hoped. "You have 23 new messages, 5 are urgent." A mechanized female voice instructed me to press six to listen. It had taken three cups of espresso and a raised glazed donut to generate enough motivation to pick up my phone and address what was under the blinking red messages waiting light.

Urgent message 1 from Dr. Tara Anderson was received at 1 am today: "Mik. Where are you and why aren't you answering my page? You won't believe what has happened. Shit! It's my pager. I'm on call. I'll call you back later."

Urgent message 2 from Dr. Tara Anderson was received at 2:30 am today: "Mik it's me again. Edward is blaming me for what happened to that young girl and Lizzie told me that you saw her mother today or I guess yesterday by now. I need to know what's going on" Tara's voice was sounding shaky as if on the verge of hysteria. "Call me. Call me as soon as you get this."

Urgent message 3 forwarded by Dr. Burke was received at 5:30 am today. That meant he was working in the early hours of the morning again. "This is a broadcast message to the Department of Psychiatry providers to inform you that the Computer Entry Diagnostic Rates, otherwise known as our CEDAR statistic, was only 85% for the month of August. Our goal has been 95%. The following therapists achieved 100%: kudos to Sarah Stewart & Rachel Bernstein. Ranking at the bottom with less than 70% are David Bowman and James Feinstein. If you need help in increasing your rate, the regional office has CEDAR completer assistance at extension 6500."

This message was urgent? And a "CEDAR completer?" A full time person to help providers enter data? Some of the more lucid individuals might think this an administrative Dilbert moment, but a closer look at the bottom of the psychiatric Petri dish would show the rapid production of a green substance formed into presidential faces---there was money attached to this madness. Omission of an electronic diagnostic entry meant reimbursement at the lowest rate when more money could be obtained by the really good diagnoses such as Major Depression, Bipolar Disorder, or Anorexia Nervosa. I should have hit "skip" or "delete" once I knew it was Edward. His urgent messages generally reflected only his urgent need for sadistic pleasure at amping up his staff's adrenaline. I deleted his message and skipped his next urgent message.

Urgent message 5 was from Tara at 6:45 am: "It's me again. I'm starting to get paranoid that you're avoiding me. I am in my office. Come by as soon as you can." I decided to listen to the rest of the messages later, before Tara became more frantic and showed up at my door.

I walked through the hall maze to Tara's office and knocked. No answer. I knocked louder but no response. I then gently pulled the handle of the door. It was unlocked. I opened it slowly so I wouldn't startle her. As I did I could see Tara lying face down on the industrial carpet with her trench coat draped over her like a blanket.

"Oh my God!" escaped my lips which resulted in Tara raising her head a little as she looked up at me in a daze. Realizing it was me she rolled to face me trapping her in the coat like a straight jacket. "Geez, Tara. Did you sleep here?"

"What time is it?"

"7:15. What happened?"

Tara struggled for a moment, then extricated herself from her coat and stood up, starting to pace. "It is completely awful. I can't tell you all the details now but Edward left a message for me implying that I may be suspended or fired for Jessica Brauer, that 16 year old patient's suicide. I guess her mother left a letter for him. I know you talked to the mother. What did she say? Is she going to sue? Did she name me specifically? I wasn't the only doctor or therapist who saw her you know. I know I wrote the prescription for the antidepressant but it was on Edward's recommendation. He said he screened the patient and he asked me to do him the favor because he had already left the clinic and I was in the evening clinic, so I wrote the prescription and faxed it to the pharmacy. We do that all the time. After I heard what happened I read the chart and he never did see her. He did a phone screening. Now he's saying I violated legal procedure that inevitably led to the patient's death, that he told me to see the patient first, and then prescribe."

"But, Tara-"

"And that this is part of a pattern of negligence and poor clinical judgment, demonstrated by the previous incident of Billy Sanders' death and the lawsuit."

"Tara, look at me" I grabbed her by the shoulders to face me. She stopped pacing for a moment. "That sounds like Burke. He is trying to torture you. He wouldn't follow through with something like that. How many suicides has this clinic had in the past year and no one was fired."

I wasn't certain at all that Edward would not fire her but at this stage a glimpse of reality would have escalated Tara's fears.

"He will fire me."

"What makes you so sure?"

Tara sat down with her hands covering her face.

"What is it Tara? What else has happened?"

There was a long silence. I could barely hear her when she started to speak.

"Remember that conference for the managers last spring when we were all comped hotel rooms for the night?"

"Yes"

She still could not make eye contact with me. "I downed several manhattans. You know I love the cherries in the sweet vermouth."

"Get to it Tara. What happened?"

"The long and ironically the short of it is I had sex with Edward. Only sort of stroking each other and then I gave him a blow job. I was so drunk. He had been drinking too, but not as much. I didn't even know he was straight. Although I'm still not certain he is. We haven't talked about it since but you see how he has treated me over the past several months. I was too disgusted with myself to say anything to you, or anyone. Not even my therapist knows." She finally looked up at me.

I can count on two hands the number of times I have been taken by surprise at someone's disclosure. Patients or friends. I was stunned. At the same time all the odd pieces of behavior related to Tara and Edward now seemed to fall into place with a thunderous thump. The sound of someone's career hitting the floor.

"Are you insane? Sex with the Chief? What were you thinking? Obviously not about your credibility, or violating TWF's rules of physician conduct, or any future advancement. It's professional suicide." I realized I was saying all the wrong things but I could not stop myself. This was beyond bad judgment. It was self-destructive. And Edward ---the thought ----ugh---no---I couldn't even let that image enter my mind or I knew that my entire brain would fry.

"You think I haven't said all those things to myself? But there is another aspect to this, and please don't go off on me. Eva Baker was Jessica Brauer's therapist and she told me the patient had said Edward had been inappropriate with her on the phone, that when he talked about medication with her he told her the antidepressant might decrease her sexual drive and performance, he said 'Which sometimes is a real problem for little Lolitas like yourself' and this was after he asked her lots of detailed questions about her sex life. Not the usual ones we have to ask but Eva said the patient felt he was getting off on it. I saw the note that said Jessica had asked for only female therapists dated after her assessment by Edward, so I believe it's true."

Good Lord. This was only spiraling deeper into what most of us had speculated was part of Edward, but that he usually was careful enough to either keep under others' radar or to make certain the situations would have, he always said laughingly, plausible deniability. He would point out in an arrogant tone that he is a respected psychiatrist with TWF Healthcare for 10 years, a published and sought after speaker, and that his word would always be taken over a lesser known staff member or patients whose reality testing was suspect, simply because they were psychiatric patients.

The Lolita comment rang true. A couple months ago, I had been referred a patient requesting a female psychologist who had been triaged by Edward. The case was a woman in her 40's who had had multiple surgeries for ovarian pain that had not been necessary. When he referred her to me he said "It will be interesting to see who she was raped by----her father or her uncle?"

I had responded that contrary to popular psychoanalytic belief not all female gynecological pain was the result of incest or hysteria. Later that day I saw the patient who in fact had been raped beginning from age eight by her stepfather. I went back to Edward and told him he had been correct this time and told him the specifics. He then responded "well then the next thing we should know is if it was really rape or if she had contributed by being a little Lolita."

"I need to check my messages." Tara was trying to pull herself together and achieve some sense of normalcy.

"Look Tara, go home. You don't have patients until the afternoon. This is your evening clinic day. Get yourself together and come back. Use the remote access code and check your messages from home. If there is anything urgent call me and I'll take care of it. Then you can follow-up this afternoon when you come back. We will sort this out later, I promise." Tara nodded, grabbed her coat and purse, and left out the back exit. I walked back to my office.

I had a few minutes before my first patient, and I reluctantly returned to listening to my messages, beginning with the second urgent message of Edward's that I had previously skipped. I listened with mounting dread. Edward was convening a special quality patient review meeting for an UNO [Unusual Occurrence] to evaluate if there was any deviation from the standard of care in the treatment of Jessica's suicide. Tara was right. He was wasting no time in beginning to make his case. He included me because of my contact with the mother.

Although I was often asked to be in these types of meetings, it was not as the therapist being reviewed. My peers saw me as "someone with spine" because I was not intimidated by authority, although David chose a less gender neutral term to describe me that involved the addition of certain male anatomical features. I checked the time and knew I had to begin seeing patients. The rest of the messages would have to wait. I reviewed my schedule on the computer screen.

My first patient was new to me. Damn. The referring MD was Brach, a long time internal medicine "pool" physician in evening Urgent Care. The pool docs either did not have the requisite medical skill or were queasy about the amount of e-coli exposure from the ass-kissing it took to become an owner in the corporation. In Brach's case it was a little different. My hope was that the patient had caught him on one of his sober days.

His note read: Husband of patient jumped off the Bridge two days ago. Requesting sleep med. Gave patient 10 temazepam, 15 mg, and scheduled appointment in Psychiatry. It appeared that the patient had a little luck in the midst of her current devastating circumstance. Brach indeed was back on one of his recovery tours.

"Mikelena!!" A head popped in around the door molding as Lizzie pushed my office door open enough to see I was there. Trying to contain herself and maintain the proper therapist boundaries by not just walking in but not quite succeeding in her efforts. "Did you hear?

"Hi, Lizzie. Hear what? I have to see a patient in a minute." Lizzie entered the office and set the morning Bay Times on my desk in front of me.

MOTHER OF SUICIDE VICTIM CLAIMS MALFEASANCE IN PRESCRIBING PRACTICES AT TWF HEALTHCARE

"Shit."

"Can you believe it, Mik?"

I was still a bit stunned and distracted after hearing Tara's story but did not want that communicated by Lizzie, who was the good intentioned Paul Revere of the department or perhaps Chicken Little a more apt parallel, who would pass the information on to every other person she talked to today with her whispered request "to keep this in confidence, of course."

"Lizzie, you know the Bay Times is an Enquirer wannabe. They know going after managed care companies is like going after the tobacco companies. People want to hear David and Goliath stories. I think they have a guy on retainer who looks through the trash and hangs around hoping to hear patients' 'TWF Healthcare killed my family member' stories. They didn't waste any time in getting this to press, and I mean including taking the time to check facts."

"I can't believe you're defending TWF Healthcare." Lizzie looked at me more puzzled than offended.

"I'm not. This kind of reporting gives us all a black eye and makes it harder for those patients who need care to contact us for treatment. That's all I'm saying. Let's talk later. I have to see this woman. Her husband suicided off the Bridge and he was a patient of one of the new psychiatrists, James."

"As long as it wasn't one of mine." Lizzie tossed back at me as she exited my office.

Now that was a universal therapist thought. Not my patient. Not on my watch. Any time one of us heard on the news or learned that a patient suicided or God forbid killed someone else and themselves. Each of us would worry to varying degrees that it might be one of ours. Not only for the lives lost, but also the potential impact of license and livelihood lost if the State Board judged one of us negligent or incompetent in the treatment of the patient. Professional self-preservation was as high a priority as professional competence in our field.

I had allowed the session to run long – over an hour. The patient left my office after the visit somewhat shored up. I hoped. As a new patient to me, I had to figure out how stable she was before her husband suicided, and then allow her to talk about it sufficiently to feel some relief. She did not use one tissue – no tears, but able to talk about what she felt. No anger yet but that would come. It had to, for any of this to resolve as completely as possible. The scar from this deep a wound would inevitably remain. She requested to continue with me and I agreed to take her into my case load and scheduled a return appointment for next week. I could never transfer a patient to another therapist after they had talked with me when it was this kind of tragedy. It seemed cruel to me, although it was not uncommon anymore at TWF. The therapist completing the formal initial intake assessment would refer the patient to a different therapist for treatment. Forcing someone to start over telling this type of story, when the pain was so fresh was unacceptable to me. Rachel, Charles, and Lizzie all felt the same way. I started writing notes longhand for myself about the session, specific words the patient used and some of my hypotheses about her emotional underpinnings. The type of notes not appropriate for a medical chart, but helped me reengage more quickly in the next visit. Life is in the details. As is death.

A quick knock and a forceful push of my office door. And there he was. Jackman. Walked in and stood right next to my desk. "Mikelena" his voice volume always in the red zone. I pushed my chair back but it only moved a few inches before it was blocked by the edge of my desk and I was stuck where I was.

"Glad I caught you. I need to talk with you. You met with Mrs. Brauer."

"What?"

"I heard you did crisis intervention with the mother of a former patient."

"You mean the Dr. Brauer whose daughter Jessica suicided. Whose family is suing Tara and Burke?"

"Oh yes," he said, "She does make a point of that doctor of education degree. She is a family friend. It was unfortunate that her daughter died when I was on vacation."

While he was on vacation? I thought. Erik's often used phrase "Blow me" came into my mind. Jackman's self-centered focus was extreme and tiresome. It took much more time to get to whatever was the important patient information, but I couldn't just ignore him. "What do you mean? While you were on vacation?"

"Not only is she an acquaintance of mine but I had effectively treated Jessica for her pain conditions. If I had been here when Mrs. Brauer came into the clinic, I'm certain I could have prevented her from going to the papers. Although I'm sure you did your best." He stepped back but only to place one foot up on the ottoman by my chair so that his crotch was elevated to within a foot of my face. A typical Jackman pose – everybody who started working with him soon learned to arrange their office furniture to prevent this, but today I was unprepared. My response to Jackman shifted from annoyance to loathing.

There was a rumor that Jackman's first wife had a "Boogie Nights" fixation on large physical attributes, so Jackman had a penile implant to accommodate her. Two years later she left him and his implant, and his residual habit of frequently adjusting himself. There was not a chance I was remaining in a subordinate position to Jackman or his implant to discuss this.

"Excuse me, Bruce." I picked up a file and stood up which forced Jackman to move back, and my 5'8" height with two inch heels added meant he was no longer in the dominant position and I would not have to be the object of his everyone should admire me world stance. Jackman's physical appearance always seemed off somehow in a way difficult to explain. He had a square jaw, long chin. His head was too big for his body. He appeared as someone who tried too hard to sculpt himself and ended up looking artificial and disjointed. His face was almost handsome in a Batman "Bruce Wayne" fashion but with his short legged body he had a Tasmanian devil look. Cartoon characters. The fact that cartoon characters described him most accurately reflected the oddness of his persona. Jackman brought in so much money and positive press for TWF Healthcare that he was untouchable.

Although many patients loved him, when he received a complaint, the interpretation was always the patient's misunderstanding or personality disorder. A few years ago one of his female physician's assistants filed a complaint against him with Human Resources for his inappropriate comments about her body, including a statement he had made one day after lunch when she came in from the unusually high summer temperature outside with her face flushed, that she looked "like a heifer in heat ready to be mounted" and he "had the right sized equipment to take care of her."

Jackman denied that he had made the statement about the physician assistant's body, saying she was angry with him because he had turned down her advances to him. He explained the specific heifer comment as her fabrication using the public statements he had made about his time as a cowboy on a cattle ranch outside Houston to make it look believable. There had been no witnesses, or more accurately, no witnesses willing to risk their job for someone else's. TWF Healthcare's investigation concluded it was a personality conflict and simply encouraged Jackman to be more sensitive. The staff member was transferred to another department, and Jackman hired one of his former female assistants who thought he walked on water and life went on as usual. Jackman's vulgar statements about women's bodies became expected. We all tried to avoid it. It was like stepping on gum stuck to a sun heated sidewalk. It wouldn't harm you, but it was disgusting and difficult to fully rid yourself of the sticky residue of expectorate.

"I have a patient arriving soon and I need to read the chart. I discussed this already with Edward, and as I understand it, he has taken care of the political issues. I am more concerned about why the young women died and what we could have done to prevent it."

Jackman's interpersonal veneer was already wearing through. "Of course that is what we all want to know. Although you realize that if someone wants to kill themselves, there is nothing anyone can do to stop them."

"Glad to hear we are both working toward the same goal." I extended my hand to indicate the conversation was over. Jackman took it, gave it a firm shake, and walked out.

I grabbed my neutral lip gloss in my desk drawer, and started to run it over my lips. What was that smell? No scent from the lip gloss container, but my right hand smelled odd – perhaps a spice I couldn't identify. Jackman. I shook his hand and who knows what he ate for lunch, or for that matter whatever activity he had been engaging in prior to entering my office. He also used various "heat" type gels with his patients and for his own chronic pain from some old knee injury. I didn't want to know what it was. I grabbed the hand sanitizer in my drawer, and thoroughly removed any possible Jackman contaminant. It was a relief to return to focusing on the chart of my next patient.

The last patient of the day was Stacy. A woman in her late 20's who had been referred from a friend. I had seen her once before. She was thin, pretty, single and considering becoming a nun. She wore an oatmeal colored cotton dress with low heeled shoes and she arranged herself in the chair so that her presence was as small as possible. There was a certain emotional heaviness to her, as if she had been burdened from the beginning of her life. She talked with almost no inflection, no change in tone. She needed to have her decision to become a nun be an emotionally free one, to embrace it if she chose but not because it was the only future she could imagine being able to survive in. Her depth of sadness was compelling to me as a therapist, wanting to help her but knowing I could not help her here. Not in the short term treatment of the TWF system. She required three to five years of individual therapy. This often sounded like a prison sentence when I said it. It was hard to explain that this kind of change was similar to the learning that occurs in college. Although it made sense to people to spend years in college, years of therapy was perceived as an indulgence or luxury. I hated this part of working at TWF. I had to tell her that I couldn't provide what she needed. That it isn't her, it's the health care system. I had to do it today. Prolonging it would be - what had Edward once said? It was like delaying cutting off a gangrenous leg when you know it had to be done. That gruesome analogy stayed with me partly because I knew it was true. Twenty minutes was left in the visit.

"Stacy, we need to talk about your next step in treatment."

"What do you mean?" She started chewing on her thumbnail.

"Remember when we talked before about what TWF covers and doesn't cover – that it does not provide long term therapy. The coverage is only for brief work?"

"Yes, but you also said we could see what we could accomplish together."

"I did and I can tell you now that what I can provide in TWF is not what you need. You need consistent longer term work. Longer than six months. I believe you will feel happier and making your decisions and your way in life will be less difficult. You will begin to have a feeling of freedom in your life."

"But I trust you. I know you can help me."

"I know this is disappointing and frustrating, but there are other therapists who can help you. I would not be doing the right thing by you if I continued to work in brief therapy when I know you need something else. You have spent your life around people who were supposed to do the right thing in caring for you but they didn't. I am not willing to be one of those. There are a number of good therapists in the community" I reached over to my folder with lists of private practice therapists and sliding fee clinics. "I will continue to see you until you connect with one of them that you feel comfortable with. This is a list of those who I know are competent."

Stacy's tears and runny nose were continuing unchecked, a liquid suspension bridge starting to form from her chin to her top of her dress. She wiped her forearm across her face, grabbed the list from my hand, and walked to the door without speaking.

"Stacy, there is still time left in our visit."

"No, there's not. Thank you." She shut the door behind her.

My chest tightened as though someone had dropped a hundred pound sack of grain on me. I was suffocating. Would Stacy be okay? I wasn't certain anymore in the way I had been; there is a confidence born of ignorance and arrogance early in a therapist's career. If you have a talent for the profession you become more skilled, more experienced, and make better decisions over time. And you become less certain. Because you know so much more of what is out of your control. I believe Stacy will be okay. In the same way I had believed Billy Sanders would be okay. And I had been wrong. But you can't save everyone. Or anyone. People save themselves. Was that true or a rationalization therapists use to help them sleep at night?

Careers function like many marriages. After 7 to 10 years most people want something different, even if they don't know why or what it is they want. Just not what they have. Some stay. Some leave. Others leave emotionally but stay physically. Was that happening to me or was it the TWF system? Maybe, but I had an immediate problem of patient charting to complete. I entered an electronic reminder note to call Stacy tomorrow check on her status. In her first visit she said she had once heard someone say that 'happy endings are just stories that haven't ended yet." She asked if I believed that. I told her I believed there were, but that life was more a series of chapters, beginnings and endings. I don't think she was convinced.

I continued with my charting until I finished the formal notes. I needed to get out of my office. Even for a brief diversion. I thought about the legal issues with Tara and Lizzie's recent reactions about the TWF bad press. I decided to engage in a bit of counter phobic behavior, or I like to think of it as the only thing my tennis coach had been able to teach me in my few ill-fated tennis lessons. I can still see his huge hairy thighs and hear his frustrated voice: "Stop running from the ball. You are supposed to move toward it. For God's sake, step into the shot." As instructed, I would step into the shot. I decided to stop by Edward's office. I had not talked with him since our encounter at Erik's fundraiser. I took a deep breath and started in Edward direction. When I arrived at his door, it was closed, although I knew he had no patients scheduled. As I leaned forward to see if I could hear voices, the door opened and David walked out, eyes down, face red. No acknowledgement that I was there. Edward then appeared with a little self-satisfied smile on his face.

"Mikelena, what can I do for you?"

I had a flash of Tara, on her knees in front of him, his long fingers grabbing her hair and moving her head back and force. That image could sell equally well as an appetite suppressant or an emetic.

"Edward. Did you see this?" I pulled the paper out from under my arm. He did not change expression. Not a flicker. Immune to the crime show trick of confronting the unsuspecting guilty party to elicit a reaction.

"Mainwaring in Legal and Schwartz in PR are already handling this. And I'm certain you've seen my e-mail by now." He said this as he adjusted his name badge more centrally. It now covered the little designer emblem on his jacket. As if the suicide and lawsuit were mere nuisances, easily dealt with and dismissed. I had not yet read his e-mail. I also did not feel up to acknowledging any lack of compulsiveness in reading my e-mail. Edward always had his e-mail inbox open right behind his TWF Healthcare schedule on his computer screen, and had encouraged all his staff to do the same. There was no point in responding to him.

"You know," Edward continued, "I recently started a new lifting regimen at the gym and have found it quite energizing. Doing my part in the fight against obesity. I feel it is often more powerful for patients to see that I practice what I preach in preventive medicine than to simply tell them what they should be doing. Wouldn't you agree?" Edward shifted his focus to me as if he had just noticed I was there.

That question didn't deserve a response. I glanced at my watch. "I better get to my next patient. See you." I started to walk back to my office with Edward's words in my head. The cut of his biceps as a thinly disguised contribution to the "obesity epidemic." I always knew he was arrogant and self-centered. But as he continued to gain power in TWF, he no longer had any use for compassion or other human qualities, as if there was a finite amount of space in his psyche and the parts that made him human were being deleted.

CHAPTER NINE

The e-mail from Edward with the prominent CONFIDENTIAL stamp in the subject line had been sent at 2:00am. He had sent it to me, Tara, Eva, Tiffany (one of the new crisis triage staff who was unlicensed), James (psychiatrist), William, who was the Designated Psychiatry Quality Representative, Bruce Jackman, as Chief of the Pain Program, as well as Gary Brown, lead counsel of medical legal risk management for the facility.

A mandatory UNO peer review meeting has been called for Thursday at 9am to 11am, regarding the patient JB, Quality #57690993. We will meet in Conference Room 2. You are required to attend.

Hmmm, I thought, a little redundant. Required to attend and mandatory. Edward was in one of his increasingly frequent controlling "I am in charge and you will do what I say" modes. He was acting quickly to clear up the mess around Jessica's suicide and make it go away, particularly with all the bad press coverage.

Please bring all materials in your possession related to this patient or her family. Thank you in advance for your participation in examining this unfortunate incident.

Had Tara seen the message yet? I called Tara's number but her voicemail came on immediately, meaning she was on the phone. As I hesitated, wondering whether to hang up and call back or leave a message, there was a knock at my door. I stretched the phone cord as I opened the door, a technique I had perfected so that I could open the door enough to see who was there. It would look like I was on the phone so that if it was someone I didn't want to talk to I would place my hand on the receiver, tell them I was on the phone but I would call them and then just motion them away. It kept away many of the terminally chatty new hires who "wanted to connect and get to know me," because their schedules were not full yet. It was Amanda, who knew this ruse and simply pushed open the door and walked in. I hung up the phone.

"Mikelena, what's wrong with Tara?" Never one to observe social convention, Amanda stepped over the usual introductory 'How are you?' fake niceties right into what she wanted to know. I usually liked this about her.

"What do you mean?"

Amanda looked irritated. "Why don't you tell me you don't want to tell me? I think someone needs to do something because three of her patients asked me if she is ill. You know Tara's patients generally love her, and they didn't want to get her into trouble so they asked me and didn't go to Patient Services to complain."

"Did they say why they were concerned?"

"Not at first, but I asked of course."

Of course she did, I thought, particularly since Tara was not high on Amanda's favorite person list. Tara had been the person to report her a few years ago for her side business of facials on company premises, and although Tara had tried to mend the rift Amanda did not forgive certain transgressions, particularly where money was concerned. "And?"

"Well, two of them said she seemed distracted and not listening. Another said he thought she was asleep in the visit at one point, but when he said something she said she found it useful sometimes to close her eyes to focus more clearly on hearing what he was saying. I don't think he bought it although you could tell part of him was flattered that he thought she was doing that because he was special."

"How has she seemed to you, Amanda?"

"She doesn't seem herself, and I thought if you didn't know, you should." Her expression communicating she already thought I knew. "Someone needs to talk to her before she gets in trouble."

"Did you tell Edward about the patient concerns?"

"Not yet. I though you could give me some direction."

Now I got it. Amanda didn't want to take responsibility for narcing on Tara, but she knew that I would do something if there was a concern about patient care. Amanda had done this same thing to me a number of times when she was first hired. In my naiveté and zealous Dudley Do-Right attitude I had at the time, I responded like the proverbial Pavlovian dog. She rang the bell and I salivated in the prospect of "doing the right thing to save patients.'" The therapist she was concerned about was generally chosen based on who had most recently "done her wrong" and were usually minor problems embellished to appear serious. She got to be the good guy and I looked like the clinic police. I learned not to respond and I generally encouraged her "to do what she thought was best." But this time was more complicated and the stakes much higher for Tara.

"I know Tara has had a couple of nasty viruses that have hung on so I know she has been more tired." I wondered if Amanda knew I was making it up as I went along. I always looked directly at the person when doing what I call embroidering the truth, and most people would believe me. However, I knew it was a risk with Amanda and as I looked at her I could see she wasn't buying it.

"I know what people are like when they're sick, Mikelena. I told you in the beginning you can just tell me you can't tell me what's going on."

Right. Then Amanda can spread there is something going on so serious Mikelena refused to talk about it. Something about this was like the "When did you stop beating your wife? question. "I don't know. It's kind of you to be concerned, Amanda. There are many potential stressors in this clinic. For all of us. And speaking of that, are you feeling okay these days Amanda? How's your back?" Giving free rein for Amanda to discuss her aches and pains was too enticing for her, and she immediately launched into her latest MRI, her new areas of pain in her feet, her knees and neck. Overriding for the moment her wish to dig up dirt on Tara and spread it around the clinic.

CHAPTER TEN

"Let's try that new restaurant End of the Alphabet that William was raving about last week." Every few months Lizzie encouraged our first Wednesday of the month lunch group that consisted of Lizzie, Tara, Rachel and me to experiment with a new restaurant.

"I'm in." I was ready for something different.

"This time it's okay, as long as we can go back to Rose's Cafe next time." Rachel never wanted to try a new place.

"Great. Let's go." Lizzie handed me the address she had already written down in case we agreed to her plan.

"Thanks. Rachel and I will meet you there. I'll call Tara on her cell to make certain she knows where we're meeting."

Rachel and I arrived first. "The End of the Alphabet" was furnished with basic geometric shaped furniture in primary colors, and large letters of the alphabet scattered about. We ordered at the front, and were given instructions to take our designated letter to the table and we would see it start blinking and play a brief melody when the order was ready. I ordered the bacon, grilled tomatoes, fried egg with melted mozzarella on thin slices of toasted bread, with a large cup of coffee. Sandwiches, salads soups – a solid lunch crowd gamble.

It only took minutes after we sat down for the letter Y to start blinking in three primary colors and we heard a MIC KEY Y because we like you portion of the Mickey Mouse club song. Tara had not yet arrived, but we were used to one or more of us arriving late or sometimes not at all.

"This restaurant owner has a developmental problem of early childhood, or a peculiar attachment to their kindergarten teacher," Lizzie gave her opinion between large bites of her multi layered vegetarian sandwich, adding "However, I am in love."

"With the sandwich or the place," I asked.

"Both. You know I am not monogamous in my food or restaurant relationships."

"Not monogamous? That is, at best, an understatement."

"Are you calling me a food whore, Mik?"

"Are you calling yourself a food whore? "

"I'm thinking that being surrounded by the trappings of kindergarten induces regressive states such as the 'I am rubber you are glue. Your words bounce off me and stick to you' type. So what are this week's headlines? I'll start."

We had a short amount of time so we established the practice of each giving the top two personal or work highlights or lowlights of the week. Sometimes we talked more about them or not, but it helped us stay connected as friends even when we hardly spoke to each other at the busiest times at TWF.

"I wonder if Tara's going to make it" Rachel checked her watch.

"I thought she was coming today. She's been so busy with the big guns of TWF, I rarely talk to her. She left me a message earlier today saying she would be late, but not this late. We have to get back in 20 minutes." As she talked, Lizzie stuffed the end of a dill pickle in between the final bites of her sandwich.

"Speak of the devil." We checked out where Lizzie was looking. Tara was visible through the glass front door, and with her long strides she quickly reached our table.

"I didn't think I was going to make it."

"I'm not certain you did. I don't think you have time to order and get back on time"

Tara looked at the cubed shape clock with its Crayola crayon hands located on the wall immediately to the left of our table.

"I have a half sandwich I am not going to eat and I was planning to give it away anyway so you can have it Tara," Rachel handed the napkin wrapped sandwich to her.

"That's great. I'll get a cherry coke and be right back." Tara gave the clerk a $5 bill for the $2 drink and dismissed the change offered with a wave of her hand, returning to the table. Rachel had already pulled up a chair and arranged lunch for Tara.

"Thanks, guys." Tara started to hand Rachel a ten dollar bill, knowing Rachel would never accept it, as she didn't today and Tara put it back in her billfold.

"What happened, Tara?" Rachel handed her a napkin.

Tara looked around the restaurant, to verify there was no one in the room from TWF. "This is a great choice. No eavesdropping colleagues or managers."

"Or patients" Lizzie added as she continued to clear her plate, pressing her fingertips to the remaining crumbs on her heavy plastic plate tilting it to the light to make certain she did not miss any.

"This is confidential. You can't tell anyone."

"Yes, Tara, we know. What is it?"

We were all paying attention now. Those of us who were the non-MDs, as we were labeled in TWF, were kept out of the closed circle of power and we were always looking for an opening, or peephole to view the inner workings. With Tara we had a glimpse at times. But when she was enraged the view to forbidden sights was the size of a wide screen TV.

"We just had a psychiatry TWF owners meeting. Burke is still barking about the finances and that we all will have to perform at a higher standard to demonstrate our value to the organization. I'm letting you know we are going to have to work harder, see more patients, especially crisis patients. But this will be good for our patients and the future of TWF, which is our future too."

Lizzie was rolling her eyes at this.

"What do you mean work harder?" Rachel sounded frustrated.

"Rachel, you're working hard but not everyone is and not everyone is diagnosing properly so we are losing money, and we're required to see crisis patients within two weeks. We can't be on the bottom third of the medical centers."

"Wait. We need to perform, demonstrate our value?"

"Keep your voice down, Lizzie."

"Don't tell me what to do. Don't tell any of us what to do."

"I'm not. You want me to tell you, but then you get pissed off at me."

"I don't want to be fed the corporate line. You're supposed to be our friend. This is the same bullshit we got from Burke in the staff meeting. Have you started drinking the Kool-Aid at those big TWF partners meeting? Or have you and Burke become joined at the hip? Or perhaps joined by other body parts?"

"Wait, Lizzie." I tried to prevent where we all knew this was going.

"No, I won't. It's your bonus, Tara that is on the line. Your profit sharing. You and the rest of the TWF MD psychiatrists get bonuses while the non-MD therapists in the Department get no money and more work. Ever since you became Assistant Chief, you've been different. What happened to you? You don't give a rat's ass anymore about the patients or us."

"Stop it. The two of you." I stood up between them. "This is not a battleground. You're on the same side. Act like it."

"I have to leave anyway." Lizzie moved away from the table and then grabbed the jacket off the back of her chair. "I'll see you later." She didn't look at Tara.

"Sorry, Tara" Rachel had picked up her purse to leave. "You know Lizzie never means what she says. She's stressed and overwhelmed."

"She's also a bitch." Tara was furious. "Can't you talk to her, Mik? She won't admit it but she still thinks I had something to do with her ex coming on to me at the Christmas party last year."

I had had enough. I didn't need this kind of drama on my time away from TWF. Tara had become oblivious to what the rest of us knew. Lizzie was the one expressing the feelings of most of the non-MD therapists. Her anger had nothing to do with her ex and the party, but everything to do with what Tara represented in TWF. And Tara didn't want to see that.

"Let it go, Tara. I'm leaving now, too. Are you coming?"

"No, Mik. I think I will stay awhile. Maybe order dessert."

"I'm sorry I can't stay, Tara," Rachel was reluctant to leave.

"It's fine, Rachel. I'll be fine. I just need to decompress. "

"Then we'll see you back at the clinic. Call me if you want to talk," Rachel added.

Not something I would have offered, but Rachel often stayed upset when her friends were upset, and liked to have closure. We drove in silence back to the department. I was grateful the rest of the day went by quickly with no further drama. I knew the UNO meeting tomorrow would likely provide more.

CHAPTER ELEVEN

The sign on the conference room door could not be missed:

DO NOT DISTURB
UNO Peer Review Meeting 9am-11am

In 36 point type font in the dark green color of the TWF Healthcare signature tree brand. Edward was the only one in the room, seated at the far side of the round table. Psychiatry chose round tables for its conference rooms to represent that we all were equal in our value and were all part of a circle of care. I regularly wished that if management could put as much energy into patient care as they did in their symbolic choices of colors and furniture, things could change. A stack of papers and charts were to Edward's right. The black folder on his left. Always a black folder. The color of death. It contained the coroner's report and police report. Six empty chairs were at the table.

I was always early, though never as early as Edward. I nodded to Edward, and chose a seat a few chairs to the side of him out of his direct line of sight. I had thought about meeting Tara for coffee this morning to help support her. I had even tried a couple of times to reach her but her line had been busy. Probably better I couldn't get in touch with her. I would not be any good to her in this meeting if it looked like I was supporting her out of friendship and not in an objective clinical way. It was a balancing act. Even though I was not on the chopping block, I still felt a sense of dread in the pit of my stomach. Maybe I could catch Tara at her office. I pushed my chair back when I heard voices in the hall. Those of Tara and Eva I recognized. The third voice was louder and unfamiliar.

So much for my plan. The door opened and the person entering first was a tall woman in a black pin stripe suit with what I always still think of as a flight attendant rolling luggage cart with brief case and a box of materials stacked on it. The clear indication of legal involvement. Tara entered after her with Eva. Tara was calm and dressed to kill. I greeted her and looked at her with the obvious question on my face. What was going on? Tara looked away and walked up to Edward.

"I would like you to meet my attorney, Natalie Heaton of Heaton, Sheraton and Blaine. She is here to protect my rights, since you requested TWF Legal counsel attend this meeting as well."

I had never seen Edward surprised. Until now. He recovered quickly from the lapse in his usual emotional rigor mortis, ignored Tara, and extended his hand to the attorney.

"Ms. Heaton, I believe you have been misinformed. Let me clarify. Today's meeting as you can see, he motioned toward the sign visible on the still partially open door, is a peer review regarding an unfortunate incident with a patient. It is not yet clear what happened or if there was any problem whatsoever with the care. I can't tell you more than that or it would be a breach of confidentiality. I also hope that no TWF Healthcare information regarding one of our members was passed to you, since that would be a breach of patient privilege. And that we do take most seriously. Such behavior, if it occurred, not saying of course that it has, would be actionable."

As Edward was talking the rest of those required to be in the meeting had filtered in, including TWF Healthcare counsel, Gary Brown. "He's right." William and Brown said simultaneously. William wisely deferred to Brown who continued, "We also cannot allow unnecessary exposure of information to an outside party. As I'm, sure you know, Ms…"

"Heaton. Having a memory lapse Gary? The name is the same as it has been in our previous meetings."

We were all aware of Heaton's reputation for representing Psychiatry staff in the past. Her area of law was labor law and particularly well known for her sexual discrimination suits against TWF. She won more than she lost, and she was known for her tenacity. Brown took the hit, cleared his throat and continued, "That would be a violation of federal HIPAA regulations, the Department of Managed Care Corporations' standards and state laws governing patient-doctor privilege."

It was clear to Ms. Heaton that there was no point in attempting to intimidate or bluff at this point. You could see that she was attempting to reconcile what Tara must have told her, with the evidence in front of her, but as with every attorney I have known, not at a loss for words.

"I appreciate your clarification. And of course Dr. Anderson would never breach confidentiality. I do want you to know, however, that if you have misrepresented this situation, or take action detrimental to my client without my knowledge, those breaches are taken seriously by me and my office. As you well know, Mr. Brown." Before Brown could reply she extended her hand again to Burke, nodded to Tara and leaned over to whisper something to her. Then artfully turned the luggage cart and walked out the door.

Edward picked up the conference room internal phone attached to the wall, punched in the number for security. "There is brunette woman in a navy suit, Ms.Heaton, an attorney, on site. Can you please make certain she finds her way safely to her car? Thank you." True to form, Edward was taking no chances that the attorney might take a wrong turn and find herself in the patient chart room.

"Well, sorry for the delay. Let's get started. Everyone know each other?" We all nodded.

"I've outlined the process for today," Edward handed out copies of the agenda. "First, let me say what a tragedy it is when we lose a patient. And particularly someone as young as Jessica. I am certain there are feelings that need to be processed, but this meeting today is a formal review and Jerold, who you all know as our employee assistance psychologist, personally assured me that he will make himself available to assist any staff member who would like to discuss this more. Any questions related to emotionally processing this event? If not, then let's continue. We will review both the paper and electronic chart data, as well as include the pharmacy information in the PHAD computer system. Eva, if you would go next, review you contacts with the patient, then Tiffany on her crisis service, Tara, Mikelena, a brief summary from Bruce since his recent involvement is minimal – mostly to contribute history of the pain treatment, and then we will hear from Gary as to his legal risk assessment and conclude with any questions, discussion and a plan for next steps. Is this acceptable to everyone?"

Edward did not wait for an answer and was already putting up a chart of the electronic visits and diagnosis for Jessica. The more I looked at it, the more it looked wrong to me. But I couldn't figure out why. Was it because it had been enlarged from 8 and a 1/2 x 11inches to 3 feet by 4 feet? Even though I only saw her history once and that was with an emotional mother in the same room, my visual memory was usually good. I also had been told you couldn't alter the electronic record. You could amend it but not eliminate it without something showing up. Tampering with the medical record? If that had happened, then there was something damning that someone, perhaps Edward? had to hide.

I knew it had happened in the past with a patient's paper chart. I knew it because I had been part of it. Not something I was proud of. When I first started at TWF Healthcare I had been compulsive about my notes being done correctly with the proper diagnoses.

But one time due to overload, distraction, sleep deprivation, I never knew what, I mistakenly wrote the diagnosis of Bipolar Disorder in my initial intake note instead of Adjustment Disorder with Depressive Features.

Months later the patient's records were subpoenaed in a custody battle lawsuit. It had been William, who had been treating the patient's child, who came to me with the discrepancy, before the chart was to be copied. We both knew how disastrous it could be for the patient to have the much more severe diagnosis of Bipolar, given that it could potentially be used against her. We decided to "fix" the record, to make it accurate. I rewrote the entire intake note with the correct diagnosis, and since this was before the electronic record, replacing the original note with the new one took care of it. Ten years ago, William and I were the two therapists most often identified by our peers as adhering most rigidly to the ethics and laws dictated by our license. Each of us was often sought out for consultation on complicated cases for direction, sometimes even by the Chief. Later on, after the case we had altered was settled, but needed to be reviewed more pro forma due to the legal issues of the custody hearings, William and I sat across from each other as we answered the questions put to us, on the record, about the diagnoses, documentation. William watched as I lied and I watched as William lied, each of us aware we were considered moral exemplars for the other staff. It becomes a slippery slope when you begin to pick and choose which ethical principles you will follow. The case was resolved. It remained our secret.

"I know this is a professional meeting but I thought everyone could use a little help with the stress so I brought in the left over brownies I had made for my church's bake sale last night." Tiffany smiled as she passed the plate of frosted chocolate chip brownies to

William on her left who eagerly snagged two of them, placing one on a piece of paper next to his coffee cup. As Tiffany began her description of what had happened on the crisis desk, I looked more closely at the others around the table. No one was listening to her, which was the usual response to her, brownies or not. Tiffany was not yet licensed, operating under Lizzie's license with the Behavioral Sciences Board. I often wondered why they had chosen Tiffany to hire. I knew she wasn't the only candidate for the position. Perhaps it was because she looked like a Dresden doll, or that she fawned over her supervisors and Edward, and every day brought cookies she had personally baked "for her special team." I glanced over at William focused on licking the last bits of frosting off his fingers. What was I thinking? Of course that would be reason enough. My main difficulty with her was that by the time information had gone through all the daisy petals, little hearts, and smiley faces inside her head, it almost never resembled the initial data. As a result, I was always double checking my referrals to the crisis desk to make certain the patient received the appropriate care. And her assessments of patients she referred to me from the crisis desk, I read, but fully reassessed each patient.

Tiffany was concluding her initial contact with Jessica, "I remember thinking she was such a sweet girl, but troubled and with no family support. That mother of hers was so mean to me over the phone. I can't imagine how that girl lived with her. And then I gave the patient information sheet to Dr. Burke, since it was a request for medication for an adolescent. That's all I have." Tiffany started to get up from her chair. "Oh, I hope it's okay if I leave now. My little daughter Ashley is sick, and I have to pick her up from my mother's and take her to the doctor." No one responded.

As she left the room, Edward began his part of the review. "I read through the chart and her electronic data and then spoke to the patient directly, and determined that medication might indeed be useful. I reviewed the possible side effects with the patient, directed her to talk to her mother also about the medication, identified the pharmacy that was most convenient for the family, and then referred her to be seen in evening clinic for further evaluation by Dr. Anderson, as you can see by the dated entry."

"I'd like to clarify that entry" Tara cut in, "That was not the discussion we had, Edward. My note indicates you requested a prescription for the antidepressant to be sent to the Lincoln pharmacy, not for me to see the patient. And since you had said you had seen the patient, I thought it was a covering psychiatrist request to prescribe, not to evaluate again."

Edward gently leaned forward toward Tara, looking concerned and puzzled. In a tone he usually reserved for his patients age six and under "Now, Tara, you know that's not accurate. I am aware you have not been up to your usual exceptional level of care recently, and there has been concern for you expressed by your colleagues and patients. Particularly with your large panel of complicated patients coupled with the nasty viruses you have had in the past few weeks. Perhaps that has clouded your perception or memory. I know I have been clear that we have to see patients before we prescribe, particularly after that unfortunate lawsuit in the Pear Valley Region."

I felt my face flush as I realized Amanda must have taken my conversation with her regarding Tara to Edward, practically word for word. I could not believe Amanda would be that vicious. She must have been really pissed off. She simultaneously nails Tara and takes a swipe at me. How frighteningly efficient of her.

"Viruses? What are you talking about?"

"Well, that's what I had heard from staff. You did go home sick the other day after you had been on-call? Isn't that correct?"

"Don't you remember Tara?" Eva spoke up for the first time. "I saw you in the hall and you said you thought you might have a touch of the flu and you were going home."

Tara's looked blank for a moment. Her newly reconstituted defenses started to strip away as she realized it wasn't only Edward but other staff who were questioning her judgment. Now I started to wonder. What if Tara had not heard Edward's message correctly? What if he was telling the truth? Tara believes she heard what she heard. I believed that. She wasn't lying. But maybe she got it wrong.

"Well there appears to be a difference of opinion as to what happened at the point of the prescription that does not appear we can resolve at this time. Let us move forward. Dr. Jackman, please provide us with your contact and history with the patient."

"Certainly. As you know I have been working with young athletes in the chronic pain and orthopedics department. Which is how I had contact with Jessica. She was quite typical of the overachieving young women who have high expectations of themselves in all areas, including athletics. She also had a stressful family life. With both parents quite demanding and critical. I knew the mother because of a family connection, but we were not close friends. I saw Jessica for regular pain management along with a physical therapist for a period of about four months. She made progress. I did not track her after that. Treatment ended six months before she committed suicide."

"But she was still receiving the pain medications, the neurontin, and vicodin?"

"I always release the patient to the internal medicine or family practice physician or psychiatrist as relevant when the patient has completed the formal program. It prevents the 'too many cooks spoiling the stew' phenomenon."

"Thank you Dr. Jackman. Your part of the treatment seems quite straightforward. Let's move on." Burke continued with his review of the patient's chart. Eva gave her usual vague description of her treatment. She was never outright dangerous in what she did with patients but always seemed on the verge of incompetence. Tara was listening, taking notes. She was holding the pencil so tightly her fingers were white, but she said nothing. The meeting continued with each person providing information including my brief description of the interaction with the patient's mother.

"I will need to take the summary of our meeting to the Facility Management Quality Group for their final decision regarding any violation of quality of care standards. I will contact anyone I feel needs to provide additional information. Thank you." The meeting was over.

CHAPTER TWELVE

"Mikelena, Mikelena" Lizzie called down the hall as she tried to speed up her petite form to catch me before I shut the door to my office.

"What, Lizzie?"

"What happened in there? I saw the attorney and I can't believe Tara pulled a stunt like that." Lizzie's dismay had a hint of satisfaction to it. Schadenfreude. One of my psychoanalytic supervisors called it. Webster defines it as "Satisfaction or pleasure found in others misfortune." Lizzie's face displayed it.

"The meeting just finished. Didn't Tara tell you about this?"

"No. I know why the meeting was called but Amanda said she saw that attorney leave the clinic. The one who represented those two therapists against Burke and TWF Healthcare for unlawful termination."

I unlocked my file cabinet, and began checking my schedule on the computer. "Lizzie, my patient light is on. I can't talk now. I have a patient waiting."

"I have a patient waiting too. Let them wait. This is more important. And as David always says 'If TWF Healthcare patients want better treatment they should get a better health plan.' You know why Edward is doing this to Tara, don't you?"

I paused in my reading through my waiting patient's chart. Did Lizzie know something or was she fishing? "What do you mean?" I looked up and held Lizzie's gaze, trying to detect signs of a bluff.

"You're kidding, right? Amanda told me she was sure you knew what was going on because you were so defensive the other day when she told you about Tara's patient complaints."

This clinic is a confidentiality sieve. "Does absolutely everything leak through the walls around here?"

"So you do know…"

"I didn't say that. Why don't you tell me what you know since you seem to be better informed?"

"OK." Lizzie had clearly been hoping for an excuse to spill what she knew. "You know all those conferences where Bruce, Edward and Tara have been presenting TWF Healthcare outcomes data and Better Care Pathways?" I nodded. Everyone in the clinic knew about their research collaboration.

"Well," Lizzie leaned forward and lowered her voice, "Burke and Tara have beenhaving an affair for over 3 years, since that first conference in Dallas."

"That can't be true."

"It is true."

"You can't believe Amanda. She's been mad at Tara since Tara ratted her out about her facial business on site."

"Do you know how I know it's true?" Lizzie looked at me with a superior air.

"I'll bite. How?"

"Because I saw them."

"What? When? Where? I don't believe it."

"At the Chicago conference."

"Chicago?"

"Yes. Remember I told you I was running short of time and I needed the continuing education for my relicensure so I had to go and attend for the full three days. Even though I knew Burke and Jackman were going and I didn't want to run into them but", she finally paused to take a breath, "I couldn't sleep the first night so I went down to the bar around 2am and saw Tara and Burke. At first I didn't recognize them. They both looked so different but it was them."

"What do you mean they looked different? Maybe it wasn't them." There was more hope than conviction in my voice.

"I don't mean they were in disguise. Tara wore this emerald green colored dress with a slit up the side, make-up, the works. And Burke had on a form-fitting long sleeved obviously expensive, though still grey of course, shirt and I could have sworn he had a diamond earring in his right ear. Doesn't which ear you have the earring in designate something? Doesn't left mean you're gay and right not? Or…" She stopped as she noticed my irritated look. "OK, I got off track. Anyway, he had his arm behind her on her chair and Tara was sort of nuzzling him, whispering in his ear." Lizzie looked at me with satisfaction.

"That's it? That's your evidence of a big affair? More likely they had too much to drink and were engaging in that kind of inappropriate, acting out sexual behavior therapists are prone to do at conferences because they have to be contained and analytical the rest of the time."

"I knew you would say that. I wasn't interested in watching that," she grimaced. "I sat by myself in a different area of the bar for a while. When I decided to go to the ladies' room which was downstairs, I heard a kind of clanking or pounding sound from the men's room and I stopped outside the door and listened. You could hear them banging against the wall and Burke was saying or more accurately grunting, 'You filthy whore.' He kept saying it, over and over. I was frantic to get out of there, without them knowing I overheard. I ran up the stairs and took the nearest elevator to my room and never looked back." She shivered. "It still makes my skin crawl."

"Did you see them or talk to Tara after that?"

"No. Never. What would I say to Tara? 'Oh Tara I hear you and Burke are doing it. Was he any good? Does he have a big cock?'"

"Why didn't you say something to me? And how do you know it was Tara? It could have been someone else."

Lizzie looked at me with disdain. "Your loyalty is admirable but your complete denial is ridiculous."

"Yeah, OK. How do you know they have been having an affair for the three years since?"

"You can tell."

"Oh, please. You're psychic now?"

"Don't you think that it's true? Something happened and now he's trying to undermine her credibility so she can't file a sexual harassment lawsuit again him?"

I thought for a moment. "I hate to admit it, but that makes more sense."

"More sense than what?"

I realized I was comparing this to Tara's story. "You know, the whole persecution thing Burke is doing. It seemed more personal that his professional ego had been wounded." Not that that hadn't been enough in the past. Lizzie and I both knew that.

"See?" Lizzie looked pleased with herself. "I told you. Now what do we do about it?"

"I don't know. I'm not certain there is anything to do now, but I'll see what I can figure out." I looked at the clock. "Oh, shit. My patient has been waiting for 15 minutes." I stood up from my chair.

"I have to do my group now, too. Let's talk later." Lizzie opened the door, looked right and left in an obvious "don't want to get caught this late for my group for no reason" concern.

Chapter Thirteen

I parked my car in my usual spot. Far away from the 4x4's, ¾ ton pick-up trucks, and the 8 to 12 cylinder ground hugging long nosed cars that populated the small lot behind the brick building with no windows on this side. I grabbed my bag and headed to the front, nodded to Derek the owner behind the counter and signed in.

"Erik." I waved to my brother who was setting up to the left of me.

"Hi Mik. You're late."

"I know. I had a last minute crisis patient and I-"

"Spare me. It's always the same story. Just shoot."

We both securely placed our ear protection that prevented the hearing loss from the blasts of Erik's 9mm Glock and my 357 Magnum as we each shot at the target. We had 22's we most often used for practice. But not today. We each looked at the other's target. Mine were all dead center.

"Too bad little brother."

"I can tell you're all broken up about it. Plus that was just a lucky start. What did you think of those job postings I e-mailed to you?"

Eric had some time ago become unwilling to hear TWF disaster stories, but in the past few weeks he had apparently made a decision to find another job for me. He had never thought it was a good idea to join TWF. An academic research or teaching position, or a public service job at County Mental Health matched his ethics and TWF's corporate structure did not. I saw it differently. I joined TWF because it was an opportunity to treat a diverse and interesting patient population with a team of colleagues who were clinically talented and hard working. There was a component of structure that I liked as well. My positive history with TWF was what kept me there, even though it had changed a lot in the past year, including Burke's sadistic management style. I kept thinking it might change back. Erik stopped letting me get beyond the first sentence of a TWF story after Billy Sanders died. At this point in our lives, Erik and I now had two main common areas: target shooting and poker.

No one at work knew about the shooting range. Therapists are generally anti-gun and anti-death penalty. I had no problem with either. Certain crimes forfeited the right to live. I opposed automatic assault weapons but otherwise gun ownership was the same as car ownership to me. For responsible use by fairly sane people.

"Mik, did you get my emails about the University positions?"

Erik wasn't letting this go.

"I'm not looking for another job."

"You will be. Trust me."

"Are you a prophet now? Or perhaps a psychic?"

"At some point there will be a major lawsuit by thousands of TWF patients for larceny by false promise."

"You've been saying that for years now. Larceny by false promise, a criminal act defined as TWF stealing from its members by not providing the healthcare it says it provides. Got it."

"It's become more than stealing. It could now come under the heading of homicide."

"You are neither a malpractice nor criminal attorney. In fact, you don't even practice law which I still find odd for a lawyer."

"Okay. Truce. I did talk with Ryan last week and he has been thinking of leaving Alextra Pharmaceuticals."

"Ryan leaving Alextra? His cash cow pharmaceutical company head counsel position? He's been there as long as I've been at TWF. I can't imagine he would find another job that pays over a half million a year."

"I know you think Ryan's moral compass always points towards money, but I think their unethical price gouging tactics are becoming intolerable to him. He's looking into a couple of criminal defense firms that work mostly on capital murder cases."

"That's surprising, although he was a criminal defense attorney before he changed to pharmaceutical counsel. In thinking about it, Big Pharma companies are types of criminals so maybe it's not so different. Or perhaps you're trying to distract me so you can win today."

"Perhaps. Who is the target today?" Erik asked. We often chose a specific target of the week. "Is it the usual? How about BJ? The consummate blow job? "

"Not that I disagree with you, Erik, but keep your voice down."

"I can't help myself. Jackman is such a jack off. He's my choice for you. I don't think it's by accident the initials of his name are the same as who he is. BJ the blow job."

Erik was making me laugh and unable to steady my hands to shoot properly. Erik had met Jackman at a caucus about a bill for assault weapon gun control with Jackman on the pro assault weapon side. In addition to my stories, Erik had his own fill of Jackman in one meeting. At another time, Ryan's wife Ashley, a work of plastic surgery art herself, had disclosed to Erik that Jackman had had his nose done, a chin implant, and calf implants. The chain of information was all confidential preventing me from telling anyone else. Although many at TWF knew about Jackman's penile implant, no one knew about the rest. Keeping secrets usually wasn't difficult for me, but keeping this one was an ongoing struggle.

Erik and I finished our 30 minutes. We signed out.

"I'm in New York for the next two weeks but I am available through the usual avenues." I knew he meant e-mail, text, voicemail.

"It will be same old same old for me."

"See you Mik. And check those e-mails."

I watched him stow his gear in the trunk and drive his Aston Martin out of the lot. He seemed a little double O at times. Thankfully, he didn't drink martinis shaken or stirred. I was the superior shooter, but Erik was better at poker. I read people well, but Erik could bluff like few people I've seen. I felt great. Shooting for me had the effect that yoga or meditation had for my friends or colleagues. A feeling of peace, calm, finding my center. Repeatedly hitting the target did that for me.

CHAPTER FOURTEEN

It was Friday. I checked my schedule for the day. A new patient, Cyntheya Stevenson, had been booked by the crisis team. I checked to see if there was a misspelling but no, it was Cyntheya. The child of a generation who thought that by giving standard names an unusual spelling their child would somehow be more special in the world, when more often it was another interpersonal burden to have to correct or confirm that yes my name really is spelled that way. It was similar to my own over practiced response to the discomfort of strangers trying to decipher the pronunciation of my Danish first name. I began my usual new patient ritual. Checking the computer for all past visits, previous psychiatry providers and meds, visits to the ER. Age 18, a high school senior, transferred to the adult service from the child team when she turned 18, a designation of maturity by law if not in fact. There were a number of visits to child team therapists, a couple of evaluations for meds in the past by Burke, Tara and Sid, who retired last year. Physical therapy and sports medicine appointments with Jackman. Our medical center was the designated center of excellence for sports medicine, so we had more than our share of over worked adolescent and young adult athletes. Cyntheya was likely one of them. Consultation with Jackman and a couple of follow-ups in the acute pain center. Although most of the therapists thought Jackman was an ass, many patients loved him and sports medicine brought money and positive publicity to TWF.

I read the most recent note: 18 year old high school senior living with her mother, advanced placement student attending community college while still in high school. Has anxiety, sleep disturbance - awakens at night with difficulty getting back to sleep, tingling in arms and legs [neurological and orthopedic consults ruled out medical origin]. Denies abuse. Some weight gain in past few months. Not suicidal. Family history: father alcoholic and out of the picture, mother with history of depression.

That was odd. Not the history, which was run-of- the-mill, but the note did not sound like Tiffany. I double checked the therapist who had conducted the assessment. Rachel had been filling in on the Crisis team. No wonder the evaluation was thorough. I checked my office to make certain there was no confidential patient information visible anywhere. My diplomas and two impressionist prints on the wall, neutral furniture, a crystal snow globe, a few sea shells and interesting stones. I glanced at the mirror behind my door to make certain there was nothing between my teeth and walked to the waiting room.

"Cyntheya Stevenson?" I looked around the room to see if I could identify my patient based on demographics. Not today. Too any young adult females in the waiting room. "Cyntheya Stevenson?" I waited. Still no response.

"Someone's in the bathroom." One of the patients volunteered.

"Thank you." Great. The "I'm here but not here because I am (a)ambivalent about treatment (b) know you are the designated authority but want to make you wait so you know who is really in charge (c) socially oblivious [oh, were you waiting for me?] or (d) completely self-absorbed 'oh is there someone else in my universe?' Take your pick. It was one of my pet peeves, which I had tried to change over the years. But it was still there, etched in the granite part of my psyche. A young woman with long red hair entered the waiting room from the hall.

"Cyntheya?" She made brief eye contact, gave one short nod in my direction and walked toward me. She was wearing new jeans and a long baggy vintage t-shirt branded with the trademark tongue of the Rolling Stones. Hands in her pockets.

"I'm Dr. Mikelena Pearson."

"I know."

I directed her back to my office. "Please have a seat." She looked at my office, made eye contact with me and then sat down cross-legged on the floor in the center of my office, pulled out her cell phone and began what I assumed was texting someone.

Patients frequently tell me about themselves without saying a word. How close they sit. What they comment on in the office. The most diagnostic item I have is a crystal snow globe; inside it is a picture of the black Labrador retriever I had as a child. My unofficial study has determined that patients who in the first visit pick it up and shake are almost always have either borderline or histrionic personality disorders. Of course, occasionally, it will be someone who loves snow globes.

Cyntheya was acting like a court ordered treatment patient, I'm here because I have to be but I won't cooperate. At age 18 she could choose not to be here. I decided to operate on the assumption that she had something to tell me, but either had to test me to see if I was trustworthy, or that she wanted to tell me but didn't know herself what that was. There was something about her that reminded me of Billy Sanders. The tough persona of "don't fuck with me", one of Billy's favorite phrases when he first started treatment, combined with a sensitivity and vulnerability that was heart breaking. I had a choice. I could comment or be quiet. My gut told me to wait. I sat. She texted. I waited. Ten minutes remained of the visit and I wondered if I had made the wrong decision.

"I knew her." She was still focused on her texting.

"Her?"

"You know. Jessica. You talked to her mother. That's why I chose you. I was on the gymnastics team with Jessica."

"I want to know what she meant to you, Cyntheya, but I can't say anything about other patients even if I did know them, because of confidentiality.

"But she's dead. Everyone knows she's dead." Her voice was irritated.

"I know it sounds strange but alive or dead I can't legally say anything about her even if I knew her. But I do want to know more about your feelings and thoughts about Jessica."

"You can't tell me anything. Hmmm. Oh, that's right. I did hear you were one of those who followed the rules." Cyntheya put away her phone, stretched out her legs, and leaned over to rub her calves. "Spasms again, damn it."

"How often do you get the spasms?"

"Sometimes. The drugs help."

My patient light went on. It was strategically placed so that I could see it but patients who sat in the chairs could not. However, Cyntheya could easily see it from her vantage point on the floor. A couple minutes remained and I wanted to use them. "Drugs?"

Cyntheya shrugged. "Didn't you read my chart?'

Not enough time left for me to work with her so she could realize she could trust me. "I'm trying to make certain the chart reflects reality." She smiled a bit at that.

"Time's up. I'm out of here." Cyntheya got up, opened the door and walked out without looking back. No follow-up appointment. No question this was a test. I grabbed one of my business cards and a pen, and stepped into the hall. She had reached the waiting room door.

"Cyntheya!" She stopped.I walked to her, wrote the date and time on the card, and handed it to her. "See you next week, Cyntheya." She took it and I rapidly walked back to my office before she had the opportunity to reject it.

"How did you get Cyntheya?" William had materialized from his office, munching on a handful of M&Ms.

"How do you know her, William?"

"Saw her on call one night, and then she had been in the pain program with Jackman. Same face. Different color hair now. Kids these days. It's hard to know what they really look like."

"What did she look like when you saw her?"

"Blonde, thinner. Quite the little hottie. Too bad you can't check out her Facebook page or some other social media site – I bet she has pictures on it of how she used to look."

"You're right, but I'm not willing to risk my license being suspended for an ethical boundary violation. What did that recent article say? Internet searching a patient is similar to entering a patient's house to get more information."

"Particularly since Big Brother TWF tracks our internet searches now," said William.

"And pretty much everything else. See you later, William."

CHAPTER FIFTEEN

4am. It was my cell phone. Every time I was on night call, I hoped that I would not get called. The same way that every time I bought a lottery ticket I hoped I would win.

"Dr. Pearson, it's Dr. Satterfield in the ER. We have a 40 year old male we need you to evaluate. He has suicidal thoughts and we are waiting on the tox screen. When can you be here?"

"In about a half hour."

"Good." He hung up.

Each therapist in the Psychiatry Department was on call one night per month and weekend every 2-3 months. As health care had changed and more people did not have insurance, we saw more patients in the ER. And legally they had to be assessed whether they were TWF Healthcare patients or not.Inpatient beds were at a premium with fewer psychiatric hospitals and the County was always overflowing. I hoped I would not have to hospitalize this guy, as much for my sake as his. There was always a psychiatrist on back-up call, particularly with medications becoming the primary intervention. There had been advances in psychopharmacology, but the main reason was that pills were less costly for TWF than therapy. Satterfield was one of the best ER docs. At least that part was lucky. He would not have called me if it wasn't necessary.

The adrenaline from being called for a crisis guaranteed adequate cognitive function so that I could quickly dress in the clothes I had placed out last night, grab the file I kept with essential contact numbers, and be out the door in minutes. We were required to be there within an hour of being called.And to be sober. This meant no social events, no glass of wine in the evening, no trips out of town when we were on call.

I parked my car in the designated on call space and sprinted the short distance to the hospital. I keyed the code in the staff door to the ER. Gone were the days when you simply walked through the unlocked door designated STAFF ONLY. I made my way to the doctors only room in the back, and used one of the lockers to store my purse, and pulled on a white coat. We all used white doctors' coats in the ER. Whether we were medical doctors or not. Our first initial with our last name and degree were embroidered on it. The full first name was missing in an attempt to prevent patients from using it. In the ER or hospital, it was white coats. The only places where the mental health non-MD providers wore them. Some of the therapists thought it was too clinical, too medical, and too much of a shield that created distance between them and the patients. But that was the purpose. To communicate at first glance, this is a professional, this is someone equipped to take charge and take care of you. Or at least that was the TWF administration explanation. It never made a difference to me. Only William, by virtue of the length of his TWF tenure always wore a sport coat. And Burke because of status as Chief got away with his trademark collarless zippered jacket.

I logged onto one of the computer terminals in the little kiosk areas to check the history of the patient before I sought the current information of what brought him to the ER. As I scrolled through the chart, I realized I was sitting right around the corner from the point where the door opened from the staff room to the waiting room. The same corner containing the patient bathroom. The bathroom with a smell of human excrement, vomit, and some fragrance infused chemical cleaner. No matter what the time of day or how many times it was cleaned, it always smelled the same.

"Mik, what are you doing here?" It was Burke.

"I'm on call. Why are you here? Are you the back-up psychiatrist?" He sat down in the chair next to me and looked at the information on the screen.

"Sorry, but they called you in by mistake. I didn't realize Satterfield didn't call you back."

"What's the problem?"

"No problem, but the nurse did not see the alert on the chart that this is one of my clinical research patients. If at all possible I'm the one to see the patient in the circumstance, not expected of course, that he or she is in the ER or comes in to the crisis service."

"That's fine with me. Is he all right?"

"Yes. Only a panic attack. He's fine now. Gave him a little clonazepam and his wife is taking him home. Unfortunate you had to come in."

"Thanks, Edward. I will check to see if anything else is brewing while I'm here and if not I will head home. See you." That was lucky for me. I didn't mind the trip in, if I didn't have to assess a patient and possibly spend hours trying to find an available bed for a psychiatric hospitalization. Burke, with all his flaws, was a workaholic, and always did more than his share of the clinical work, which was his best quality. I checked with the triage nurse and no potential "customers." The rest of the night was uneventful.

CHAPTER SIXTEEN

The next week at TWF was routine, a welcome change from the recent drama. Cyntheya had shown up for her appointment today and she was willing this time to tell me a little more about her history.

"Dr. William had asked me if I thought I needed to be in the hospital. I asked him what his salary was. He told me I was avoiding the issue. I said I wasn't, but if I was the one who was going to decide if I should be hospitalized and do the job he was on call to do, then I should be paid for it."

I couldn't keep a straight face, and one of the fastest ways to lose trust with a system savvy young adult like Cyntheya is to be fake. She seemed pleased with her ability to elicit the response she wanted. She appeared more relaxed, even though she again sat on the floor. This time she did not bring out her phone or use anything else to communicate she was unwilling to be present when present. A little progress.

"I have this dream."

Have. Indicating present, recurring. "What is it?"

"I'm not sure. It is never all clear to me."

I waited.

"I'm in a room, and it's like I'm being wrapped in a blanket, warm and snuggly. I try to see who is with me but all I see is blue like the ocean or the sky. I hear what sounds like some kind of machine, I can't tell. I smell something like french fries. And smells like the cleaner that my mom uses in the bathroom. When I wake up I feel relaxed but my body feels sore and my mouth is dry. Feels like I ate dirt or something and my throat is sore." As she was talking she had pulled her knees up to her chest and was sort of hugging herself.

"How long have you been having the dreams?"

"A while."

"A while?"

"Yeah."

"You seem like someone who would know pretty much exactly how long it has been."

"What makes you think that? You hardly know me."

"You're right. It isn't based on knowing you because this is only the second time I have talked with you. Call it my clinical judgment. Or an intuitive hit."

She watched me. Took her time. Waiting for something. Perhaps some sort of "tell." She looked down. "They started six month ago." No elaborating. She was going to make me work for this information.

"Did something change at that time? Or something happen? Positive or negative?"

"Like what?"

"Different events affect people differently. I don't know what it could be for you. Think about the past six months to a year and tell me what comes into your mind."

"What comes into my mind? Sure you're not Freudian?"

"I'm not asking for free association. I'm asking for data mining."

"Okay." She looked up at me and her eyes seemed as if a window had closed between us. But her voice was filled with distress. "The truth is out there." She waited for some sort of understanding or recognition on my part.

I was in conflict. Was this a reference from the 1990's X-Files show resurrected in movie versions where no one but Fox Mulder knows there are alien or paranormal activities? Or was it something else? I took a risk. "I want to believe."

She nodded.

I still wasn't certain what that meant to her but it apparently had been an X-Files reference. I could only assume there was something she felt threatened by that the "authorities" would likely not believe. And she wanted to know if I was one of them.

CHAPTER SEVENTEEN

"William, you have an announcement?" Tara asked. She was methodically moving from one agenda item to the next in our weekly adult services team meeting. In these small clinical meetings she was organized, insightful and supportive. Reasons most of the adult team was so loyal to her.

"Yes. As you all know, I have been with TWF Healthcare for 20 years and have been talking about retirement for the past few years. My wife and I discussed it and decided that in four months I will end my journey here and retire to our family home in Utah."

"Congratulations William. You will be missed by all of us." Tara spoke for the team and there was nodding by team members but no one else said anything. We had been anticipating his announcement for some time. I admired William because he had a rare level of compassion for those who could not afford the high cost of prescriptions and co-pays. He was willing to step outside our ethical code, which required us not to cross over the boundary from therapist to good Samaritan. He had, on a number of occasions, sent cash anonymously to his elderly patients who he knew could not afford the medications they needed. I was the only one in the clinic he had told, and although technically I should have reported it, I didn't. It was something I often wished I could do for patients in need but knew I couldn't cross that particular line. If it had been reported, he could have his state license suspended.

I have friends who aren't therapists, who don't understand the therapist-patient boundary issue. They get their information from movies and television series where therapists socialize with their patients or end up having sex with them. My ethical and legal principles are viewed as some sort of pretention, rigidity or self-importance. But boundaries are essential for the patient's emotional safety, particularly those who were abused by the people who were in a position of power or caretaking. Parents, spouses. And although there is some flexibility in the boundaries, we are ethically and legally required by our licensing boards not to cross the line.

William pushed the boundaries in ways I admired. I will miss him.

"Lizzie, you're next." Tara was already moving on to the next agenda item.

"I have seen this 19 year old young woman eight times over the past three months."

"Patient identification number?" Tara was taking notes.

Lizzie gave Tara a little salute, "Aye Aye Captain" provided the number and started," I saw Zoe for the first time on referral from her medical doctor, who thought she was having adjustment problems to college, symptoms of insomnia, nightmares, weight gain - the freshman 15-"

"These days it's more like the freshman 20," William interrupted, referencing the common phenomenon of women gaining weight in the first year of college.

Lizzie gave William a look of irritation. "I was talking about her symptoms. Sleep problems, nightmares, weight gain, decreased interest in her friends and school. She is in the advanced placement program at school. Her IQ was assessed as 145, in the top 2%."

William again interrupted, "She sounds depressed. What is your assessment, Lizzie?"

"And what exactly is the question?" David added.

Patient presentations that were mostly intellectual meandering by the treating therapist to impress the other members of the team were a regular hazard, and neither David nor William had the patience for it. But Lizzie was an exceptional therapist, and I knew if she was discussing a patient it was important.

Lizzie responded, "I want your thoughts about this first before I give you my hypothesis, so that I can see if what I am thinking is a reasonable conclusion. Let me read you guys what she wrote. She describes her dreams." Lizzie pulled out three typed pages and starting reading to us, "I have a lot of dreams but this one is the one that I have a few times a week. I'm lying on a beautiful white sandy beach and I look up and see a blue sky bright with a few white puffy clouds. The sand is warm and supports me and makes me feel protected. I hear the sounds of the waves crashing on the shore."

William snorted. "That doesn't sound like a 19 year old. Lizzie, are you sure this is her writing?"

"Yeah," Charles added, "it seems made up."

"Wait everyone. Let me finish. I want you to listen first and then give your opinions. This will require more than the usual superficial TWF McTreatment response."

"But Lizzie, doesn't it sound familiar to you? In fact almost identical to a relaxation or self-hypnosis script? The kind most of us were trained with, and TWF sells on CDs in the TWF Healthcare member store?" I spoke up because I felt there was something off about this. Lizzie shot me her well known "shut up" look and I decided to listen to the rest.

"I am going to continue. 'I feel warm all over as if I am being lowered into a warm bath or hot tub. The next thing I notice is that I feel tired, my muscles are sore, my jaw hurts and my mouth feels dry but also sort of sticky. When I wake up, I feel bad, kind of depressed.' I asked her what else she remembered. She said it was like lucid dreaming."

"Lucid dreaming? She said 'Lucid dreaming?' She is yanking your chain." William could not contain himself.

"Yes, she searched the internet, trying to find the meaning of her dreams and she came across the LaBerge theories of lucid dreaming, and it resonated with her. She said she thought she heard a soothing voice telling her everything would be okay."

"Male voice?" Tara was focused on the case, interested.

"No. A female, She said older female which to a 19 year old could be 30 or 80. Perhaps a mother figure countering the negative part of the dread, the fear. What do you all think?"

"I'll tell you what I think," Tara began. "Most likely this is a young woman who has been molested or abused in some way but by whom, when and what happened is unclear. I agree with Mik that the description she gives is almost exactly the same as the relaxation or pain management scripts that many of us were trained to use and that can be obtained these days in almost any large bookstore or downloaded off a number of internet sites, including TWF Healthcare's. Her description of her physical sensations is most interesting to me, and leads me to believe something did happen to her that she is not fully able to retrieve, either because doing so would overwhelm her defenses and she is unconsciously protecting herself or because she may have been drugged. Rohypnol, or another anterograde amnesiac sedative hypnotic so easily accessible these days, and labeled the "date-rape" drug for good reason."

There was a feel of fortune telling, almost psychic reading in the way we sometimes had to piece together the patient's story and look for what caused the pain or problem. Intuitive leaps, not unlike the "gut instincts" of a good cop, were essential to help the patient figure out what was happening. It also supported my theory, not accepted by most of my colleagues, that the best therapists were born not made. Graduate programs simply provided the maps and tools to assist with the innate ability.

Tara continued, "The female voice of reassurance may be the beginning of internalizing Lizzie as a protector or good mother, or alternatively could be the voice of the perpetrator as a way to quiet her. I can't tell which but I lean toward the reassuring good mother."

What Tara said made sense, but I was having a déjà vu feeling while listening. Something was familiar and not because in general this story and type of abuse was not unusual. Some of what Cyntheya had said was similar. Did this mean they had been at the same party, or they had talked with each other, or was there a chat room somewhere both were accessing?

Tara was wrapping up her conclusions, "Lizzie, I think continuing to see her individually for a short time will be most helpful. She trusts you and more time will allow additional evaluation. You've seen her several times already so I would start thinking of referring her outside TWF. She will likely need longer term therapy that we can't provide. The clinic doesn't have a therapy group that fits her, so for now I think that's all that we can do for her. If there are no other thoughts, let's move on to the final item."

After the meeting ended I returned to my afternoon schedule, but the patient's dream remained with me throughout the rest of the day.

CHAPTER EIGHTEEN

"Where is he?" Jennifer, our part time receptionist, was at my door as I was reviewing my schedule for the day. She was waving a patient registration slip.

"Who, Jennifer?"

"Dr. Burke. He has three patients registered and his 8:45 has been waiting for over 20 minutes. I called his office but he's not there. Is there a Chiefs meeting somewhere? Did the scheduling department forget to close his schedule?"

"Did you page him?"

"I have his pager. He didn't pick it up this morning. And you know he refuses to use a cell phone for work."

"Try paging him overhead. Maybe he's in pediatrics or the ER."

"I will. But can you please talk to his 8:45? The name on the registration slip is Walter Phelps."

He was the real reason Jennifer had come to me. She was quite familiar with the paging system but did not want to deal with Mr. Phelps, a wealthy, bright, chronic pain patient, quite dependent on Burke for pain relief both psychological and narcotic. And he could talk your ear off. I sighed. He generally refused to see anybody but Burke. I could hear the page for Edward overhead which meant the patients could as well.

"Mr. Phelps?" I caught his eye across the waiting room. He folded his newspaper methodically, and picked up his cane, a beautiful piece of craftsmanship with the head of an eagle in antique silver as the grip.

"Yes, miss? Is the doctor here? My appointment was for 8:45 and it's almost 9:30. I have a 9:45 in orthopedics. Dr. Burke has never been late before. You could set your watch by him. I brought him an article about PTSD and veterans. That's where I met him, you know, at the Veterans Hospital. He helped so many of us."

"I'm certain Dr. Burke is taking care of an emergency which is why he is late. Wait here, Mr. Phelps, and I'll check into it and see what I can find out. I'll be right back so we can get you to your orthopedic appointment." I walked back toward Edward's office and saw James in the hall. As one of the psychiatrists he would have a Master key. Only MDs had Master keys, another indication of the TWF caste system.

"James, come with me." I took him by the arm and directed him down the hall.

"What's going on?"

"Edward's missing in action and I have his distraught patients in various stages of decompensation in the waiting room. You have a Master key in case we need to get into his office and figure out where he went."

"I heard the page." James pulled a set of keys from his pants pocket. "I need to ask Edward something anyway, so the sooner we locate him the better."

We had reached the office door. I knocked firmly and said in my best urgent therapist voice, "Dr. Burke, please come to the door. I need to speak with you." No response. No sound. I tried the door. It was unlocked. I looked at James who nodded. I pushed the door slightly ajar. "Dr. Burke?" The motion detector light came on as the door opened and I saw him. Lying on the floor. On his back. Facing away from us.

"What happened? Is he unconscious?" James walked to where he could see Burke's face but then stopped short, covering his mouth. "Oh my God." He reached down to check if there was a pulse, shook his head, and then turned away, starting to dry heave.

I put my arm around James and moved him away from Burke close to the door. "Call 911, James." I walked to where James had been standing. Burke's eyes were open but vacant. He was dead. Then I saw what James had seen. On Burke's torso sat a doll. Not a complete doll, but the upper body of a doll. Burke's jacket had been zipped up to fit tightly below her. I felt pulled into some bizarre vortex, like Alice falling through the rabbit hole. I knew this doll. It was Malibu Barbie. But her legs were not visible. They were inside Burke. Six inches of plastic replaced with blades sharp enough to slice through his flesh and organs. Sharp enough to cause the blood from Burke to ooze past his fitted jacket bottom to create the dark red pool visible against the ivory color of Burke's office rug.

James was now frozen in place by the door, staring unblinking at Burke. "I called 911." He sounded flat, detached. In shock. But no longer dry heaving.

I walked over and placed myself between James and Burke, forcing James to refocus. I placed my hand on his arm. "James, what did they say?"

"They said to stay calm. And try to keep everyone on site until they arrive."

"James, can you go call security and find Amanda so she can notify everyone? I will stay here to make certain no one else has to see this." James nodded and left.

I locked the door from the inside, making the decision not to generate attention by standing guard outside Edward's door. There was nothing to do but wait. I had been in the room with dead bodies before. One time at the passing of a terminally ill friend, and another with my grandfather. I had even dissected a body in an anatomy class. It was not at all the same. This was a projective. A room-sized Rorschach card with its splash of red right in the center. The red a focal point of someone's penetrating rage. There were sparkling lights beginning to surround Edward's body as I wanted not to look at him but couldn't stop myself. The room was starting to become painfully bright. I was on the verge of passing out. I reached back and grabbed at Burke's desk, my hand making enough contact with his computer keyboard to allow me to sink slowly to the floor. I placed my head between my knees to move the blood flow back to my brain. My usual response to the sight of blood had only been delayed this time. I closed my eyes and slowed my breathing. I couldn't look at the body or blood anymore.

I sat and waited. Waited and went over everything again and again in my head. Trying to avoid looking at Burke's body and the blood. It was unusual that the door to Edward's office had remained closed after 9:00 am, but rarely was anyone ever willing to disturb him when his door was closed. Working late. Coming in early. He was almost always the first one and last one on the site.

Where was James? It seemed like hours but when I glanced at my watch only minutes had passed. I stood up. I must have hit the Enter key when my hand landed on Burke's computer. A therapist's schedule had appeared. The date for her schedule was a month from now. The six point type was difficult to read on this particular screen but I could see there were no blank appointment slots. I read the patient's names, with the reason for the appointment listed next to the name:

9:00am	Edward Burke	Suicide
10:00am	Edward Burke	Suicide
11:00am	Edward Burke	Suicide
12:00pm	Edward Burke	Suicide

"Oh my God. Oh my God." Any strand of calm I had been clinging to was now ripped from me. I stepped back from the desk. I could hear pounding.

"Mikelena. Mikelena. Open the door. Open it or I'm going to use my key." It was James. "I couldn't find Amanda but Jennifer is informing management and calling security. The police will be here soon." James arrived pale and breathing in short bursts. "They want us to leave the room, then secure and guard the door so no one else comes in here. I'll do it."

"Mikelena."

I looked at James. I pointed to the computer.

"You look sick. Sit down before you pass out."

I pulled James over to the computer screen. He glanced at it, then put his arm around me as much to steady himself as me. "What the hell? What is this?"

"I don't know. But we have to get out of here, and you and I need to make sure no one else comes in here." I could not tolerate one more second next to Edward's body. My thoughts kept shifting between the reality in this room and my disbelief. As if I expected Burke to stand up, rip Barbie off his chest, tell us this was just a test, a role play or psychodrama, and then begin critically assessing our crisis response.

"I'll stand guard now. You go back to your office and get away from this."

"I will, James. Thanks. But make certain no one else comes in here, and don't say anything about any of this to anyone." James only nodded. Eyes now glazed over, staring straight ahead, standing his post. I could hear Jennifer paging Mr. Arnold urgently to the reception area. Our code for security equivalent to 911.

CHAPTER NINETEEN

The local uniformed police arrived within a few minutes. Our reception staff led by Jennifer, and Patrick from security had done an unpredictably effective job of closing down the clinic and handling the patients. Therapists had been told to wait in their offices until it was clear what the next step would be from the local authorities. The situation was as taken care of as it was going to be, and I needed to get back to James. I didn't want to leave him alone too long. And I knew the police would want to question James and me. I began to shiver, at the same time feeling the sensation of perspiration soaking through my bra under my armpits. I found James and stood next to him, neither of us speaking.

"Dr. Pearson?" I had been too engrossed in my thoughts to notice the two uniformed police officers now only a couple of yards from me in the hall.

"Yes?"

"I'm Officer Aronson and this is Officer Wilson."

"Dr. Pearson and I have met." Officer Wilson extended his gloved hand to me. He was a college hall of fame linebacker who 15 years later still had the look.

"Yes, Officer Wilson and I have spoken about a few cases in the past, and he has helped out the Department with crisis cases." My words were an accurate description as far as it went but I could not keep the distaste I had for him from creating a flatness of tone to my speech.

"Too bad about that Sanders boy though. And now this." His tone was not one of condolence or sympathy. I chose not to respond to Wilson's little jab, the look I gave him said "Back off." We had argued in the past due to his belief that there was no such thing as domestic violence or hate crimes. He had been reprimanded after I made a complaint to his Captain. Usually he was not a first responder to a 911 call from our Department.

"The receptionist up front said you found the body."

"We did." I pointed to James. "This is Dr. Benson. We were together when we found him---he—Edward—Dr. Burke's in here." I turned to reach for the handle of the door.

"Wait!"

The officer blocked my arm and hand. I stepped back and looked at him. Control issues. What a surprise. "What? Are you concerned about fingerprints? I already opened the door as did Dr. Benson, and who knows how many other people."

"We need to wait for the crime scene unit and the detectives."

He was right. "What would you like us to do?"

"Let's take this one step at a time. Dr. Benson, is the office as you found it?"

"Yes, it is." James's only words since he had been at his post.

I started to nod, but stopped. No, that wasn't quite accurate. My expression was not lost on Officer Wilson, whose disdain for me was now offered a legitimate opportunity for expression.

"Did you touch something Dr. Pearson?"

"I hit Burke's keyboard with my hand when I was trying to steady myself. That's all."

"Let me get this right. You hit the keyboard after you found Dr. Burke? "

"Yes."

"After you found the body?"

"Yes." I debated for a moment with myself. I hated to disclose any weakness to this officer but now was not the time for a pissing contest. "I was unsteady because I was going to pass out from the sight of the blood. I only hit the enter key on his desk."

Officer Wilson chose not to let this opportunity be taken from him. "So you almost passed out. Women tend to have that response. Don't worry. We're here now to take over and the crime scene investigators and detectives are already en route. Anything else you would like to tell us? Anything else you found?"

I paused at this point, unable to ignore the expression on his face. Suspicion? Smugness? Was I now a suspect? "The computer screen showed that Burke's name was entered several times into a therapist's schedule with the word suicide after each entry."

"Was it your schedule?" Officer Benson was still not ready to let this go.

"No, of course not."

"Of course not. Make certain both of you stay away from the crime scene. Don't touch anything for any reason. Either of you. We will take a full statement from each of you. The crime lab will process the crime scene and evidence. We will need your fingerprints. To eliminate you from any prints that we may find. You touched nothing, Dr. Benson?"

"No, I found Dr. Burke with Dr. Pearson here, checked him for a pulse, and then I went to call the police and alert the staff."

As promised, the crime lab technicians came down the hall. I overheard one of them mention to the officers that the homicide detectives were also on site.

"I understand there are other staff members who were on site. We will need to talk to them as well. We will get your statements after we secure the rest of the witnesses."

"Certainly. This way." I led them to the staff offices and conference area. Relieved not to be interrogated anymore, at least for the moment. Feeling as if I was guilty of something. Guilty of something more than contaminating a part of the crime scene. And there it was. The reason psychoanalytic institutes are still churning out Freudian true believers. How many times in the past year after a couple of glasses of wine, had I said to my friends that the increasingly sadistic Dr. Burke was making his way to my top ten list of those I wanted more dead than alive? I realized that I was stunned, shocked, horrified at his death, but not devastated. I was guilty. A part of me had wished him dead.

CHAPTER TWENTY

I continued to sit in the group room where I had sat with the officers as they reviewed my statement and James'. Dazed, not certain what to do next. Or even if I had the energy to move to my office. I knew that an officer had remained in the waiting room to assist with the notification of today's patients. I also knew that the information would be all over the news and on the internet. At least some form of what happened.

"Mikelena." I felt a hand lightly touch my shoulder. "Mikelena, it's Luke Sustern."

I looked at him but it took me a moment to recognize him. He was taller and broader than I remembered. I stood up and held out my hand. "What's happening? Are you with the other detectives?"

"I'm assisting them due to the unusual nature of the murder and the expected impact on the community. I understand you found the body."

"Yes. I did"

"I know you've already spoken with the uniform officers, but I'd like to hear about it, if that's all right with you."

I nodded. I followed him into one of the conference rooms where they were set up to take statements. I sat in one of the two chairs in the corner of the room and Luke grabbed the other chair and sat in it across from me.

"Do you mind if I record this?"

"Not at all. As long as I can have a copy."

Luke looked a little surprised. "We can provide you with one or a transcription."

"Then go ahead."

"My liaison role between the police and the community includes emergency situations where there are potential victims or victims of violence. James appears to be in shock currently and unable to tell us anything right now, so I wanted to talk with you. As painful as it may be," he reached over and briefly touched my hand "and I am sorry to have to ask you this, but I need to know as much information as possible while it's fresh in your mind. Is there anything else you can tell me about what you saw or what happened when you entered Dr. Burke's office?"

"Yes." I went through all of it again with Luke listening intently, nodding, encouraging with expressions of compassion. Luke touched my hand again. The brief stabilizing contact therapists often use in grief and tragedy. To stay focused, connected.

"That's good. You're doing well."

I wished I had never been in that office at all. I could feel myself starting to shut down.

"Is there anyone you know who would want to hurt Dr. Burke?

"Frankly, lots of people. Staff. Disgruntled patients. Fired staff. The list is long."

"Okay. Anyone you know who ever threatened Dr. Burke?"

"Directly?"

"Or indirectly."

"I'm not certain I feel comfortable giving out people's names who may have been momentarily pissed off at Burke. He was arrogant and abusive. Ask anyone."

"I believe you, and I will. But right now I'd like to know what you think."

"Well, I will have to think about it. At the moment, no one in particular comes to mind," I lied. I could hear irritation in my voice although I was mostly exhausted. I crossed my arms and sat back in my chair. I felt like one of my sulking adolescent patients who wanted connection, wanted to be heard, but was too irritated to actively respond when the opportunity was right in front of them. I didn't want to continue talking about this. I had now entered the red zone of critical emotional overload. My tone registered with Luke, primarily evident in his looking down for a moment and his mouth tightening. I guessed he was assessing whether he should continue or back off. His voice was soft and coaxing; he must have understood the meaning in my tone but made the decision to continue regardless.

"Are you certain you can't give me any idea of who may help us find the killer? Or any other detail? Anyone you saw before you entered the office. Whatever it may be even if you think it insignificant, may be helpful. Take a moment to think about it."

I began to wonder if there was something I was supposed to be saying? Did he know something that he wanted me to corroborate? What did he think I knew? I pushed back my hair hoping to also clear my mind. Was I so drained and distracted I was becoming paranoid? No. I wanted to help Luke and the investigation, but I was done. I hadn't killed Burke and I had no idea who did. And if wishful thinking was reality, I wouldn't be working for TWF Healthcare. I would be driving a Gallardo Lamborghini and taking vacations in a tropical paradise.

"There is nothing more I can give you now. I'm sorry. I would like to go back to my office to check on my patient messages and anything I should attend to before I go home."

Luke paused a bit and reviewed his notes, then nodded, "Of course. Your patients need you. Thank you for going over all of this again." We stood up at the same time, shook hands and then almost as an afterthought. "Do you have a number where I can reach you, Mikelena, if there is anything else?"

"I do." I reached for one of my TWF business cards I always kept in my jacket pocket when I was at work, and used Luke's pen to add my cell and home numbers. "Here's all my contact information."

"Thank you. I know this is very difficult for you, but you have helped." He was putting my card in his wallet as I turned and started walking back to my office.

It had taken hours for the police to take all our statements. I had checked my voicemail, and now I was waiting for Rachel since she had asked me to connect with her before I left. Rachel and I had been together before when disasters occurred. We were at TWF during the 7.5 earthquake, and we were driving together to a conference last year when a major storm hit the area and knocked out the electricity in half the city. Now Burke's murder. I had wound down enough to stop standing or pacing, finally sitting, my head on my crossed forearms on my desk, feeling overwhelmed, burdened. I was agitated, running everything over in my mind. Finding Edward and the sense of all of this being so unreal. And seeing Luke. Luke was tougher than I expected. Tough and compelling. It was one of the emotional aspects of crises. It intensified transference. Intensified whatever was present, whether it was attraction or repulsion.

"Hey sweetie" Rachel put her hand on my shoulder and I raised my head. She looked as exhausted as I felt. "I'm finished. You ready to go?" I nodded. "Will the clinic be open Monday? What will happen to Burke's patients?" I had been wondering the same thing.

"I don't know. But patients need to be treated."

"My guess is they will move us to the trailer where we use to be. It's still vacant. Have you eaten, Mik?"

"No, and I'm finally getting some appetite back. We should stop somewhere. Where do you want to go? Rose's Café?"

"That sounds really good. Anybody else around?"

"I saw Tara and Lizzie leave a little while ago. I don't know about anyone else."

"Let's just go. I'll meet you there in 10." We separated at the door to get our cars. We were both attempting to return to some sense of normalcy. And this was a time when we needed the comfort of the familiar. A reliable friend and filling reliable food. Antidotes to the bizarre reality of our recent experiences and a welcome break before having to confront it all again in a couple days.

CHAPTER TWENTY-ONE

The sun had set and there was barely a pinkish orange haze on the horizon by the time I returned home. I poured a glass of cabernet, put my mail to the side, and checked my home voicemail. Sixteen messages. Friends and family who had heard about the murder and called me. By now, there was probably a new blog with minute by minute updates of speculation, viewpoints, commentary on the latest horror to happen at TWF Healthcare. Anything like this was also catnip for the news entertainment networks. What was the old newspaper saying? "If it bleeds, it leads." I had left Erik a message earlier today while I was still at TWF. My father was doing his reclusive missionary work somewhere in South Africa. I didn't want to worry him and knew he checked messages about once a month with one of our cousins who was tending the farm. I told my cousin not to use the emergency access to him but to let him know when he called in. There was nothing he could do anyway. I also messaged my good friend Alexandra in Florida because I knew she would be hysterical when she saw the news. She was my best friend from undergraduate school and although we didn't talk often, as she always says, our friendship transcends time. We were able to pick up where we left off as if months of time had not passed.

I wasn't certain if I wanted to listen to the messages left for me. Voicemail is similar to other items of technological convenience. It is a tool, not a weapon. You have free will and are not required to respond or even listen to messages left for you. These are statements I repeatedly tell my patients who are unable to set limits with the increasing technological onslaught of new ways people can access each other and enter their lives. Too bad I don't often take my own advice. I pressed the "play" key. The first was Alexandra: "Mik, I got your message. I can't believe it. It's so ghastly. This after that psychologist out here was hacked to death in her office, and that therapist out there last year shot to death as he walked out of the clinic. You must be in total shock. I know you have support there but call me when you can. Lots of love from me and from Robert," who was her third husband. Most of the rest of the messages were the same. Friends offering support and echoing the horror of it. Mostly not knowing what to say.

No one knew about the Barbie doll aspect except the police, James and me. Keeping that secret as well as the knowledge that Burke's suicide appointments had been booked in the computer was harder than I would have expected. The police were the ones trying to decipher what this all meant and no one was talking to me.

I had thought about a few professions before I entered my doctoral program, but never crime investigation. But now looking at what the detectives and investigators did in examining the evidence, figuring out where the lies are, asking tough questions, drawing conclusions, with the hope of solving the problem or crime. It wasn't that different. This thinking process was not helping, although the cabernet was. The phone rang. I decided to answer. I didn't want to add this person to the list of people I had to call back.

"Mik? I've got to talk to you." David's voice was strained. "Is this a good time?"

"Sure, David. Go ahead."

"No. Not on the phone."

"Why? What's going on? Are you okay?"

"Are you alone?"

"Well, yes, but-"

"Good. I'll be over in five minutes."

I had no idea what had happened but David was someone who in spite of his tendency for self- absorption could be sweet and funny at times. And harmless. I wasn't certain I wanted him here after all that had happened but I also didn't want to call him back and say 'Don't come over." Mostly I was now curious about what was going on. I hung up the phone and made sure I and the place were presentable. Ten minutes later the doorbell rang and it was David.

"Thanks for seeing me." His eyes were bloodshot and his face was pale.

"Sure David. Sit down. Would you like a drink? Wine or water or soda?" I pointed to my partially emptied wine glass on the table.

"Thanks. I'll take wine."

David moved the pillows and chose to sit at the end of the sofa. He crossed and uncrossed his long legs, adjusted his socks, and stretched back to tuck in his shirt which was edging out of his waist band. I handed him the wine and he took a long drink.

"What's going on, David? I could assume this is a social call but after Burke's murder I think that's unlikely."

David stood up and walked to the mirror that was on the other side of the room, reflexively checked his image and then returned to sit, this time choosing the chair right next to me.

"Have you ever heard anything about Edward and me? Why am I asking? You wouldn't tell me anyway. But you must know something. A couple of months ago I heard your friend Lizzie make a joke about whether Edward loved my work or "loved my work' in that lewd tone of hers. We weren't involved—not technically. But we were involved in all other senses of the word. I was getting to care for him. Maybe I shouldn't talk about this." But he couldn't stop. "You know how when two people have chemistry between them it becomes more and more intense. You find ways to keep brushing against each other, you look a little longer into each other's eyes. Anyway, that's what was happening between Edward and me. It was months ago. Over at my place. We were having a glass of champagne to celebrate his success. He confided in me that he had been told that week he would be receiving a $50,000 bonus for cutting cost for TWF. $50,000 for bringing the psychiatrists in the region into line to use citalopram as the first antidepressant prescribed for TWF patients. You know he is the Pharmacy Committee Chairperson."

David was starting to become detailed and tangential, his default mode when anxious, and although another time the monetarily compromised morals of Edward and TWF Healthcare would have completely captured my interest, at this point I was becoming impatient for the other shoe to drop.

"I know Edward's the chairperson, David, but what happened?"

"Sorry." He stared at the tassels on his shoes. Long enough for me to be aware they were exactly the same as Edward always wore. I shuddered. "I need to know you will keep this in confidence. And you have to believe me."

"Of course, David. I assumed you came to me because you know I will."

David moved forward on his chair and gazed intently at me. Another long pause. I watched him holding his breath as though he was deciding whether and how much to tell me. Then he started.

"That night we toasted and Edward asked me if I wanted a special treat. I wasn't sure what he meant but at that point I was up for pretty much anything and I was already helping him spend that $50,000 in my head. He handed me a couple of oblong white pills. I wondered if it was ecstasy which I had always wanted to try but had never had the nerve or frankly the opportunity. I took them, and didn't even ask what they were, but pretty soon I felt fabulous."

"Edward did drugs?"

"Of course not. He gave them to me." David ignored my empathy lapse and continued. "I started dancing provocatively having a blast while Edward was watching me and smiling, making certain my glass was never empty. I started moving closer to Edward, dancing next to him and then I impulsively reached over, stroked his hair and began to pull him toward me starting to kiss him. He jerked away and struck the glass from the hand. Do you know what he said to me?" David stared at me. I slowly shook my head realizing he was waiting for some response. He said "You faggot. You're drunk. You disgust me. Get out!' He grabbed me by the arm and pushed me out into the hall." David was clenching his fists and tears were beginning to form in his eyes.

I was sickened by what Edward had done to David. I reached over to touch David's hand. He held my hand and continued. "I did something afterward that I shouldn't have. It was stupid but I was so angry and I didn't want to call him because I know he screens his calls and wouldn't answer or would answer and hand up on me. I sent him an e-mail."

"You sent him an e-mail to TWF?"

"Of course not. He had given me his home e-mail. But I'm afraid I said things I shouldn't in the heat of the moment and now I'm freaking out. I can't believe I did something that stupid. But I didn't kill him."

"David, you're right. That was stupid, but I know you didn't kill him. I don't understand why you are telling me all this? What do you think I can do about it?" I didn't trust David's motives and now was questioning my own judgment in allowing him to come over.

"What was that?"

"What, David?"

"That buzzing sound."

I had fixed my 1950's doorbell myself a couple of weeks ago and now it was barely audible and sounded more like a bumble bee. "My doorbell." We simultaneously moved back in our chairs.

"What now?"

"Sorry, David. I need to get that."

"Are you expecting someone?"

"No, but only my brother or the neighbors drop by, so it's all right. Either one I can tell to come back later."

I went to the door and checked the viewer. "Shit!"

"What, Mik?" David sounded even more anxious.

"David, you need to stay calm. It's Luke Sustern, the homicide detective."

"Are you kidding? Did he follow me here? Did you tell him I was coming over?" David was now beginning to decompensate into a puddle of paranoia. Beyond reassurance or reality testing.

I took him by the shoulders. This is why people get slapped across the face in old movies when they are hysterical. Talking alone doesn't seem to penetrate. I shook him. "David. Stop it. I am getting the door. Sit down." I set him on the sofa and walked to the door. The doorbell buzzed again.

I opened the door a foot. "Luke, hi, sorry it took me a moment to get the door."

"Are you busy? Is this a bad time?" I could see Luke trying to scan the room behind me.

"Well, a friend is over. Has something else happened? Can it wait until tomorrow?"

"I would prefer to speak to you tonight."

"Well, let me think. How about this? I will meet you in 15 minutes at that coffee shop, Joe's, about six blocks up the street. They're open 24 hours."

"Sounds good. See you there." Although Luke had remained the professional that he was, something showed through briefly in his eyes. Questions? Surprise? Or perhaps disapproval? Whatever it was, it made me a little anxious.

I could hear movement in the room behind me and David's strangled whisper, "They know something. Why did he come to you? You can't tell them what I told you. What am I going to do?" David was becoming more paranoid and less functional by the moment.

I decided to attempt the verbal equivalent of slapping his face. "You can stop acting guilty and pull yourself together. You need to contact a lawyer to find out what to do. I won't volunteer anything but I also won't lie. This is murder, David, not some traffic violation. I don't know what to do but I know what not to do, and that's run around leaking guilt, and spilling emotion and information everywhere."

David stopped pacing and blinked rapidly. It worked. He now appeared mostly like his usual self. "I'm going home. I 'm going to eat, take an Ambien, and then figure out what to do in the morning." He grabbed his coat and started for the door. He stopped, almost as an afterthought and hugged me. "Thanks, Mik. Thanks."

I locked the door and scrambled to get ready. I only had 10 minutes left and did not want to increase Luke's suspicion or questions. The kind of clear headed calm crisis response I had now was hard wired. It was present my entire life, even as a child and adolescent. I was the one who, at age 15, took my father to the ER when the hay baler crushed his hand, bones sticking out from underneath his skin. But it was a double edged sword. It was useful most of the time, but mental health professionals were supposed to be more emotional, especially women therapists, and it made me stand out. This was not always good. It had tended to increase suspicion in people who didn't know me. In whatever the situation. I had to leave now. Not the best idea to keep a detective waiting. I grabbed my jacket and as I closed the front door behind me, I said a silent prayer for any help available in this nightmare.

I ran down the steps, caught the edge of my shoe on an uneven piece of concrete, and felt my left knee hit splitting the fabric but caught my fall with both my hands. Great. No time to go back and change. I didn't want it to appear I had something to hide. I brushed off the grit, dirt and continued on down the street. The coffee shop had a large front window facing the street.

Luke was sitting with his back to the door. I slid into the booth and sat across from him. His hands were resting on the table. His fingers lightly touching the white heavy ceramic coffee cup. Luke's shoulders were broad with his white cotton shirt sleeves rolled up and tight across muscular arms.

"Hi"

"Thanks for meeting with me"

I was out of breath. My arms and hands were tingling. "It sounded urgent. What is it you need from me?"

He kept eye contact with me as he raised the mug to his lips.

I narrowed my gaze and leaned forward, "Luke, you asked me here. I thought it was only therapist types who did the stay silent and let the other person's anxiety make them talk trick."

He smiled. "First, I need to be clear about my role in this case. I am not officially a detective on the Burke homicide. I was on the scene as a police trauma community liaison. I checked in with my captain and he agreed that it would be inappropriate for me to be a formal investigator in the murder, for two reasons. First, I had been working with Burke on the county suicide prevention committee and second, I have an acquaintance with your brother. And of course, there is a potential third reason."

It was my turn to be silent.

"You're frowning."

"What is the third reason, Luke? If you aren't investigating why did you ask me to meet you here?" He looked down. There was something else going on with him. Embarrassment? I couldn't quite tell.

"You're the third reason. You're Erik's sister and since you found Dr. Burke's body, there could be potential complications."

"I'm still confused. Even if that's true, why did you ask me to meet you here?"

"Erik called me when he heard about the murder, and he is concerned about you, but you know he is on one of his political junkets, so he could not see you himself. He asked if I would stop by. He said if I called you, you would say you were fine even if you weren't. So, I apologize for the intrusion.

But I was concerned myself, particularly since you and James found the body. I don't know if you heard but James had to be fairly heavily medicated. He wasn't able to cope with what he saw."

"Oh my God. No I didn't know." As a new psychiatrist, James was not someone I knew well, and I had no idea how vulnerable he was.

"Are you all right?"

"I haven't had time to make sense of all this. But you don't have to worry. I'm not like James."

"I am aware of that. Not only how you handled my interviewing you but others said the same. I think the words 'unbreakable and iron will' came up."

"Did Erik say that?"

"No. He said you were an odd combination of high sensitivity and empathy with a core of steel. And he was still worried."

"That sounds like Erik. And you said you were concerned, too?"

"I did. I have seen too many collateral damage victims from this type of violence. Vicarious trauma."

"It's still unbelievable to me. It doesn't seem real. Every cliché imaginable about this kind of violence is running through my head. Who would do this? And why?"

Luke's deep green eyes held warmth, sympathy. I could see why he was good at his job. A person felt he cared, and that he was some sort of emotional superhero. With a special power to remove the horror, even if the relief was temporary.

"Thank you Luke. And I'll probably thank Erik later, when I am not irritated with him for calling in the police."

Luke smiled again. My train of thought was momentarily derailed. I shook my head. "Who could do this?"

"I don't think anyone knows yet. As you saw, this was an organized well planned murder, done by a meticulous person."

"A well organized, meticulous person with a burning rage. And it was personal to Burke."

"I would have to agree with that. I do have a question though. What do you know about David Bowman?"

"Why do you ask about him?"

"I saw him come to your place tonight."

"He's a colleague."

"A colleague, not a friend?"

"Are you now asking me in some official capacity? Or as a regular person?"

"I'm interested, that's all. And you don't need to tell me. Plus, I shouldn't be taxing you with more questions. You need to get some rest. "

"Thanks for that. Nothing he said would be useful to you anyway."

"Good to know." Luke put $20 on the table and we both stood up at the same time, with little space between us. He handed me his card. "Thank you for meeting with me. I know Erik will be relieved. This is my cell phone number. Call it any time, day or night."

I took his card and shook his hand. A handshake that was held by both of us more than a moment too long.

"Good night."

"Good night Mikelena. Can I walk you to your home?"

"No thanks. I think I'd like to be by myself."

"Are you certain?"

"I am. I have your number if I need you."

"Good night, then."

Chapter Twenty-Two

I returned to my apartment, exhausted but tense. Erik had sent out reconnaissance. Not the first time Erik found a way to check on me. What I needed was a quick fix. I nuked the ice cream exactly 15 seconds to make it mud pie consistency for immediate consumption. It was now almost 11pm. I opened my e-mail. I wasn't going to sleep much tonight anyway. I scanned the list of new e-mails. One caught my eye. "TWF Healthcare Gravesite" read the e-mail subject line. I opened it.

TO: Dr. Pearson

Doesn't it make you wonder?
Does TWF always lie?
Connect the dots, if you really care.
And you will find the lies.

What was this? Some angry, marginally creative, disturbed patient was my first thought. I did occasionally receive the equivalent of "TWF Healthcare Sucks" e-mails that made it through my spam filter. This one was sent a few hours after the murder. I looked at the pictures in the e-mail. They were several photographs of pairs of TWF doctors. Edward was in most of them and Jackman. A few of Tara with Edward. Nothing out of the ordinary. All generic business type or conference functions. A couple of pictures of Edward and people I didn't know. They could have been taken from conference or TWF websites. I didn't get the connections. And that phrase, "connect the dots" what did that mean?

At the bottom was a link TWF HealthcareGravesite.com. I closed the e-mail and accessed the site. "Welcome to the TWF Healthcare Gravesite. Please feel free to post your own stories." There were pages after pages of newspaper headlines, including the story Lizzie had shown me. There was a side panel of numbers of graves to date: "340 and counting." What was this? Who would send this to me? None of my friends would do this. Not even Lizzie. A patient? Maybe. I was familiar with the website because I had found it years ago when I was searching for news articles on TWF Healthcare. The site had an ongoing grave count that was added to every time someone felt TWF had been responsible for a family member's death. I was surprised that the corporate attorneys had not made the owners of the site change it, but apparently there were still first amendment rights that couldn't be eradicated by TWF Healthcare legal. Was I a target? Or some kind of ally for the person who sent it?

This had to be related to Burke's murder. I wanted to talk to someone I knew before I called the police. I picked up the phone, and then stopped. I ran through my list of TWF friends. Who was a night person who was not reactive, and could keep their mouth shut? Lizzie's strength was analysis of situations but could she keep her mouth shut? Sometimes she could, but probably not at this point. Tara might, but at the moment she had her own emotional fallout from her relationship with Burke and his death. William? No. James was the only other provider who knew the details of Burke's murder and might be helpful, but after talking with Luke, it was clear that James was completely out of commission and likely to be that way for the foreseeable future. I could call Rachel and risk waking her, and her ER doc husband who worked for the University hospital and regularly repeated his disgust for TWF or any other managed care company. Plus he hated Rachel's friends calling the house at night anyway. Not worth the cost. I needed to conserve the after 11pm calls there, in case there was a real emergency.

As I finished my ice cream, I became calmer, but still debated whether to call someone or not. The e-mail wasn't threatening to me. I didn't want to overreact to this. But it felt like one of those movie scenes where the heroine is ignoring something important and everyone is thinking "why doesn't she do something?" I decided to call Erik. Family was required to be there in these situations, and since he had sent Luke, he should be expecting some sort of contact from me anyway. I called his cell. "Are you there? Can you pick up? If you get this in the next few minutes can you call me right away? It's not an emergency but urgent." As I was re-reading the e-mail, my cell rang.

"Hello."

"It's Erik. Are you all right? I have been picking up my messages hourly in case you called." I was not surprised. The brother-sister connection. He had always been there when there was a crisis, even though he knew I had a "family" of close friends.

"I'm doing okay. Thanks. This will be quick and it's confidential."

"I get it, Mik. Talk."

"I received a strange anonymous e-mail re TWF with pictures of TWF Healthcare MDs. Here is what it says." I read the poem. "What do you think?"

"I'm not certain. There is no threat to you or anyone in particular. But given Burke's murder, the police should know about it. Let them tell you if it is relevant or not. Or you could call Luke Sustern first. I have his number."

"So do I, since you sent him out to check on me. But he left already."

"Oh."

No Apology. Or explanation. Typical Erik. Always assumed he did the brotherly right thing.

"How did the person even get your private e-mail address?"

"I don't know. Anyone can pretty much get any information now. You know that. But I don't think I'm a target."

"Of course you don't. Counter phobic. I believe that's the term your friend Lizzie calls you?"

"Thanks, Erik. For the advice, not the psychological interpretation. I won't keep you any longer. Maybe I will call Luke first, then the police. "

"Do it. He is a night person like you, and even if he is home now, I bet he's still awake watching some science fiction channel. Do you want me to call you later tonight?"

"No. I'm fine. Thanks."

"Bye."

I entered Luke's number.

"Sustern"

"Hi. This is Mikelena Pearson. I received a strange e-mail tonight on my home computer regarding TWF and I don't know if it's important but I thought I should check with you and the police."

"You did the right thing. What does it say?"

I described the content and pictures.

"Can you print it out or better yet forward it to me?"

"I can try."

"I'll stay on the phone while you see if you can."

"Damn it. It won't let me copy or forward."

"Let me contact the department and see what they think. Leave it as it is. There is no direct threat or mention of the murder itself so it could mean nothing, but it's best to be thorough in these situations."

My landline phone rang. I let the voicemail pick up. "Mik, this is Tara. Are you there? I need to talk."

I picked up the phone. "Tara. Hi. I'm in the middle of something. Can I call you back in 10 minutes?"

"Yes. Thanks."

"Sorry, Luke, another call."

"Look, I'll check into this. There is no direct threat and with all the media coverage there may be more craziness. Be careful and vigilant. I will report this to the investigator so it will be part of the file. They will decide if the police need to follow up with you. We don't know what we are dealing with yet and there could be another victim."

"I know. And I will."

"The police will call you back tonight if there is anything else you should do, and I will call you tomorrow."

"Thank you, Luke."

"No problem. That's what I'm here for." He hung up.

I hit 3 on my speed dial. Tara answered. "Thanks for calling me back, Mik. What was happening?"

"I was talking to Luke Sustern the detective. How are you?"

"Not good. David told me Sustern was there. What happened? What did he want from you?"

"It's a long story. But why did David call you? I didn't know you two were friends."

"Well, we sort of bonded recently after Burke humiliated David in the department meeting. We have that in common."

"So you called to find out what was happening?"

"Well, that and frankly I am completely overwhelmed by all of this."

"Is anyone staying with you, Tara?"

"My daughter, you know Brittany, is coming out tomorrow to stay with me for a while. I guess she sensed what a basket case I am. And I think she can connect with me now as another victim."

Tara had told us about her daughter Brittany. She had been estranged from her for years. Tara's second husband had molested Brittany, and although Tara had divorced him, there was still some sense from Brittany that Tara should have known and blamed her. Tara had tried to reconnect but with little success. I was relieved that Brittany could sense Tara's desperation now and provide her with support.

"I don't know if I told you but Brittany is recently licensed as an attorney, family law not malpractice, but she can still help me and won't cost me a fortune like Natalie Heaton."

"That's good, Tara."

"The other reason I don't need a heavy hitter like Heaton is that Edward indicated to me after the meeting that he believed me about the case, and that maybe he wasn't as clear as he thought he was about seeing the patient versus sending in the prescription. And now he's been murdered."

I wasn't certain I believed Tara, but I didn't want to push her on this or hear any other self- disclosures tonight. I also didn't want to tell her what David told me, although now I wondered if Tara had been the one to suggest David contact me. That fit better than David deciding to confide in me. I did, however, want to ask her about the pictures of her and Burke in the e-mail sent to me but my instincts said not to.

"Earth to Mikelena."

"I'm thinking. Wait a second." I could hear Tara blowing her nose and then clearing her throat. "Are you crying?"

I have these waves of sadness. I can't believe Edward is gone. Even though he was an ass, I still cared about him."

"I know, Tara."

"Enough of self pity. So are you refusing to tell me why that detective was at your home?"

"No. But you know he is not officially investigating the case because he worked with Burke and the department on community initiatives like the Bridge suicide project. He is a consultant more than anything else. I also met him first at the opening of Erik's restaurant so we are sort of acquaintances."

"Speaking of secrets..."

"Who was speaking of secrets?"

"No one. That's what makes them secrets. Now you have one about this detective. I can hear it in your voice."

"Don't be absurd." I sometimes hated Tara's ability to be highly attuned to the unspoken when she applied it to her friends to obtain information she wanted, but with my emotional containment ability she rarely picked up on what was going on with me. Unfortunately, this was one of the rare times.

"Oh my God! You're involved with him."

"No, I'm not, Tara. He's a friend of my brother's."

"Crises intensify sexual connections, Mik." It was a little disconcerting to hear her repeat what I had told myself earlier. "You know that. Especially you. I will admit he radiates sexuality. Amanda said something about he could handcuff her anytime. Does anyone else know about this?"

"There is nothing to know. I told you I am not seeing him."

"Yeah, right."

"I am done talking about this, Tara. And talking in general. I know you want to divert your attention from what happened today but it's not going to be speculating about my romantic life. Will you be able to sleep tonight?"

"Yes. I always have medicinal backup in emergencies like this. Courtesy of the Lexisystem pharmaceutical company. Not that you heard me say that." Tara was one of several MDs who had no ethical problem with accepting medication samples from pharmaceutical sales reps for her personal use.

"I didn't hear a thing. And who cares about that after what happened today."

"You're right. I hope you're all right Mik. Call me if you need to talk, or if you could use something to help you sleep. Otherwise I know I will see you at the department crisis debriefing meeting Monday morning."

"Thanks, Tara."

CHAPTER TWENTY-THREE

I awakened Saturday morning, mouth dry, and ice pick migraine on the left side of my head. Good choice of image. Particularly since I had awakened every hour trying to get my breath after seeing a life size Barbie lurching forward, walking on knife blades toward me. Like some sort of deranged circus character on stilts. I shivered. Shook myself more awake, and decided to get moving.

I usually loved those weekend mornings when I could sleep in. I made my way to the kitchen, got out my grandmother' white enamel coffee pot and proceeded with my Saturday ritual of making egg coffee. Mixing the coffee grounds with egg, then adding them to the water, boiling three minutes and then pouring the mixture through a strainer. I never knew why we always put the egg in it but in true Scandinavian form I began drinking coffee at age nine and shortly after that, started making it for the family, neighbors who stopped by to visit, and the men hired for seasonal work on the ranch. I smothered my toasted English muffin with butter and wild blueberry jam before I realized I had no appetite. I forced down a couple of bites, dumped the rest in the garbage disposal, and went to retrieve the morning paper from outside my door. I wasn't ready to check the latest phone or e-mail messages. I had contacted my inner circle friends and family, and the rest could wait until I was ready to face the questions, their fears, or the inevitable "How can you work there?" The police had been thorough and the interactions with David, Tara and Luke now seemed like extensions of my bad dreams.

The fact that Burke's murder had occurred on a Friday was the silver lining on a dark thunderstorm cloud for the administration. It gave them time to figure out the media spin and contact patients. For the rest of us it was worse in some way having to carry all of this until Monday. "Renowned Psychiatrist Murdered at TWF Healthcare." The headline of the Chronicle led the front page story. I scanned through the story, looking for details or my name. "Dr. Burke's body was found in his office by two colleagues." At least someone had the good sense to leave out my name and James. Most of the article focused on Burke's history and career. More of an obituary than a crime story. However, the author did include the stories of other mental health providers who had been murdered in the country in the past few years. It concluded with the usual "police are exhausting all possible leads and pursuing a number of persons of interest." No other details. No Barbie doll reference. A TWF spokesperson was quoted as reassuring the patients and community that TWF was safe, secure. However, out of an abundance of caution, additional security measures were being implemented and if anyone had any concerns to call the 800 number they were providing 24/7 for patients to talk with someone from TWF who could address their concerns.

Luke had called back. Apparently there had been over 1,000 e-mails received by several TWF staff and administrators but there was not enough manpower to investigate all of them. Mine was in the low risk category administrators, so other than save it for now, there was nothing else that needed to be done. It would be checked later. Several blogs related to the murder had also been created by individuals, some by TWF members but many weren't. The corporation was regularly targeted by the press, former or current employees, and patients. Sometimes it was warranted. The malpractice war chest of TWF Healthcare supported a double digit number of attorneys as well as retaining others specific to types of cases. I was relieved that the e-mail was low risk and that I had not been singled out.

I figured I would get through the rest of the weekend by simply maintaining my routine and connecting to my TWF friends as we provided support for each other. I hoped to gather as much strength and emotional reserve as possible before the chaos of Monday morning arrived. I had provided all the information I knew about Burke and the murder to police and Luke. There was nothing more that I could do now.

CHAPTER TWENTY-FOUR

It was Monday. We were all to meet in the large conference room. In the same building where Burke had been killed. Some administrator had decided not to move us into another building but simply close off the hall by the crime scene, Burke's office.

"Wait! Wait" I could hear Tara's voice almost wailing. She was at the far end of the fall outside her office. I stopped walking and faced her.

"Hi Tara."

"Mikelena." She grabbed me and wrapped her arms around me as if she was drowning. "I can't believe it. I still can't believe someone killed Edward." I stepped back and took her arms off mine, holding them at her sides to try and calm her down. She was red eyed and puffy-faced.

"I know. I know. No one can believe it."

"Lizzie said you found him. You were in his office. Why didn't you tell me that when I called you?"

"I did find him. James and were together when we found him." The image of Edward's body was still present whenever I closed my eyes, and sometimes when I didn't. Like the retinal afterimage of a flashbulb too close or when you look directly at the sun.

"What happened?"

"What do you mean?"

"The media say he was stabbed to death but no one will say exactly what happened. Was it one of his patients?"

Someone had leaked to the local network news that Burke had been stabbed, but thankfully no other details. "Tara, I can't tell you and neither can James. The police told us not to talk about it. You know I would tell you if I could." It was hard not to talk about it, with the hope that talking would diminish its emotional impact. All of us who worked with trauma carried within us emotional storage areas that contained the dark, unspeakable residue of the experiences that our patients shared with us. It changed you. At a certain point it could become toxic.

Therapists were, by the requirements of our chosen profession, or by who we were that made us choose our profession, looking for the back story, the reasons people are the way they are and why they do the things they do. We listened to the stories of victims and perpetrators every day.

There was brilliant Lawrence Dupree, IQ of 176, who I treated during a training stint in a residential treatment center for the criminally insane. He was there because after school one day, his first day in second grade, when the baby sitter was absorbed in a call to her best friend, Lawrence cut up a half ream of paper with his safety scissors, stacked it on a pile of his mother's clothes, bound and gagged his four year old brother and placed him next to the pile, poured a bottle of rubbing alcohol over it all, and lit a match. He locked the door to his brother's room and braced the door handle with a chair he dragged over from the hall, so the door couldn't be opened from the inside. He then went downstairs to the family room to watch his favorite movie. His brother was saved by the smoke alarm and a fire department station located within minutes from the house. When the first psychiatrist to see Lawrence asked him why he did it, he said simply, "He wouldn't be quiet." Attempts to understand his reasoning, through projective tests, thematic apperception tests, play therapy produced nothing further. The judge assigned to the criminal case weighed the psychiatric evaluations from the defense and the prosecution, and ruled that little Lawrence had not understood the consequences of his actions. Further he agreed with the conclusion of the defense's expert psychiatrist that children of his age are malleable, that he could learn from his behavior and be successful. That the greater crime would be to assume this brilliant a young mind could not learn and could not be successful in the world. The judge turned out to be correct. Lawrence did learn and was successful. Four months later he permanently silenced his little brother by disabling the smoke alarm and selecting a longer window of unsupervised time. He was diagnosed sociopathic and placed in a psychiatric hospital for juveniles determined to be criminally insane. Sociopath, antisocial personality disorder, the most frequent serial killer psychopathology. No remorse. Aware of right and wrong but not bound by societal norms or morality. A six year old choosing to violate norms to serve his own needs.

There were only a few of us in the clinic who had ever treated or evaluated the criminally insane – the term still used because of the original laws associated with it. The McNaughton Rule. One news anchor had editorialized that obviously anyone who kills is mentally ill or "insane." That just isn't true. People want to believe that because it separates them from the "evil" in the world. But there are those who kill for basic human motives – greed, jealousy, revenge – none equals insanity. I knew all of us in the clinic were trying to figure out how this could happen to one of us. Could we be treating a killer? Could I be treating a killer?

Tara was still talking. "It couldn't have been a patient. You know that I joined TWF so I wouldn't have to deal with those free clinic type patients anymore. And I know that a social worker was shot and killed in a psychiatric clinic last year, but that clinic is out in the boonies. You expect that sort of thing in those rural areas where there are too many guns powered by too few brains. And it was after hours with no one else there and no security at all."

"Tara, they didn't catch the person. No one knows if it was a patient or…"

"Or staff. Or someone who hates therapists."

I nodded. "But I do remember reading that the police profiler concluded it was not likely a patient. I hope TWF will take extra security measures now."

"That's what they said. I hope you're right."

"Me too, Tara. Are you sure you're feeling up to seeing patients today?"

"Yes, I can manage. Everyone is upset. We can't all be the Nordic stoic type and I wouldn't want to be anyway. You look like you aren't even bothered by it." I ignored her comments, placed my hand on her arm, and we walked into the conference room in silence.

"There's Lizzie and Rachel. They're headed into the meeting. Are you ready to go in?"

Tara brushed her hair back. "Do I look all right?"

Either she had chosen not to wear any makeup this morning or she had already wiped it off during one of her crying spells. "You look fine. And you're right. No one expects us to look anything other than distressed today."

"Thanks."

I opened the door for her to enter the group room where the staff meeting to process Burke's death was to be held. All clinic patients scheduled for this morning had been cancelled.

CHAPTER TWENTY-FIVE

"Most of you know me, but I see a few unfamiliar faces, so let me introduce myself. I am Jerold Manning the area EAP director. Part of my job is to help out when disasters occur. Of any type. There has been a tragic event on Friday with the death of the Chief of Psychiatry, Dr. Edward Burke. I know this is difficult both due to the loss to the patients and community of such a noted psychiatrist, but also personally to all of you. There may be those of you who are wondering if you are in danger. The police have assured TWF Healthcare that although there are no suspects under arrest, the assumption is that this incident is likely specific to Dr. Burke. However, anyone who feels that he or she cannot work due to psychological trauma or other concerns should see me at my office. I have freed my schedule for today and tomorrow for anyone who may need me. That said, I am here today to help this group cope with the loss and find ways to resume the workings of the clinic so that our members are reassured that we are there for them, which I know is what Dr. Burke would have wanted us to do. At this point I would like us to have a moment of silence in honor of and in respect for Dr.Burke." He bowed his head and closed his eyes. There was silence in the room. I watched the second hand on my watch to see how long the moment was.

"Thank you." 30 seconds had past. "Would anyone like to share feelings or thoughts at this point?" A number of staff gave brief tearful comments regarding their sense of loss and the loss to TWF. Jerold stepped forward again. "In about 20 minutes we will be joined by police investigators who will answer questions and also discuss how we can best help them in this situation. Next we will hear from our facility security manager Patrick Albe."

Patrick stood up all 5'4" and 150 pounds worth of security. Often you hear how someone appears small and not at all tough, but they are particularly skilled in martial arts or in communication.

Patrick was skilled in neither; he was, however, kind, friendly, and likable. He made his twice daily rounds of our campus with his signature uniform style. Either his pant leg was caught inside the back of his shoe, exposing curly leg hair protruding over his short black socks, or his shirt was oddly tucked in so that the hem was sticking out above his belt. He handed out a sheet of paper that outlined the security changes he planned to discuss. "This indicates the changes we have implemented and those that are planned:

Item 1. Keypad Locks have been changed to a 5 digit code instead of the former 4 digit code to secure all areas from patient access unless accompanied by a staff person.

Item 2. Everyone must wear their identification badges at ALL times. Although this has always been a security rule we will even more rigorously enforce it. Interpretation: They never enforced this – which I knew because I hated wearing my badge and almost never did.

Item 3. There will be additional security officers on the premises until further notice and the local police department is on special alert and an officer will be on campus daily for the next month."

I glanced over at Tara. She was making notes about something. I couldn't imagine what. Certainly not this drivel. There was no way to secure a building from the perpetrator when that person could be one of our patients.

"There will be a video surveillance system implemented in the next few months." Patrick continued.

"In a few months!" Charles, who rarely spoke up in meetings, blurted out what we were all thinking. "My daughter was crying this morning when I left because this murder is all over the news, and she is afraid I could be the next victim." Heads were nodding.

Jerold interceded. "We are all afraid, but we can't let this affect our judgment. Perhaps your daughter would benefit from one of the services we have for the family members of employees."

"Jerold, you may be well meaning but you're an ass." William was the only therapist with immunity from firing or consequences since he had announced his retirement. "This is ridiculous. If retail stores already have surveillance systems in place to monitor shoplifters, TWF Healthcare should be able to get off their fat financial butt and put in a system in a week, if they wanted to."

"I agree." Lizzie and I spoke simultaneously.

"I will do everything within my power to have this implemented as soon as possible." That statement might have been reassuring if Jerold or Patrick had any real authority. But we all knew they didn't.

Jerold continued in his preprogrammed role. "We all must cope with our fears and concerns and take care of our feelings and each other. There will be a designated Acting Chief and one Assistant Chief for the Department over the next three months. I have great confidence in the law enforcement services in our community, and I have the personal assurance from the Chief of Police that no stone will go unturned to find and punish the person who did this heinous and cowardly act."

I didn't think real people talked in low budget movie clichés like this. How long had he worked on this speech and did he really believe it would allay our anxiety? I looked over at Lizzie who caught my eye and rolled hers. I wasn't the only one feeling "handled" and not at all adeptly. In this moment, I experienced more of a general sense of disquiet, unease about Burke's murder than fear. Knowing the gruesome details made it clear it was personal to Burke. Not some random, disorganized killer who was targeting TWF Healthcare mental health professionals, but this person's idea of appropriate consequences for something. That something was the part I couldn't figure out.

Charles was shaking his head and entering something on his phone. Most likely making plans to transfer to another TWF Healthcare facility. He was one to take action for himself sooner rather than later. He had transferred to the San Cortez facility from the East Valley clinic because he had felt undervalued. As a good therapist who spoke Spanish and Cantonese, he was someone any clinic would want, and he could easily transfer.

Jerold was now resuming his laptop slide show that outlined the steps of the crisis debriefing process for us to implement with the patients we would be seeing over the next couple weeks. There would also be a "town hall" meeting for TWF Healthcare members Thursday evening to be co-led by Jerold and the CEO of TWF Healthcare who was a charismatic speaker and a good choice to reassure patients that all is well, and to pay no attention to the man behind the curtain. And when he spoke, people believed the Wizard.

For most of the therapists this was the first major crisis to address with patients. For a few of us it was one more in a series.

Many years ago, William and I had co-led community TWF Healthcare groups following a 7.5 earthquake in the area that had leveled homes. William was surprisingly engaging with all types of patients. He extended himself to many patients, and did phone follow ups for some of the more fragile people who did not have insurance coverage, but needed to talk. One more reason I will miss William.

Jerold continued with the list of expected patient responses: patients not showing up for appointments, going to another clinic, showing up and being angry or scared or bewildered, or those who were in such denial they acted as if nothing had happened and would not even raise the issue.

"I have forwarded to you on e-mail information on coping with a violent death in the workplace as well as outlining patients' reactions expected and some suggestions in addressing this. The primary talking point for TWF Healthcare is that this is a tragedy, but one that could have happened anywhere. Although we are instituting more security procedures we have always met the community standard for the safety of our staff and patients."

Each time I saw it in an e-mail or heard TWF Healthcare administrators utter the phrase "talking points" I cringed. How do we spin this for damage control? See the answer in the five listed "talking points."

"Next, Dr. Burke's cases have been reassigned and an encrypted list for each of you has been sent in the electronic chart. Although many patients will have already heard about Dr. Burke's death, when you contact the patients, I would operate on the assumption that they do not know."

"Are you saying no one has contacted the patients?" Lizzie interrupted.

"We tried to contact patients and some we were able to, but those we were not we did not want to leave this kind of message, so there are a good number of patients who have not been contacted. This kind of message cannot be delivered to patients by clerical staff. Every effort was made to be equitable in the distribution, although if a therapist has been co-managing a patient with Dr. Burke, that therapist was assigned to the patient."

In recent years, TWF Healthcare tended to think of the best patient care and ethics when it meant the therapists were the ones to do the extra work. It was hard to listen to this crap. Today of all days.

Jerold was continuing. "I know this is difficult for everyone but we have to pull together as a team and I hope we all can do that with our focus on the patients, and working as a team we can take care of each other."

Charles whispered behind me "If I have to hear 'team' one more time, I can guarantee there will be more workplace violence." I nodded in response to Charles, but Jerold saw me nod and smiled, silently thanking me for the support he thought I had given him.

"When the date for the memorial service is scheduled, I will inform you all. We are short staffed due to the absence of James who will be off work for at least the next three months and one of our social workers, who we expected to return from maternity leave has decided not to return to TWF Healthcare, and we will be posting her position as soon as possible."

The door opened and Jackman entered. Seeing the packed room with no seats available he chose a space standing against the wall with his cowboy boot heel braced against the leg of the chair in which one of the new staff was sitting. She looked up at Jackman, and he patted her shoulder. Lizzie had also been watching this display. She leaned over her lap to mime sticking her finger down her throat in a "gag me" response. I chose not to look at Jackman, but stared at my folded hands, neutral therapist face intact. I wondered how many people in the room felt true grief at the loss of Burke. Jackman probably did. At least as much as any narcissist is able to. But my guess was that he was in the minority. Lizzie, Charles, William, and me - I knew we did not.

"Dr. Jackman. Would you like to say a few words?" Jerold had reached the end of his preprogrammed Violent Death in the Workplace Presentation.

Jackman nodded and slowly walked to the center, embraced Jerold in a bear hug, and then looked over the group. "This is a tragic, tragic loss. Dr. Burke was my good friend and mentor. As many of you know we met at Harvard and we immediately bonded through our mutual goal of service to the physically and mentally ill. I am deeply saddened by his passing." He stopped, took a handkerchief from his pants pocket and wiped a tear from the corner of his eye, gave a couple short snorts into the cloth, carefully turning the used sections to the inside and then the sections into triangles, not unlike the required method of folding the American flag. "I echo Jerold's words that Dr. Burke would want us to serve our patient population rather than dwell on our own grief. In serving our patients we are honoring him. The dedicated, accomplished, compassionate Dr. Burke."

Jerold stepped forward and stood next to Jackman. "Thank you, Dr. Jackman. Would anyone else like to say a few words?"

There was now a protracted silence in the room. Not the hold your breath type of silence you experience at a theater or ballet performance right when the lights start to dim. Not a silence of expectation, but a silence of discomfort and avoidance. It was not that the audience was devoid of genuine mourners. Burke had changed many patients' lives for the better. All of us knew that. He was also one of the hardest working doctors in TWF. However, the few who were without ambivalent feelings regarding Burke had already spoken.

"Then let's each honor Dr. Burke in our own way as we go about the rest of our day. Thank you."

CHAPTER TWENTY-SIX

I knew the rest of the day would be interminable. Burke's murder had made every patient interaction, phone or in person visit, an acute trauma session. Whether the patient saw it that way or not, I had to. That meant a high level of vigilance and finely tuned empathy. That kind of constant intensity of attention was unsustainable in the long-term.

I took out the dark chocolate covered espresso beans and bottle of Coke. My emergency energy stash saved for these times. It was placed right next to my earthquake readiness kit in the bottom desk drawer.

My phone rang. The sequence of short rings of my phone identified it as an outside call. Outside the TWF Healthcare facilities. If I didn't talk with the patient now, I would have to call them back before I left for the day. Although that's a policy I had since I started treating patients, it was reinforced by one of my former colleagues, a psychiatrist. He had not called a number of patients back who had left messages for him on that particular day. He had listened to them but figured an overnight wait wouldn't be a problem. A 42 year old police officer, married with 2 adult children, someone he had seen in a few visits for panic attacks the year before, committed suicide that night with her revolver. The quality review board found my colleague had met the appropriate standards of care, but it continued to stay with him and I knew he never left work again without at least having attempted a call to every patient. I picked up the phone, "Dr. Pearson."

"Mik, Hi. It's Luke Sustern. Is this a good time to talk?"

"As good as any. Do you have any updates? Or anything you can tell me?"

"I wanted to follow up more personally, after the message I left."

"Thanks, Luke. How are you?"

"Trying to contain the firestorm. People are frightened and I would like to have something tangible to assuage their fears. But I don't. I'm keeping at it. How are you managing at TWF?"

'I'm managing. Drained but managing. One day at a time. Or more accurately, one patient at a time."

"Sounds like a good strategy. I assume you have not received any more unusual e-mails or messages."

"You're right. I haven't. It appears the police were right. It helped to talk with you at the time, and I thank you again for that."

"I want to help you any way I can, Mik. I think about you and it's important to me that you are safe. Will you call me if you need me?"

"I will. I promise."

"Take care of yourself." He hung up.

I sat for a moment thinking about the conversation. Was I reading too much into the "I think about you" statement? Was it "I am obsessed with how attracted I am to you?" Likely wishful thinking on my part, although I could feel the chemistry when I was in the room with him. He was often in my thoughts. I hadn't met anyone quite like him. Even if my fantasies were only an escape for me at this point, it was the engaging distraction I needed. I decided to keep my own interpretation of his words.

I braced myself for the messages that had been left on my voicemail. I pressed the number for message retrieval: "You have 10 new messages, six are urgent." All the urgents sounded the same. It was one of the top administrators representing TWF Healthcare Leadership with the odd voice echo indicating that he recorded this on speaker phone. It gave the staff the sense that upper management were all holed up in a top security underground cave somewhere, but wanted to let those of us on the front line know that our security and the safety of the patients were their top priorities. The next messages were from patients:

"This is Mrs. Bernhart and I'm not setting foot on that graveyard you call a Psychiatry Department. I'm canceling my appointment and I will be seeing a therapist in the Mandika private clinic."

There were similar messages from a few patients, and other messages from patients and from colleagues concerned for me as well as for them.

I made a couple of calls, then took a break, and started to brace my door open for a moment.

"They searched Edward's house and have taken all his computer files and all the hard copy data, including those binders that had all that patient information." Amanda was breathing hard from the quick trip down the hall to my office, and was now resetting the sparkly green and blue butterfly that had unsuccessfully held her bangs to one side.

"What are you talking about, Amanda?"

"The investigators, the police. Just like they took all Edward's stuff from his office."

"How do you know that?"

Amanda looked at me and smiled slightly.

"Oh, that's right. I forgot about your sister." Amanda's sister worked as an administrative assistant in the police department and was similar to Amanda in her inability to maintain information boundaries. "I'm not sure I understand the problem. It's a murder investigation."

"I know, but I am working with Dr. Jackman and I was working with Dr. Burke on that chronic pain study, and we have a patient coming in this week whose test results haven't been scanned in. Dr. Burke took them home."

I began to realize the problem. Although legally we weren't supposed to remove identifiable patient data from the premises in hard copy, we all knew Burke did, regardless, as did a few other staff. The work load was too much, and at times it was easier to work at home on weekends than to come into the clinic.

"We need that information. You know how irritable those chronic pain patients can be."

I did know. It was annoying that Amanda did not see herself in that category. "Wasn't William working with Burke and Jackman?"

"Only the patient recruitment in the first six months of the project. He hasn't been a part of it for the past few months. You know he hates research design and data collection."

"I do. Boring bean counter work, I believe he said."

"Right. So can you help?"

"I'm not sure how I can help you. I didn't have access to that data. Can't the TWF Medical Legal Department get that released?"

Amanda was silent for a second. "Well, I heard you had an 'in' yourself with the cops."

"I don't know what you mean."

"You know. I heard that the detective who was here the day Dr. Burke was murdered is a friend of your brother's and maybe he could help release the data. I know Dr. Jackman and you don't get along that well, but the work is terribly important to the patients."

I looked at Amanda, trying to choose my words. She could not tolerate the silence. "Why do you hate him so much? He's so caring with the patients and does all that research. I know you think he is a macho pig, but don't you see how he dotes on his wife Maria. Why last Christmas he gave her a beautiful diamond and emerald bracelet that must have cost a fortune."

I was still figuring out how to respond. Frankly, the expensive gifts we all knew Jackman bought for his wife always seemed like some sort of compensation, bribe, or maybe payoff. It never looked like caring or love. And there was no way in hell I would impose on my brother or Luke for the likes of Jackman.

Amanda was tapping her foot as she furrowed her brow, and gave a frustrated sigh.

"Oh, forget it. You should trying bending your ethics or whatever that is that you follow and help me out. I know I will never convince you how wonderful Dr. Jackman is. I was told he may be taking over as Chief of Psychiatry, in addition to his other roles, so maybe then you'll change your mind about him." She left with a little dismissive wave of her hand. I was grateful that my silence was more effective than anything I might have said. I also hoped that it was a rumor that Jackman might become the Chief of Psychiatry, but I had more pressing concerns at the moment.

I continued seeing patients and made more phone calls. Once that was completed, I scrolled down the page of e-mails from colleagues from other facilities, e-mails with news media updates, and more TWF "talking points" as the story showed up in various places.

This one looked worth opening. An e-mail from William with the subject line "talking points." I opened it.

"I would like to join with administration in **TALKING** about doing our best to work as a team in this difficult time. Along that line, I suggest that we have a pool. Who do you predict will have the most patient no shows and cancellations over a week's period of time and by how many percentage **POINTS**? The winner will have his or her drinks paid by the rest of us at our weekly happy hour for the next month." He had copied the e-mail to the usual group. There were times when William's irreverent humor was what we needed; right now it was welcomed in the midst of patient after patient trauma response, what we were doing, and what we knew we had yet to do over the next few weeks.

CHAPTER TWENTY-SEVEN

The next day was less chaotic. My patients were all showing up. That included Cyntheya.

"I see him. A big man. Across the room. Sitting at his desk in a worn leather chair. Legs spread apart. I watch him take the piece of twisted rope of grey material and hold it right under his nose. Close but not close enough to touch his skin. He inhales deeply, sliding the tip of his tongue in and out at the corners of his mouth and then he swallows, tilts his head back and closes his eyes as though he tastes the smell. He moves his hand down, unzips his pants, and pulls out his cock. He turns towards me so I am forced to see all of him. I am unable to move or run away. He smiles and stares at me as he jerks off. Finally he stops, places a glove on his right hand as he finishes the job, his whole body stiffens and then relaxes. He never touches me. It is as if I am there but not there. He cleans up and walks out the door."

"Cyntheya, what are you feeling?"

"Why are you asking me that?"

"Because you read your dream to me as if it is your algebra assignment. No emotional connection."

"Do you think I am making it up?"

"Making up what?"

"The dream."

"Did someone think you made it up?"

"My mom. She said I was either psychologically disturbed, or headed for a career as a writer for bad porn movies. As if there is some kind of good porn. She called me a 'drama queen.'"

"What do you think?"

"I don't know. I did what you told me. I wrote this down as soon as I woke up so I wouldn't forget l like I do most of the time. But I don't remember any of it. It's like reading something someone else wrote. I don't like it."

"Dreams are a creation of your mind. They mean something. We will figure out what. What I do know is that you are carrying painful feelings. They show up in your anxiety and sleep problems, and bad dreams, or a better word would be nightmares. Do you feel anything now as you read what you wrote?"

"Just feeling weird, as if in some way I knew him but not really. And that I couldn't leave the room."

"Keep recording what you dream. We'll figure it out."

After the session ended, I decided to call Lizzie for a consultation. Lizzie was the most experienced of all of us. She "had done hard time" as she put it by working 10 years in an acute inpatient unit at the State Psychiatric Hospital as well as 25 years in private practice, long term work with abuse and trauma victims. She also didn't respond to TWF Healthcare patients with the "treat 'em and street 'em" philosophy of the newer therapists. Maybe better for me to do a face to face versus phone. The advantage of having a resource like Lizzie right down the hall. I checked her schedule. Looked like she had time open but that was not always accurate either because patients were squeezed in or she was sometimes having phone sessions with her private patients. I knocked on her door and heard the familiar "It's open" greeting. Lizzie rarely got up from her chair unless she was forced to.

"Hi. You have a minute? I need a consult."

"Sure, hon. Sit down. I have a couple of minutes." Lizzie loved giving her opinion.

"Thanks. I have my notes with me so I could do this as quickly as possible."

"Before you get to that, Mik, did you hear?"

"What now?"

"David quit. He turned in his resignation effective immediately."

"What? Why? Does he plan to get another job somewhere?"

"His family is loaded. Didn't you know that? His mother is a pathologist and researcher who invented some sort of special patented medication administration system."

"I knew he had expensive taste, but I never knew how he afforded it. I thought he was designer dressed all the time because that's where he spent all his money."

"I didn't mean to sidetrack you from your consult but I couldn't see you and not tell you."

"I'm surprised but I don't have time to talk about it right now. I need your thoughts on this so I will review my notes with you. I want to look at the underlying themes so let me go through all the information first and then I'd like to hear what you think." I read through the recent session. "What do you think?"

"I don't think there is any question this girl was abused. Do you?"

"No. Anything else?"

"I'm disturbed by the vividness of her descriptions and the dissociation from them at the same time. I'm guessing it is more recent or possibly even current rather than earlier childhood abuse. You said she has been having symptoms in the past year. There is the combination of details with an overall sense of vagueness."

"I'm not certain, Lizzie. There's something else about this I can't quite put my finger on."

"What's your plan for her treatment? She seems to be moving in the right direction."

"I thought I could keep seeing her until she goes to college. Unless you would be willing to take her into your practice? Do you have any scholarship slots available?"

Lizzie had made a commitment to providing therapy to those who were either disadvantaged or who were uninsured. She had a few slots in her private practice for the low fee patients. Some paid only $20 per session, less than their insurance co-pays would be if they had insurance.

"I don't know if I will have a slot opening up in the next year since I took two new low fee patients last month, but I will keep you in mind if something changes. You didn't ask but definitely I think you should keep seeing her for now. She clearly trusts you and to me she seems close to accessing the trauma." Lizzie turned back to her computer. "Sorry, Mik but I need to make another call before I see my next patient so I have to kick you out."

"No problem. Thanks Lizzie." I mulled this over as I returned to my office. A less satisfying consult that I had hoped. Maybe there wasn't some other connection but there was still a sense of something missing that I should be able to identify. I also knew that these types of unconscious connections were similar to creative efforts. You couldn't force them to happen. You had to let them percolate and emerge when they were ready to, or prompted by the next bit of information from the patient.

I reached my office without having my thoughts disrupted by one of the other staff. The phone rang as I opened the door.

"I got it!" It was Lizzie. "It bothered me when we were talking but I couldn't quite connect it. You know what Cyntheya, that patient Jessica, and Zoe, the patient I presented have in common besides the obvious abuse issues? Burke was the psychiatrist for all of them."

"This is your epiphany? Burke was the psychiatrist for thousands of patients."

"Humor me. They also all changed from Burke to a female psychiatrist."

"That reduces the number of patients to a couple hundred females who wouldn't return to him."

"But what if he did something to them in his office. All those late hours or even more likely on those Saturdays when he worked by himself here."

"Right. I would be more likely to give your theory credibility if it wasn't the fifth Burke theory of perversion you have proposed since I have known you. I prefer the one you had that he used hypnosis with patients for pain management so that he could suggest they give him high scores on his patient satisfaction forms."

"I was mostly kidding on that one, but this time I can feel it's true."

"I'll consider it, Lizzie, but I'm ending the call now."

I knew Burke was emotionally sadistic. That was glaringly evident with both David and Tara. But a sexual predator of young female patients? The murder weapon was a Barbie doll. Obviously that meant something to the killer. Lizzie didn't know about it so she wasn't using that reference to link together these patients in her theory. She was eerily intuitive at times as well. On the other hand, we saw so many young women who were victims of sexual abuse that these patients may be no different. And Cyntheya had not mentioned Burke's death in the session, but neither had a couple other patients. I was certain the police had to be pursuing the vengeance motive given the type of murder. Lizzie's theory could be correct, but at this point I had to choose between being a therapist or an amateur detective. The choice was made for me. My next patient was already registered and waiting.

CHAPTER TWENTY-EIGHT

The day was over. Our group decided to meet at Zack's Bar, at Charles invitation. But not for our usual competition. Tara, Lizzie, William, Charles, Rachel, and me. No one was late this time.

"To Dr. Burke" William raised his glass and looked around the table at the rest of us. Lizzie was already in the middle of a long drink of a cosmopolitan. The rest of us were silent.

"Are we toasting to his demise?" Lizzie asked with an innocent look on her face. "Hail, Dorothy! Or whoever the liberator is. The wicked witch is dead."

"Lizzie!" Tara and William appeared shocked.

"Don't act offended. Especially you, Tara. Burke's death gave you a 'get out of jail free' card - so to speak." Everyone was silent.

"What are you talking about Lizzie?" Tara's voice was filled with tension.

"You were on the chopping block, Tara. Don't deny it. Particularly when you had been screwing the guy who was going to really screw your career."

Tara was glaring at me. She assumed I had been the one to betray her secret.

"That's enough."

"No Mik, it isn't close to enough."

"What do you mean, Lizzie? Or maybe I should ask Tara." Charles was always slow to be involved in gossip but Burke's murder seemed to have opened a number of doors that were usually closed. And padlocked.

"Okay. Maybe I went too far." Lizzie set her glass down. "Let's see. Will all those who have not had the thought 'I feel like killing Burke' please raise your hand." Rachel's hand was the only one raised. No one else moved.

"All right then."

"All right what?" Tara asked.

"Practically everyone felt like killing Burke at some time. There is no point in acting all bereaved when we all know the truth. But I am willing to remove those at this table from the list of possible suspects. I do regret that I didn't think of the murder solution myself. However, stabbing is much too up close and personal. Messy. I have an idea. Let's bet on who did it. A patient, employee, ex-employee, patient's family member, scorned lover. Who else could have a motive?"

"I think it's someone who worked at TWF." Tara spoke without looking up.

"Worked? Past tense."

"Worked----e d. Someone who works here would not be so stupid as to kill him on site. What about Bob Albright? He swore he would get Burke for firing him. I think Bob is capable of harboring a grudge and he was devastated."

"Naw." Lizzie dismissed this. "Ten plus years is a little long for delay of gratification for being fired."

"Perhaps someone killed Burke to send a message. Not just to Burke but to TWF Healthcare in general." Charles was now engaged in the discussion.

It was too enticing for any of us to stop the ghoulish process and redirect to something more appropriate. Too compelling to wind our way into the darkness that existed in everyone and that we searched to find. We were all involved in this particular psychological autopsy.

"The message would be what? Besides the obvious 'die you morally bankrupt sadistic scum.'" William signaled the server for another round.

"What about that Billy Sanders' family? Or the mother of that young woman who suicided?" Charles appeared to be considering these possibilities for the first time. I was certain they were already on the persons of interest list.

"Sanders' family settled, remember? And that other situation was resolved." Tara interjected.

"Yeah, but the Sanders weren't that happy with the no fault nondisclosure agreement they had to sign for the monetary settlement. Maybe one of them took matters into their own hands."

Charles stopped for a moment and looked from Tara to me. "Oh that's right. You guys were both involved in that."

"Well, not Mik." Tara corrected. "Anyway, Charles, there was no assignment of fault. You know how patients' families are. They can't accept that either the person was that disturbed, or that they could not prevent it and need someone to blame. Five providers and Edward were named. I was not the only one."

The lawsuit named you but didn't find you at fault?" Although Charles was looking at Tara it was as if he was talking to himself.

"That's right, Charles. And I wasn't at fault, not just legally but in reality." Tara placed emphasis on her statement by gesturing at him with the toothpick she had cleared of the three olives from her dirty martini.

"Geez – don't get defensive. I was simply trying to figure out how this all works."

"Everyone stop it. I think we are all upset about Burke, and we are taking it out on each other" Rachel spoke up. "Burke's death is not part of a game. I know he was tough on people but he still helped a lot of people, including my sister's son. He was the only psychiatrist to diagnose him correctly, so he could get some help."

"My money is on a former employee." Lizzie continued, ignoring Rachel's attempts to change direction. "Revenge is still a dish best served cold."

"Too well planned and too much inside knowledge to be either a stranger or a patient. I'm afraid they won't catch the guy," said William.

"Why assume it's a man?" Lizzie interjected. "It could be a woman."

Charles looked at his watch and then pulled out his wallet to place a $100 bill on the table. It was late and it was time to stop the discussion of "who done it." We all needed to get home.

"I want this to be my treat." Charles announced.

"Ooo-big spender." I placed on hand on Lizzie's arm to prevent her from continuing.

"Thank you Charles from all of us." I gave him a quick hug.

"Yeah, thanks pal." William gave him a pat on the back.

No one said anything but we all knew his request to meet at Zack's was his good bye to us. His paying for our drinks was an attempt to partially absolve him of his guilt at abandoning us and the clinic. We knew he would transfer within the month. We were all too emotionally fatigued to address it. And no one blamed him for his decision. Many would envy his escape. Escape not from someone who might kill again, but from the collateral clinic damage the murder of Burke had created.

"Mik, can you give me a ride home?" Tara had ridden with Lizzie, and was not willing to be subjected to any more of Lizzie this evening.

"Sure. My car is this way." We walked in silence the first couple blocks.

"Did you tell Lizzie about Burke and me?"

"Of course not. She knew."

"How?"

"You should ask her. And I never told her what you told me or confirmed I knew."

"Really? Thanks. But why didn't you tell me she came to you?"

"Because of this crap. Who told who what, and I didn't want to know any more about what you did with Burke. To be honest, it disgusts me."

"You?? What about you and Ryan?"

"I didn't say Burke disgusted me because he has a personality disorder like Ryan's, but because Burke's a sadist. A whole other level of slime."

"This is a complete mess. The police talked to me like everyone else and I admitted having a past sexual relationship with Edward because I figured it would come out and it would look worse for me. I don't need one more complication."

"Tara, I wish you had told me the truth about your relationship with Burke."

"What difference would it have made?"

"You've known me for over five years Mik. Why wouldn't you believe me?"

"Maybe because you have known me for that long, but didn't feel you could tell me the truth. You didn't trust me, Tara. That makes me wonder why. And wonder if there are other things you aren't telling me."

"Like did I kill Edward?"

"What?"

"You heard me."

"Of course not. I know you could never do something like that."

"Do you? Couldn't any of us if pushed too far or if the stakes were high enough?"

"You sound like Lizzie."

"Lizzie is not a stupid woman."

Tara and I had talked before about this. We did agree that although we hoped we were evolved, morally intact enough to never step over that particular line, we also were not certain we would not. In the right set of circumstances. Tara and I had been close friends when she started in the clinic, before she started her climb up the administrative ladder. The fact that she was smart, supportive and kept confidences made her one of my best friends. It was during that time that Tara with the disinhibition of at least a bottle of wine, had disclosed that when she was married she had thought and even planned to kill her husband (now ex-husband) after she learned he had molested her daughter Brittany. Poison, she had said, was the method she had decided upon. An overdose of an undetectable drug. Two times she had saved enough drugs to kill him and each time she flushed the pills. Only once did she consider taking them herself to end her own pain, but knew she did not want to abandon her daughter or herself. She had tried therapy a number of times but like many mental health professionals results for her were mixed. She had spent, she estimated, $80,000 in therapy. I had overheard her tell Lizzie at one point, "I should have bought a Mercedes with the money instead." But it may have helped her more than she knew, because when I met her she had a steely strength I admired, even with her times of emotional ups and downs.

Did I think Tara might have killed Burke? I did consider it. But I also had seen the crime scene. The Tara I knew had difficulty containing her emotions for an extended period of time, and that crime scene was meticulously executed, contained, a result of calculated rage. Maybe that was a part of Tara I didn't know. We had reached Tara's house.

"You're right Tara. Your business is your business."

"Thanks, Mik."

"Don't take Lizzie too seriously. You know how she is. "

"I know. All bark, no bite. See you tomorrow."

I drove home, parked my car in the garage and sat for a moment.

CHAPTER TWENTY-NINE

So little time had passed since Edward's murder, but in some ways it felt like years. His office had been painted, recarpeted, new furniture. The few personal items Burke had kept were either in evidence with the police or in his stepmother's possession. A new computer. Burke's name plate removed from his door and the waiting room staff listing. Years ago, management had decided to use removable name plates for our office. So that if someone needed to share an office or a pool doctor was working, it would appear more professional to have that person's name outside the office where they saw patients. It also added to the ease of eradicating any indication that a particular staff person had ever worked there. As it did with Burke.

I opened my office door for a minute to eliminate the prison cell feeling my small office sometimes had by the afternoon. Space was always at a premium in TWF Healthcare. Never certain why that was. Either they repeatedly hired grossly incompetent planners or it was cheaper for TWF Healthcare to squeeze providers as well as patients. Economics. Always running right underneath the TWF Healthcare "We care" veneer like a sewage line.

William appeared in my office doorway. "Hi William. I see it's yellow day." William held up the yellow peanut M&M before he popped it in his mouth. One of Williams's rituals. We all knew that at the start of each week, he bought a five pound bag of peanut M&Ms and separated them into colors. He then had a specific color designated for each day. If it was a short week, he threw the rest away and started over the next week with a fresh bag. It was his only visible obsessive compulsive feature, and in sharp contrast to his usual easy going persona.

"Hi Mik. I came by to see how you are doing. You know, checking in."

"Are you telling your patients yet that you're retiring?"

"Not yet. Frankly, I haven't even formally filed for retirement."

"Why not?"

"I'm not sure. It doesn't feel right to make a big announcement to the patients so soon after they hear about Burke's death."

"You're right. William. And it's a selfless decision on your part."

"Well, I'd like to say that's my only motive, but it has turned out to be a bigger psychological step than I expected when I got to the point of doing it. And the longer I stay the more money when I do retire. I'd also like to be around when Burke's research is finished to make sure I get my name on the publication. You know how they tend to 'forget' authors when they aren't around at the stage the article is submitted to the journal. He stared at the M & M, turning it over and over in his palm."

"Makes sense, William. All of it."

"Ah, but you cleverly turned the conversation away from yourself. A well known Mikelena trick."

"Well, I hope you stay as long as possible. I don't know if I can cope with another green therapist who believes the psychological world can be conquered one cognitive behavioral technique at a time. Did Amanda ever talk to you about the Jackman and Burke research data?"

"She did. But I wasn't involved in the data collection. I helped out Jackman at Burke's request because I thought it was a follow up to Burke's first studies. Between you and me, I think it was part of a bait and switch scam to get the patients to participate."

"What do you mean?"

"The usual. Jackman told me it was a pilot to see if certain drugs were better than physical therapy for atypical chronic pain, but I got the sense there was some manipulation of the information or design, because they cut me out of the loop when I started to ask questions. You know how Jackman is proprietary, may I suggest paranoid, about others being involved with his patented traction/pain management devices."

"I know."

"Surprise. Surprise. I was never contacted again. I assume I will receive some tiny footnote acknowledgment with five other 'helpers' when it is published. I did feel a little wounded that I was suckered into the whole thing. But you know my TWF Healthcare survival philosophy."

"I do. 'Go with the flow, but bail at the sign of rapids or waterfalls'." I recited this like a school child.

"And the corollary?"

"Never believe it if an administrator tells you it's only a Level One rapids or there is no waterfall on the river, unless you have nonbiased confirmation."

"Precisely." William was now munching the last two or his yellow M&Ms. "Back to the coal mines."

"Thanks for stopping by William. Keep me posted about the retirement status."

"Oh I will."

CHAPTER THIRTY

The end of another day. My last scheduled patient had no showed. An 80 year old retired Army Colonel whose wife of 60 years had died three months ago. He was doing fairly well, the antidepressant originally prescribed by Burke was helping, but it surprised and concerned me that he had not shown up for his appointment. He had a gun, which I knew he would never give to someone for safekeeping, although I had asked him to, and he said he would think about it. I didn't think he was a risk. But Burke's death threw a wrench into the usual psychological workings of a suicide or homicide assessment. I called his home and left a message. I needed a break before I tackled the rest of what I needed to do before I could leave for the day.

I walked into our lounge – the little room with the basic work life essentials: a coffeemaker, refrigerator and microwave, along with an old fashioned cork bulletin board where staff could post pretty much anything they wanted as long as it didn't violate obscenity laws. Cartoons, pictures of children, pets, Lizzie's new puppy Elvis was already up there, the new model of Ferrari was Jackman's contribution, articles of interest from financial planning to clinical seminars were posted with a tack or pushpin. Sometimes I would look at what was posted as a form of relaxation or distraction. As I did today.

"See anything interesting?" It was Luke.

"I do." I was looking directly at him. "How are you, Luke?"

"Good. I'm good."

"What are you doing here?"

"My consultant work. And as I can, I help out informally with the investigation. The detectives have their hands full, given the complications of the patient confidentiality privilege and all the media frenzy."

"And lots of patients or should I say health plan members wanting to contribute their view of how deplorable TWF Healthcare is?"

"That's not too far off base. Although, as you know, there are also many loyal TWF Healthcare patients who thought Burke was a God and who are devastated by his death."

"I know."

I saw Amanda walk by, and then glance back behind Luke with a smug look on her face, quickly licking her lips and pointing at him. "Oh Dr. Pearson, I left you a note. The Colonel called to apologize for missing his appointment and wants to reschedule. I knew you would be concerned."

"Thanks Amanda. I was. Do you know Detective Sustern? This is Amanda Simmons"

"We have met. Are you here following up with the murder investigation? Any leads? I think that's the right police term. Leads? Am I right Detective?" She struck her well-practiced chest out hand on hip pose that she had told me was infallible in capturing men's attention.

Luke appeared to be tolerating her display. "Well, Amanda, I'm not a formal part of that investigation. I'm continuing the liaison work I had been conducting with the department."

Amanda seemed oblivious to her lack of sexual impact "You know, Detective. There were some computer files on a very important research project-"

"Amanda."

Amanda glared at me, and then smiled at Luke as she carefully centered the large turquoise stone on her necklace right above her cleavage. She moved forward to plant herself inches from Luke in the physical space usually reserved for lovers or spouses. Luke, to his credit, stepped back and crossed his arms. Nice nonverbal counter.

"I wonder if you might be able to have those projects released or perhaps you know who I could talk to."

Luke was far more gracious than I would have been. "Well, I would like to help but that is not in my area of jurisdiction. You would have to contact the police department and the officer or detective who is in charge. The information that is not related I am certain will be released. Knowing TWF Healthcare they already have their attorneys on it."

"I agree with Luke, Amanda. I know you're trying to help out Dr. Jackman but there are protocols and legalities."

"Well, I'm not going to stop trying." She gave Luke a sweet smile, ignored me and walked off.

"May I speak to you a moment, Luke?"

"Sure. What is it?"

"No. In my office. It's more confidential there."

"Fine." Luke motioned for me to lead the way. I opened my office door and Luke walked in, stood until I started to sit in my chair, and then sat in the chair across from me.

"Thank you. I have wanted to ask you some questions about the investigation and Edward's murder but I wasn't certain how, and if it is appropriate." I was scrambling to find a way to check on Lizzie's theory, a way that didn't make me seem like the usual conspiracy theorist nutcase Luke must regularly encounter.

"Go ahead. I'll let you know if I can't answer."

He leaned forward and the closeness of his presence felt the same as it did every time I had contact with him. An intensity and sexuality that was distracting. Slowed my mind into a wavy distortion similar to the visual field right above a surface directly heated by the noon sun. Images of having sex with him started to float in and out. Focus. I needed focus. I didn't invite him in here for sex. Or at least not consciously."

"Is there a problem?"

"Not at all. I'm trying to think of where to start." I cleared my throat and looked down for a moment. I was able to shift back into my usual professional mode. "Can you tell me if the investigation points to a patient? Or employee?"

"Is there a specific reason you want to know this?"

"None other than watching this clinic implode on itself with fear and paranoia as therapists transfer out or psychologically deteriorate because they are scared one of us might be treating a murderer, and no one wants to be next."

"I can tell you that the police have been reviewing Burke's cases including those in the past few years. It has been challenging because of patient confidentiality issues and the complicated TWF system. There are a number of persons of interest they are investigating."

"What about the evidence? It occurred right in his office. His computer was even used." "We had hoped there would be more, but the security system was not set up for this type of crime, and Burke did allow access to his computer by a few people, even though that was against the security policy."

"You're right. Amanda, for one, had access to Burke's password as his administrative physician 'extender' as TWF called the role. Last year the computer system was hacked a couple of times as well as a laptop of one of the MDs was stolen; it had patient data on it. There have been discussions about security cameras but no one wanted patients to feel paranoid or that their confidentiality was violated. No wonder the investigators are having difficulty."

"The only surveillance cameras are outside the Emergency room. The security guards did not check the building after hours and it was only alarmed on the weekends."

"It has to be an act of revenge, don't you think, Luke?"

"Vigilante justice for something Burke did or someone thought he did?"

"Yes."

"This is not for public knowledge, but that is one theory the homicide detectives are pursuing. Do you have someone you think may be a suspect?"

"I don't know anyone who I think would commit murder, and who would choose a Barbie doll for a weapon. I have gone over and over all this in my mind and I can't figure it out, and there is no one to talk to about it. James is still disabled from all of this. There isn't anyone else."

"This has be to very difficult for you, Mikelena. You can talk to me, you know. Any time. I meant that when I said it. Anything I can do to help you, let me know."

He moved further forward to take my hand. There was a sharp knock on my door.

"Just a minute." I opened the door. It was Tara.

"Hi Mik." She started to walk in, but stopped when she saw Luke.

"Oh sorry, I didn't realize I was interrupting something."

"You're not interrupting. What is it, Tara?"

"Never mind Mik. It can wait. I'll call you tonight or you can call me."

"Are you sure?"

"Yes. Not a problem. See you. And you too Detective." She softly closed the door behind her.

"How well do you know Tara?"

"I have known Tara for years. She is a colleague and we used to socialize together. She's good with patients, and doing pretty well as acting chief since Burke's death."

"I heard there was a conflict between her and Burke regarding a lawsuit from a patient's family after a suicide. Not Sanders but another one?" Luke had shifted back to detective mode.

"There was a disagreement between them about the facts. It was shortly before Burke's death. I wasn't involved with the patient's care. Did you ask Tara about this?"

"I didn't talk with her but she was interviewed by the police along with the rest of the staff."

Another knock. This time it was a tentative one. "Come in. It's open."

"I'm sorry Dr. Pearson, but the Detective received this message. The person said it was important that he call as soon as possible." Amanda handed a note to Luke and walked out without making eye contact with me.

"Don't you have a cell phone?"

Luke read the message, and then looked at the received calls on his phone. "Damn it. I must have turned it to silent by mistake. I'm sorry. I have to return this call. I told the Lieutenant I would be here. Remember, Mik, call me anytime you want to talk."

I sat in my chair, with the lingering intoxicating feeling I had whenever he was in the same space with me. He also made me feel safe, which was rare for me. I checked my cell to see the status of the calls. I knew I had turned mine to silent, as I always did at TWF. Messages from Erik, Tara, Tara, and Tara. That interruption from Tara earlier may not have been as casual a concern. I wasn't sure whether Luke thought Tara knew something more about Burke's murder or if he was the type to gather information whenever he had the opportunity. I needed to call Tara back. Waiting to talk to her in the past had been a mistake. Now was as good a time as any. I heard the ring and her voicemail picked up almost immediately. She was talking on the phone. I left a message for her, knowing I would also call her as soon as I returned home.

CHAPTER THIRTY-ONE

Tara and I had traded messages but never connected. I was trying to finish my notes quickly so I could stop by her office and see her face when I talked to her. I wanted a better sense of what was happening with her. Everybody copes with death, stress differently but without knowing her real relationship with Burke, I could only guess what she was feeling or thinking. Speculating was not speeding up my charting pace.

"How's it going?" I looked away from my patient note on my computer screen to see William, back again, leaning against my doorway. When did my office become Grand Central Station? He held out his hand, offering me M & Ms.

"No thanks, William. What's going on with you? You have time to hang out now? Patients abandoning you first before you leave them because your retirement news leaked to the patient community?"

William took a moment, then stepped into my office and closed the door behind him. "I need to tell you something." He walked over to the chair and sat down, staring at his hands.

Now I was worried. "What's wrong?" I hit "log out" on my computer.

"I have to tell someone I trust." He looked up at me, and I nodded.

"Okay. What is it, William?"

"How do I say this? I guess just say it. Burke was involved in studies of off label uses of new drugs for treatment of trauma, posttraumatic stress disorder." He looked at me, assessing my reaction before he went on. "He started with the Veterans Administration patients in the collaborative TWF Healthcare/VA studies but it became too risky when the upper management started requiring they have more oversight into the specifics of the patients. He was getting great results with the few patients he treated. And these were patients who had not responded to other treatments or medications."

"Wait, William. You mean patients like Mr. Phelps? His adoring chronic pain VA patient?"

"I don't know who the VA patients were. And let me talk. I need to get this out."

"Sorry. Go ahead."

"He then changed to using TWF patients. He chose patients he thought would be most helped by his treatment - using a combination medication and virtual reality treatment. There has been all that publicity about researchers using different medications and virtual reality to treat PTSD in veterans and sexual abuse victims with some success. And even though MDMA or ecstasy type drugs aren't yet legal there are clinical trials using them going on, too."

"But, William, one of the critical points here is that ecstasy is illegal, and the clinical trials using it with PTSD are controversial and they are tightly controlled experiments combined with therapy. I know researchers are trying to figure out what will work for these patients because of how many are suffering from PTSD but to use both ecstasy and a drug like midazolam that induces amnesia with psychiatric patients who don't even know what medications they're getting is unbelievable to me."

"I know you're upset, but there are always initial risks at the point of a major psychological discovery when it doesn't follow traditional theory."

William never talked like this. It was as if he was reading from the marketing business plan talking points for the treatment.

"Anyway, I screened the patient questionnaires and clinical information Burke provided to me because I believed it could help and speed up the research so that more people could recover, since few treatments work for trauma. Particularly PTSD. His treatment made sense to me. The medications he was using, one that causes amnesia for the events induced with virtual reality and another that creates a receptive mood could help change the trauma memories and develop positive new ones; they could work more quickly and effectively than other methods. It's not that different from having a medical procedure like a colonoscopy where the anesthesiologist gives the person medications so that they are somewhat conscious but they don't remember the discomfort they may have experienced or sometimes they don't even remember the procedure."

"Do you know what could happen to those patients who have negative side effects to these drugs? When they don't work? Or side effects that may occur later, after the drugs wear off? Hallucinations, dissociation, agitation, disinhibition, paranoia."

"But what Burke was doing was ground breaking. He was getting around the stigma of using ecstasy and not waiting another 10 years before they approved it. He used these drugs in a controlled specific way, with a virtual reality type re-experiencing of the trauma but with a positive outcome where it isn't only use of exposure but reprogramming what happened – the patient triumphs over the situation or perpetrator."

"Triumphs? Really?"

"Yes. Triumphs." William's few hairs on his head were no longer able to absorb the perspiration that had developed. He stopped for a moment to grab a tissue and mop off his forehead. "Burke chose a small select group. He also used the standard types of self-hypnosis, relaxation imagery, and visualization most of us use, and he gave types of positive post hypnotic suggestions for patients to prolong the effect. He stopped when it was clear the results were not what he had hoped."

I was stunned but my mind was racing trying to figure out how this could happen.

"He did this on Saturdays, didn't he? When he was often the only one here." William nodded. "Saturdays and evenings I think. When no receptionist was here."

"I don't even know what to say, William. I'm only somewhat surprised that Burke would do this. His ego would have easily overstepped the lines of ethics or even legalities. But you? Didn't you realize how much harm could be done? Or may have been done?"

"I was helping. These patients suffer so much from their trauma."

"You could have killed people or made them kill themselves or someone else."

"But I didn't. I made certain the protocol was one that was no more potentially dangerous than any others."

"How would you know that for certain?"

William searched in the pockets of his jacket, and then stretched out his leg to make certain he reached the very bottom of his front pants pocket to find the last M &M. He started looking at the M & M in his hand, turning it over and over, as if he was hoping there was some message there for him.

"William? Was there someone else involved? Was there someone besides Burke who told you it was not dangerous?"

"I don't want our discussion to be more complicated that it already is."

"I'm not certain I understand what you mean. Why are you telling me this now? If the study was discontinued. Are you sure it was stopped?"

"Yes. I am."

"Did something happen?"

"No, but I started to think that maybe this could be linked to Burke's murder. If I talk to the police, I am afraid I could be in big trouble. I thought about doing it anonymously but wasn't sure if that would be the best way. I wanted to talk to you to see if you had any ideas of a way to let the police know that won't link this back to me."

"Why come to me, William?"

"You know me better than anybody here." I stared at William. Watched him as he chewed the candied peanut; the sound like the rhythmic ticking of a metronome.

"What about the legal aspect? You could be charged with a crime."

"Only if there was some negative consequence."

"Like Burke's murder."

"That was not my fault." The response was quick as though William had already considered and dismissed this possibility.

"I believe it's called felony murder. Or second degree murder. If you could have or should have known that the consequences of your actions would lead to the death of someone."

"What are you now, Mik? The district attorney? That's a little disturbing."

"That's disturbing? How about you participating in some H.G. Wells Island of Dr. Moreau experiment?"

"I didn't participate. My part was screening the patient information. And, since you are being legal with me, I could say I didn't know anything about the actual experiment because there is no evidence that says I did."

"Do you know that for certain?"

"I do. Burke wanted it that way."

That made sense to me, because Burke would have wanted his experiment to look legitimate and as if it was a regular treatment. With no evidence of what he was really doing.

"Let's go back a step, William. Back to the why. Other than your altruistic spirit. I assume there was some 'screw you, TWF Healthcare' embedded in this project for you." William shifted his weight, checked his pockets again to make certain he had retrieved the last candy. That there wasn't one more left to distract him from the question. My clinical awareness was heightened and my mind was running in therapist mode, searching for the real story. What William was not telling me. I felt like someone trying to crack a safe, listening intently while the dial turns, waiting for each click of each correct number, so that the tumblers all fall in place and I can open it and find out what is really inside. I knew why William came to me and not anyone else. I was the one who had already looked the other way when he repeatedly violated our licensing board ethics by his acts of what I truly believed was kindness, even generosity, to patients. Even more damning was our history that we had altered a record. Together. It was apparent that William was considering whether to tell me more or not. He made his decision.

"I was sick to death of TWF playing with patient's lives, screwing with their medications, doing research, and I use the term loosely. They were only trying to defend their cost cutting medication decisions and the treatment decisions. They didn't care what happened to their patients as long as they paid their insurance premiums and didn't demand expensive tests or to see specialists because that would reduce the precious bonuses of the MDs and the brain dead middle managers. Providing only 'evidence based' treatments, particularly in Psychiatry where they is no evidence for most effective treatments because they have to eliminate all the patients with more than one diagnosis, leaving only a small group who qualify to participate." William's voice was becoming more strained and high pitched and he was now pacing in a circle around his chair. "Let's talk about patients suffering, harm to patients, patients being killed. You know how many patients have suffered needlessly or even died because of this kind of crap?"

I was torn. Between the truth of what he was saying and wanting to know more about what happened, and my fear that knowing more would make it even more difficult for me to do the right thing with the information William was giving me. Whatever the right thing might end up being. William used to say repeatedly that "No good deed goes unpunished" knowing that not only did I loathe that aphorism but that I didn't believe it. But I also couldn't believe William was using my history with him of not reporting him to tell me this so he could unload whatever responsibility or guilt he felt. He knew I was his best hope besides a priest, perhaps, of keeping it in confidence. And being agnostic, William would not be opting for the priest. Another realization hit me. "Who were the patients, William? Was Billy Sanders one of them?"

"Billy Sanders? No. I don't think so. Really, Mik, I don't think he was".

"But you don't know for sure."

"I didn't have the names. Only their clinical information, so I would not be biased. I don't know who was chosen."

"Chosen? As if it was some special privilege for them. Are you lying to me, William?"

"Of course not. I came to you with this."

"It's true there wasn't anything in the legal case about Billy being part of an experiment." I was thinking out loud. We were both silent for a moment.

"But there wouldn't be, would there William, because the experiments were not part of the medical record. They were kept separate. So TWF legal would have no problem in releasing the medical records. And those drugs you are describing are short acting and not ones that would be expected or even show up in the usual tox screen."

It was all falling into place as I thought about it. "Burke would have given the medications as if they were samples, as he often did. He had to have given the medications free to the patients to eliminate the need for a required pharmacy record. And if he didn't book them into his schedule, but had them show up when there was no receptionist to register them, there would be no electronic record of any of them being seen."

I was now feeling nauseated. All of the ways we as therapists had found to get around the system to help patients were now gaping holes for evidence to fall through. To see a patient who was struggling financially for a brief visit without registering the patient prevented them from having to pay a large copay. Shit. A number of us had done that from time to time. I hoped that Billy was never included in Burke's study but it might be the explanation that no one could find or why TWF settled. Maybe someone started to look in the right direction that would have exposed all of this, and maybe someone decided Burke was worthy of the death penalty.

"Do you know how long Burke was conducting his experiments?"

"I'm not sure. A year or two maybe. But then he stopped it because it wasn't producing the degree of effect he expected. It wasn't the magic bullet he hoped it would be for PTSD."

Something wasn't adding up. I could tell there was something missing or some part of this was a lie. The detection ability I had was never wrong but it also could not tell me exactly whether it was omission, partly fabrication, or out and out lie.

"Don't look at me like that." William started to look pissed. "I did call the TWF ethics hotline even before Burke stopped because I wasn't sure if it was the right thing to do and whether it was working. I didn't want to say anything directly to Burke."

"You called the TWF ethics hotline anonymously?"

"Yes, I did. Although I didn't say exactly what he was using, only that I had general concerns about the experiments he was conducting."

"And nothing happened, right?"

"Well, I don't think they found anything wrong. Then Burke told me about three weeks later that he had stopped that experiment because it wasn't as effective as he hoped, and I wasn't needed to do the screenings anymore."

I was silent.

"What? Stop it Mik. Stop looking at me as if I sold crack to children. I'm not like Burke. I'm one of the good guys."

"Are you that naïve William? Do you think TWF Healthcare uses that ethics hotline to correct problems? I've told you this before. That 'confidential' line seems to only protect TWF. It's giving advance notice to Burke and TWF management so they can cover up the problem."

William looked shocked.

"Now you have no evidence, you are off the project, you don't know who the patients were or where the data or information is stored so no one can follow up with them. Gee, I'm not a detective but it looks like it is now your word against a respected, accomplished, and not to mention dead psychiatrist backed by a corporation that if you go up against will bury you in paperwork if they don't bury you for real."

William was beginning to appear ashen, and he steadied himself by leaning against the back of the chair.

"Damn it, William. I don't know even know what to say. There is no question someone needs to find the data and the patients, and you should tell the police and anyone else who can help you do that. You need to tell someone outside TWF, like the police. Did you talk to anyone else in TWF?"

"No. No. I'm feeling kind of overwhelmed. I guess I believed the lies I was told .....and ....and...." William was shaking his head, "and those I told myself."

William was grappling with what he did, and in another situation I would have tried to support him emotionally but I was too angry. "You had to know before you came to me, I wouldn't let this go." I felt as though I was talking to myself. "William, I will talk to my attorney to decide what needs to be done. The most important thing will be to find the patients and to make certain TWF Healthcare did stop the studies. I will keep you posted but I can't guarantee I will consult with you about what I do before I do it."

"Thank you and I'm sorry. I'm grateful you listened to me. I know you'll help me if you can. You are a great friend." He reached over to give me a hug but thought better of it, patted my shoulder, and walked to the door. He hesitated for a second, then walked out and gently closed the door behind him. I glanced at the clock on my desk. Only 15 minutes had elapsed since William came into my office. I knew what I had to do. It was how that was the question.

I scanned for Elaine Elwood's name in my contacts. My attorney. There was a time when I knew her number by heart. She was aggressive, smart, and savvy about the legal and political issues of TWF Healthcare, and 10 years ago when I was called as a witness against TWF Healthcare management, including Burke, by a few staff members, Elaine had balanced protecting my rights and preventing retaliation by TWF. I hoped she was still in practice.

I entered her number in my cell. It rang and her assistant took my information letting me know Elaine was in court but she would give her the message. I knew I would receive a call either this evening or tomorrow. Elaine was as compulsive as I was about calling back in urgent situations.

I couldn't wait. What if a patient died or became psychotic while I was trying to figure out the "right thing" to do. Or because I was trying to cover my ass and not sell out a friend. I found the number I had been given for the police department and an officer took my report and asked questions. As I told her what I knew, I realized I didn't know anything they could follow up on. No patient names, all my information was second hand, "hearsay", no evidence and if William decided not to corroborate the information, it was pretty much worthless. The officer was polite, but it didn't take psychological training to read the fatigue and general lack of interest in my information. I felt as though I was somehow confessing. To absolve my responsibility of receiving this information or some kind of guilt the information carried with it.

As I finished leaving a follow up message for William, there was a knock on the door. He was back again, with an excited look on his face. "Mik, maybe we don't have to do anything. I talked to Rafael in quality and before I could tell him anything about what you and I talked about, he told me TWF is already in process of sending out the standard follow up letters to all the research participants of Burke's telling them to contact Amanda for follow up. Plus there is that TWF 800 number they set up right after Burke died so that any members or patients of Burke's who have questions or concerns can be followed up as the normal part of continuity of care. So even though they may not be listed officially as research participants, the patients have ways to get care and follow up. No one needs to know anything else."

"You didn't tell Rafael anything about what happened?"

"No. I didn't need to because they were already doing what would be done if they did know."

"That's great, William. But I already talked to the police. I left you a message. The police will want to talk with you."

"How could you do this to me? I trusted you. You gave them my name?"

"Of course I did. You can say whatever you want. You know they have no evidence so if you want to protect yourself, go ahead and deny it. Lie. You've been lying all this time. What's the problem now?"

"I am not like that. I never thought you would rat me out Mik. You're like all the rest of them. You're trying to save your own ass."

"Bullshit. You used me. You didn't have the balls to do what was right. You told me because if I let it go you could feel absolved about what you did. And if I didn't, you could feel victimized by me. Think about it William. Did you really believe I could let this go? Especially if there was any possibility that one of the patients was Billy Sanders?"

"I don't know. I thought I was doing the right thing by helping Burke. It was his experiment, not mine."

"And it looks like he paid for it." My cell rang. "I have to take this William. I'll talk to you later." I closed my door and answered the phone. It was Elaine calling me back. Direct, almost curt, efficient. As if she was following up on a previous conversation. She took the information. Reassured me that I had done all the correct actions and nothing need be done now. She cautioned me about keeping information confidential. She confirmed that unless William chose to play ball, this would go nowhere. It was not in TWF's best interest to buy into the idea that one of their premier psychiatrists had become some sort of mad scientist, she said. And then added her current fee is $650/hour. That worked for me. I knew I could trust her and she knew me, which made $650 worth it. I felt somewhat better, knowing someone else knew, feeling less alone with it all.

I began to review my patient caseload in my head. Who might have been a subject for Burke? No one stood out. Except Cyntheya. But she would have told me. Wouldn't she? Most likely Burke would have chosen patients from therapists who regularly saw PTSD patients. William of course, Tara did, and Lizzie. Did Tara know what Burke was doing? Lizzie had such disdain for Burke she had found ways to avoid patients he had seen and almost never collaborated with him. Anthony treated PTSD patients but he hadn't been here long enough to be involved. That was pretty much it for the list. Burke didn't need many patients anyway. Just the right patients to make his study viable to prove his theory was right. That he was right. And smarter than the rest of the psychiatric community.

I went through my computer schedule starting six months ago to make certain there was no one I had missed in my mental review. No one. Thank God. I had done enough for now. All I could do. I logged off and went home.

CHAPTER THIRTY-TWO

Erik had bailed on me again. I could go to the range alone but preferred the company, or more accurately, the competition. Given what had happened with William, I needed the release. When I went alone I wore a fitted long sleeved black t-shirt and jeans. The fabric right next to my skin. A smooth slide. The way I felt when I loaded my 357. I selected the far right side, and set up. I shot a couple rounds, and then stepped outside the glass to watch. By that time, the place was deserted except for a shooter at the other side of the range where the heavier caliber guns were used. He didn't see me. I watched him. His body was in a stance that was powerful, focused but relaxed. He had a 9 mm. He looked familiar. About 6'4, muscular arms, broad shoulders, and tight jeans. His body became rigid and then relaxed as he fired over and over. He was as focused on his target as I was on him. He set his gun down for a moment and turned slightly. It was Luke. He nodded to me and I stepped back inside and we both resumed shooting.

It seemed as though only minutes had passed when Richard signaled to us the time was up. We finished at the same time, greeted each other but then walked out the door in silence together. Our cars were parked close to each other. He stored his gear in the trunk of his car and stepped over to mine. He placed his hand on the trunk of my car after I closed it, and stood inches from me. "Nice shooting, Mik."

"Thank you. I would have to say the same for you."

He moved slightly forward so that our bodies were in contact with each other. He placed his hand on the back of my waist and pulled me slightly toward him. I reached up and stroked the outline of his jaw with my hand and traced the edge of his full lower lip with the side of my thumb. Luke leaned down to kiss me and I could feel my body responding. Feeling the sensuality of his powerful body and being aware of his scent. The gun range had been more than enough foreplay. As we kissed, I reached down and felt the hardness of him under his jeans. I moved over him and slid down his body, unzipping his jeans, stroking him and taking him in my mouth. I could feel him, so hard, breathing rapidly. He pulled me up to him, pushed up my shirt and I could feel the warmth of his breath as he licked and stroked each breast. He slid his hand down my back and I could feel the roughness of his hands following the curve of my body as slid off my clothes. He pulled me to him, pushing into me and kissing me hard. We moved together, and the intensity was overwhelming. It was as if he was hard wired into my head, knowing what I wanted exactly how I wanted it. Afterward, we stayed intertwined leaning against the car, Luke softly kissing me. As we became aware of our surroundings we realized we were not alone. Richard was doing his best to be discreet but get to his car after closing down the range.

"Sorry Richard," I said.

"No, I don't think you are. Choose another parking lot next time." Richard never smiled but his stern leathered face was crinkled in amusement.

"We can't do this again. Not with the murder investigation. I wasn't thinking." I pulled my clothes on and drove out of the lot. When I glanced in my rear view mirror, I could see Luke still standing by his car.

CHAPTER THIRTY-THREE

I walked to the waiting room. This time I opened the door and Cyntheya was up from her chair immediately, before I called her name. She took a moment to sling her back pack and what looked like some type of work out bag over her shoulders. She nodded to me and walked to my office planting each foot as if she were starting a hike on a steep incline.

"I started back on my work outs and using my home traction device machine. Jackman gave me a different one to use and had me return the other. I guess it was one of his special creations that hadn't been through the final part of the patent process yet. This one works better." She opened the bag to show me the metal and rope contraption. She sniffed the air. "And it smells better, too."

She closed the bag and sat for a moment. "I think death is like our dreams." She looked at me with a haze to her as if she was seeing things not in the room.

"How do you mean?"

"In our dreams we are connected in all sorts of ways to people and events in ways that defy the properties of physics, gravity, time, distance and the limitations of our physical bodies. We can be in two places at once. We can speak to anyone from any point in our lives or the history of the world. We can connect to reality or not connect to reality. We can have whatever powers we want. We can fly."

"What are you feeling?"

"Sort of sad."

"Because?"

"I'm not sure. My friends are all talking about Burke and who killed him. My best friend really loved him. She has a section of homage to him on her facebook page with all his awards."

"What about you?"

"I only saw him once. Not connected. I feel sad for my friends."

I had to know if Cyntheya had been in Burke's experiments. Her symptoms and diagnosis would not have placed her in Burke's line of sight for his project, and nothing in her record pointed to it. But I needed to know.

"I'd like to ask you about something. Is that all right?"

"You're asking my permission to ask questions? Isn't that your job?"

"Yes. This is a little different."

"All right. Ask."

"Did you ever participate in any programs conducted by Dr. Burke?"

She was silent for a moment. "You mean was I a subject in Burke's research? I was screened but then I was excluded for some reason. Why?"

"I'm checking with my patients to make certain that if they were in his experiments they will receive follow up."

"No. I wasn't. I would have told you. They gave that phone number for patients of Burke's to call if they had questions or concerns. But are they stupid? This is the same as asking for 'persons of interest' who may have been witness to a crime. Everybody knows they're trying to locate suspects – figure out if a patient offed Burke."

"We don't know that. What would it mean if they were?"

"They should try to find the person. Even if Burke is an ass." Cyntheya was silent. I waited.

"What I never told you or the other therapists is that my mother had manic episodes when I was little. 'SuperSuzy times' she called them. She was creative. She painted murals in bright colors over the entire walls of my room and the halls. Sometimes even in the living room. She had talent. That's what everyone said. But really she was too crazy to do anything with it. She loved sewing and sewed many of my clothes I wore to preschool and kindergarten. But her sewing obsession was making clothes for dolls, mostly Barbies. Not only my Barbie dolls but my friends' dolls and she would donate outfits everywhere. Anywhere. I found her wedding dress in a box under her bed. It was a short satin wedding dress with thousands of crisscrossed tiny pearl beads. It was quite beautiful. My dad told me she had crafted it from taking apart 500 Barbie wedding dresses and sewing them together for her own perfect Barbie doll wedding dress. The beads covered all the seams. I hated dolls, especially Barbies. I hated SuperSuzy times because there was no way to stop her from starting new murals over the old ones that were sometimes only half finished. She would stay up all night sewing doll dresses, skirts, blouses, and coordinating them with the doll accessories she would find at garage sales. I could never bring friends over because I never knew what I would find."

"How awful for you. Where was your father when this was happening?

"He left early on for his second wife and provided money for me like he does now, but he couldn't tolerate it either."

"But he could escape."

Cyntheya nodded. "When my mom wasn't crazy she was great. The first time I saw Burke I freaked out when he made some comment about my looking like a Barbie doll, and I was glad when he referred me to Jackman so I didn't have to work so much with Burke. It's one of the reasons I was never enamored of him like a couple of my friends who had him for their shrink." She looked up at me and pulled a long strand of reddish brown hair in front of her face and answered my unspoken question. "I wanted my hair this color to make me less visible. I am less visible and the weight I gained also helped."

"Helped?"

"Helped me not to stand out. Not to be noticed."

"Standing out means being a doll? A Barbie doll?"

She nodded. "I hate Barbies."

"What are you feeling?"

"I just said it. I hate Barbies."

"What else? Who else?"

"You want me to say that I hate my mother but her disease is not her fault. I have read journals and books on Bipolar Disorder. And she had been on meds now for years so she is a different person."

"You can still hate what someone did even if it was unintentional. If someone runs you over with their car but didn't intend to, the damage is still real."

Cyntheya nodded.

"And if that person is the one who is supposed to make certain no one ever is damaging to you, it is far more devastating. You can love your mom and hate what she did. Both can be true. If you don't integrate the two, you will flip back and forth from one side to the other, never with any resolution."

Cyntheya started to cry. "I wanted to tell you before but I was afraid people would think I was crazy like my mother was."

"But you told me now. And that's important. It took a lot of courage to tell me."

We spent the rest of the session processing Cyntheya's disclosure that explained so much. But not everything. We came to a stopping point.

"Cyntheya, because you haven't told anyone this before you may wonder when you leave here if you did the right thing or you may feel anxious. If any of that happens, I would like you to tell me and we will keep working on this together. Okay?"

"I get it. And I will."

"I will see you at your next appointment."

Cyntheya needed time to work through her emotions about this. I hoped she wouldn't be so uncomfortable with what she disclosed to me that she didn't come back. That happened sometimes. It was easier for people to seal over again and continue as they had been, than open up and resolve what had been festering underneath. I was fairly certain she would come back. But you never knew.

As I wrote my note, I thought about the Barbie doll impact on Cyntheya. Not uncommon in this world of distorted body image for girls. And women. With Burke's death, every time I heard about Barbie it meant something different, gruesome in a completely different way than killing girls' self-esteem. And it was something I couldn't disclose to anyone.

CHAPTER THIRTY-FOUR

My brain continued to try to process all of the underlying meaning in what Cyntheya had said in her visit, long after I finished my note. I believed her that she had not been in Burke's experiment. It was difficult to concentrate only on her circumstance when there was too much information running through my mind from all the secrets emerging about Burke. After what William told me, I even thought about Lizzie's sexual abuse Burke theory. It didn't seem so improbable anymore, but it didn't completely fit either. Except for the choice of murder weapon. Barbie. Cyntheya's session made me think of that aspect even more. There was a tap on my office door.

"Come in."

"Hi Mik." It was Lizzie. "Oh my God. What is going on with TWF's request for Burke's former patients to call a special phone line?" Lizzie slipped through the opening of my door that was ajar and she was now hidden behind my door, out of view so she would not be seen by anyone passing in the hall. She placed a finger to her lips.

"What now? Your double O status revoked by M again?"

"I'm being discreet not undercover."

"What's going on Mik? You must know. Didn't you read the latest "talking points" e-mail from administration? Do you want to know what I think?"

"Not really."

"I saw the reporters on the local network making it sound as though TWF was taking additional steps to take care of Burke's patients and research participants. And that TWF gravesite website is going berserk with all sorts of speculation about way TWF is doing his."

"I don't know any more than you," I lied. "I'm certain you're right that it is another cover your ass strategy by medical legal. I hope patients aren't so terrified by the murder that they don't feel safe contacting TWF.

"That's what I was thinking. Or that they would be paranoid that this is a ruse by the police to collect persons of interest?" She was sounding like Cyntheya. "Everyone is too legally savvy these days to make themselves a suspect. What if one of them did kill Burke?"

"Would it be better if it was a staff person or family member of a patient?"

"I'm not saying that. I believe there is more to this story than TWF is saying."

"You're probably right, Lizzie. But let's wait on all the possible nightmarish stories until we know more. I think there is more evidence to be discovered. It takes more time when there is this high profile a murder and when the police have to make their way through all the confidentiality crap."

"Do you know that because you've talked to that hunky police detective of yours about this?"

"There are so many things wrong with that statement, including the ownership issue. I've talked with him, but I hardly know him." I avoided eye contact with her. What I said was true, although it was also true that I couldn't stop thinking about being with Luke in the parking lot.

Lizzie smirked and let it go. "You don't seem your usual self, Mik. You look preoccupied or something."

"I have been trying to unravel a big ball of psychological yarn."

"Something related to Burke?" Lizzie's tone perked up.

"No."

"Oh."

"Disappointed?"

"Yes, I am. It is as if we are all in a movie or miniseries where only one part of the puzzle is shown at a time and everyone is waiting for the next secret to be exposed. What if someone gets away with murder? Do you know how many people never get caught? I do. Don't look surprised. I searched it online. From the Justice Department. Did you know that there has been a 30% decline in clearance rates for murder in the past 45 years? And that 20, 000 murders per year go unsolved, including bodies that are never identified?"

"That seems wrong."

"I know it does but it's accurate. The technology is much more advanced but the criminals are even more advanced."

"Great news, Lizzie."

"It also means that the chance of getting away with murder is better than the chance that a person will improve with therapy."

"Again, thanks for that cheerful comparison, Lizzie."

Lizzie and I were alike in that both of us loved odd psychological thrillers. American Psycho as an example. Not Hitchcock's classic movie Psycho that almost everyone likes but the Christian Bale serial killer movie. Such things were horrifying to our other mental health colleagues. We both could embrace the darkness that exists but Lizzie always seemed to have a level of delight in it that was outside my range. It didn't disturb me. In fact, I envied her that at times. After Lizzie left, I scanned my schedule. Another meeting. A special convening of the Clinician Health Support Committee at lunchtime. Jackman, Tara, Elliot, who was Chief of the Chemical Dependency Services, and Jerold were requesting the managers and elected staff reps (Rachel and I) for a "needs assessment" of the therapists and MDs in reaction to Burke's death. Almost always a code for some other mission of ferreting out those who are not following the company line. Perhaps it was in response to William's disclosure about Burke's experiments. Jackman was becoming more involved in the Psychiatry Department activities. Maybe he was the heir to the Chief of Psychiatry throne and not Tara.

I had heard nothing more about the experiments. Not unusual for TWF. But nothing from William either. He was angry and I didn't know how he would respond to me. I did what I thought was right. But being right wasn't helping me sleep better at night.

"Mik. Ready to go to the meeting?" Tara. In a grey-blue tailored skirted suit and three inch heels. Hair now a rich red brown cut short but loose, softening the angular features of her face.

"Wow."

"What?"

"You know what. You look great. The hair. The suit."

"I know. I decided to stop dragging around and put a good face on it. For the staff and patients. I saw that personal stylist Christian and it cost a fortune, but worth it. As acting Chief, I decided I needed to start acting like the Chief." She gave a short laugh.

"Yes. You do look the part."

Tara seemed pleased. "Thank you, Mik."

It seemed to me this might not be the best way to command attention, but then I was never someone who aspired to "leadership" positions in TWF. Maybe Tara had it right.

"Tara, do you know the purpose of this meeting?"

"Jerold said it was to proactively identify therapists at risk for problems related to Edward's death."

"And they don't want more transfers like Charles."

"That, too.

"I miss Charles." Tara statement seemed forced. She needed to work on her sincerity or at least appearing sincere.

"Everyone misses Charles, especially his patients. I don't blame him for leaving."

"But he was always a little sensitive don't you think? Always having to be reassured, petted, hold his hand. A bit of a whiner."

I stood up from my chair. "Whiner? Tara, I have no more patience for blaming the victim. Charles is the victim of a colleague's murder four doors down from his office. I am only surprised more therapists have not left or are not out on disability. That sensitivity you bemoan about him makes him a gifted therapist."

Both of Tara's carefully plucked and colored eyebrows raised and her eyes were cold "So Charles is not the only sensitive one."

I met her gaze. Could I afford to have the "acting chief" angry at me? I really didn't care anymore.

Tara read my expression accurately and an automatic smile appeared. "Don't worry. We are all on emotional overload. Let's go." Tara walked purposefully. She seemed to have regained her emotional balance. I wondered how she had managed to accomplish that.

The meeting was scheduled for 90 minutes or 75 actual minutes. Otherwise known as "mental health time" similar to the 50 minute therapy hour. Jerold led the meeting. No surprises in his summary of events. A thinly disguised attempt to have everyone on board with the TWF talking points. I was thankful that Jackman was sitting next to Tara, Jerold, and some new upper management appointee. Jackman always situated himself at the TWF hierarchical power center. Always took up part of the physical space of whatever female he sat next to, with the exception of the few times he had sat next to me or one of the few female top regional administrators. We were the only ones who made it clear our space was not negotiable. He hated it.

"How can we prevent some of the hysteria, overreaction by providers and patients? The patients seem to be doing better than the staff. How can we assure the therapists and doctors that TWF is safe?"

"Is it safe? Can we make that assurance, Bruce?"

Jackman liked to be called Dr. Jackman in meetings, not by his first name. This is why I never did.

Jackman's eyes narrowed a bit. "Well, Mikelena. I am a little surprised you are one of those overreacting."

Jerold and Rachel almost simultaneously spoke – both sensing a potential flash fire in the room "Let's focus" from Jerold and "Everyone is stressed" from Rachel interrupted the exchange. Rachel deferred to Jerold and Jerold joined with her "Rachel is correct. Everyone is stressed and we all need to focus on the fact that worry and fear on the part of staff and patients and the community is normal. We are here today to see if we can help prevent other good therapists from leaving our medical center. "

"Like Charles?"

"Yes. Perfect example. Experienced clinician. Bilingual. High customer service scores. A significant loss for this medical center."

Discussion went back and forth for the next 40 minutes to arrive at the conclusions that had been created by upper management prior to the meeting. The meeting was held to give the illusion of participation and buy in on the part of the lower level structure, when it was a choreographed with each of us given our dance steps.

I spent most of my time drawing on the pad I had at an angle in front of me. It looked as if I was taking notes. This technique had been crafted from endless meetings in TWF when I paid attention and ended up with a migraine at the end of the meeting. Fearing that one day my head might finally explode, I started drawing during meetings and my migraines ended. The meeting came to a close. Lizzie was in the hall and walked me back to my office.

"What is happening with Tara? Did someone submit her to one of those makeover shows?" Lizzie was laughing propelling pinpoints of saliva into the air as she tried to talk at the same time.

"Stop spitting in my office."

"I can't."

"At least cover your mouth." I handed her a tissue from the box on my desk.

"Did you ever talk with Tara about her relationship with Burke?"

"Did you, Lizzie?"

"Don't be oppositional. She doesn't trust me like she trusts you."

"I don't know any more than you do. And I don't know what's going on with Tara."

"Join the club. Although I always thought she was a climber. A TWF organizational kudzu."

"What's that?"

"Those vines in the South that when planted take over everything yet they look innocent, but by their overpowering presence they kill the less aggressive plants and flowers."

"Tara is ambitious," I agreed.

"How are your patients faring?"

"Mostly as expected. I have the same feeling as when we had that major earthquake and each patient dealt with it in the way that matched their psychopathology. This is much the same. From denial, to rage, to fear, to weaving the tragedy into their own stories of violence or abuse. I even had one patient who was certain another health plan had taken Burke out because he was too much competition."

"Did you have that patient's antipsychotic meds upped?"

"Not a bad idea. But I think the scariest part is not knowing where to look for the murderer – among us? Our patients? The police have their work cut out for them. The helplessness is what drives me crazy."

"Me too, Mik. I wish we could solve this. For lots of reasons."

"Hi guys" Rachel was sipping from the cup of coffee in her hand. "I think Jerold did a good job. It has to be difficult to work with staff on this tragedy." Rachel's eyes were crisscrossed with red and she looked more tired than usual.

"Jerold's real job is as the TWF administration fluffer" Lizzie responded.

"Fluffer?"

"Yes, Rachel. Fluffer. He makes the administration appear potent even though it's all fake. The same as the person who fellates the porn star so that the guy can perform for the camera. And then what does that make Tara?" Lizzie continued. "One of the porn stars? Or perhaps Jackman with his implant hard-on and much larger ego."

"That's vile, Lizzie." Rachel was upset.

"The emotional hypocrisy in this place is vile, Rachel. At least you know what you get with porn."

"It's time to see patients." Rachel turned to walk away.

As Lizzie and Rachel left, I saw William walking past. "William!" He continued to walk toward his office. "Hey William." Still no response. I was being shunned. He was not talking to me. He would leave me work messages only as necessary. It was clear I had wounded him. But William had betrayed the patients and me. He had denied what he had told me when he was asked by the police and by TWF. He said I had confused what he was talking about. That he was talking about the experiments that had been approved by TWF – not anything else. And that he had been concerned they received proper follow up following Burke's death. As I had suspected, there was no corroborating evidence of any kind. It was termed a miscommunication, a misunderstanding generated understandably in a high stress and traumatic time. No evidence of any kind for the police to follow up on. It was scary to me but on some level not surprising. Erik had been furious. My attorney was not surprised. She was familiar with cover-ups in corporations including TWF. It didn't matter that this took place in a health care organization. Power and money equal corruption, regardless of geography, is one of her favorite phrases, off the record of course.

CHAPTER THIRTY-FIVE

I needed stress relief at the end of the day but the gun range was too risky right now. I might see Luke, and my life was complicated enough without a crisis induced sexual relationship. I changed into my running clothes and headed out to the multi-use path that wound next to the Bay. Water was soothing to me and my brain needed to detox from TWF.

I missed Ben. The true love of my life. A rescue spaniel that for five short years was my best friend and playmate. The men I dated knew they were second string and Ben took every opportunity to demonstrate that fact. It also seemed appropriate to me. Ben and I used to run twice a day, and my neighbors, a retired couple who were also "dog people" did doggy daycare for me when I worked and Ben loved them as well – his adopted grandparents. Ben was probably older than the shelter thought and five years went by so fast, until Ben started limping and the vet told me Ben was riddled with cancer. I couldn't stop crying. He died peacefully in my arms two weeks later when it became clear he was ready to go. I wasn't, but I knew I had let go for his sake. I had dogs before but not like Ben. He was my soul mate. Everyone told me the usual consolation advice when your dog dies: get another one. As if he could be replaced. It had been over a year but I was still mourning. I knew I would have another dog at some point. But not now.

The pain lessened over time but Ben was always with me when I ran. I talked to him in my head and I could see him running, sniffing and laughing. He had been my main antidote to TWF. He never burdened me with psychological interpretations of my behavior and would not tolerate my obsessing. Life was for moments of enjoyment, food, play, sleep, not stultifying ruminations about things you can't control. Ben would never have any of that.

This was the time of day I loved to run. Dusk. Twilight. Even loved the sound of those words. I watched the planes that appeared in slow motion as they turned to make their final approach to the local airport. Seeing shapes of people. Less harsh reality than in daylight. I passed a few of the lover's coves, my label for them, where making out had been replaced with hooking up, but I still saw it as romantic. Ryan and I had selected one of these places after a TWF social function. It was hot, sweaty, passionate sex with the edge that comes from knowing others can see you and with the possibility of being caught. It was sex. Not making love. It was one of the ways that Ryan and I were alike and it had been our primary connection. I thought about Luke. He had that same sexual intensity and lack of inhibition. The gun range parking lot scene proved that. He was different from Ryan. Luke had depth. He was the smoldering, lose yourself completely in him type of man. My type. But not now. I had to keep telling myself that. Repeating that I didn't need one more emotional distraction in my life while there was a murder investigation. What I longed for was peace. A quiet mind. I tried to purge the secrets, the betrayals, and murder.

The turnout coming up on the path next to a sewage treatment site was only used by the homeless when it was cold out. I slowed to a walk to allow more time to see if there was anyone back there. A black SUV was wedged between the large steel "No Trespassing" signs. It was light enough to see movement in the car but not much more than that. I switched on the little flashlight I always carried – it had a high powered beam – for light and as self-defense tool if needed. I swept the light across the car. A head popped up for a moment. Than a hand pulled it back down. I turned away and started running. Tara. It was Tara. Did she recognize me? And who was the guy? I didn't think she was dating anyone. Who was this? Maybe this guy was the real reason for the power makeover. But why would she lie about that? Other than of course the usual reasons. He was married or there was something else taboo about him – young, maybe? I finished my run.

I was frustrated with all the TWF staff drama and keeping secrets. Tara wasn't being honest about a lot of things, if that was really her I saw. I needed to talk with someone who knew Tara well enough to help me figure this out and it needed to be someone who had a dark side who wouldn't be disturbed by it. Lizzie. I entered her number.

"Yes."

"It's Mik. Do you have a minute?"

"I do but I'm going out in about a half hour. What is it?"

"I want to talk and use your analytic skills."

"A case?"

"No but I'm hoping you'll keep this confidential." I had decided that it wasn't essential that she did keep it confidential, which was why I could tell her.

"I always do."

"No, you don't."

"You're right but I am capable of it. I keep my patients' confidences."

"Please do your best to contain yourself. Agreed?"

"Okay. Just for you. This must be good. Go ahead."

"You know that running path by the Bay?"

"Sure. I take Elvis out there sometimes – even though it's not a dog path anymore."

"I was out there and I'm fairly certain I saw Tara and a man in an SUV parked by that sewage treatment site."

"Gross."

"I know. They treat the sewage but the area still reeks. I think Tara was going down on some guy in the car."

"Who?"

"I couldn't see him. I saw her head and his arm and that's it."

"I didn't think she was dating anyone."

"Me either but then I wondering if her sudden makeover was related to this man and not to her management aspirations."

"Oh my God."

"What, Lizzie?"

"Maybe it's both."

"What do you mean?"

"You know who owns an Escalade SUV? Was it black?"

"Yes, it was. But lots of people own them."

"You're right and one of them is Jackman. Or more accurately, Jackman gave it to his wife as one of his 'sorry I screwed someone else again' gifts. How ironic."

"Jackman? No. Tara can't stand him."

"Doesn't mean she wouldn't blow him. Like she did Burke."

"Her makeover and the sucking up" Lizzie chuckled to herself, "may both be related to moving up the TWF food chain. That has to be it. And Tara has been avoiding us. She has cancelled lunch with us twice, and she no longer hangs around and talks. Haven't you noticed?"

"I did but I assumed it was the trauma from Burke." And, I thought to myself, I assumed she regretted telling me about her affair with Burke and she was creating distance from me.

"Get real, Mik. In spite of what we tell patients, trauma doesn't change most adults. Children, yes. Adult simply become more of whoever they were before. Tara is Tara whoever that is. If that guy in the car was Jackman, and I am certain it was, Amanda is going to be pissed off when she finds out."

"But she's not going to find out from us. Right Lizzie?"

"I agree with you this time. I'm not certain even I could tolerate one more drama in the TWF soap opera. I have to go now though, Mik."

"No problem. Thanks. I'll talk with you later."

CHAPTER THIRTY-SIX

After I hung up with Lizzie, I sat in my kitchen and stared out the window at the long strips of bark hanging loosely off the catalpa trees. Jackman and Tara. Tara was lying about more than the affair with Burke. What else?

When my phone rang, I let it go to voicemail. I wasn't certain I wanted to talk to anyone right now. I checked the message. It was a message from Luke to call him back. In my magical thinking state, I wondered if he could sense my thoughts about him on my run. I called him back and he picked up the phone.

"Sustern."

"Hi Luke. It's Mik. How are you?"

"Good. Thanks for calling me back."

"What happened?"

"No, not to be alarmed. I have been thinking about you. In fact it has been hard for me to think about anything else. Although you said something when you were at the gun range about not seeing me, I was hoping you would reconsider."

"I feel the same, but it's too complicated, Luke."

"Will you think about it? I'll call you in a couple of days to see if that iron will has softened."

I couldn't help laughing. "We'll see."

"Then I will talk to you later in the week, Mik."

Erik's number was showing up on my phone. "Have to take this call, Luke. It's Erik. Bye." I ended the call and accepted Erik's.

"Hi Erik. Are you home?"

"I am. Back yesterday from London."

"How did it go?"

"Nailed it. Are you up for trying a new shooting range? I checked out a newly constructed high tech one that one of my clients uses."

"I'd love to."

"How about around eight? Texting the address to you now."

"Great. See you there."

The day was starting to improve. Luke calling. Erik with a new gun range. I stretched out on my sofa, allowing myself a rare moment of do nothing time. My mind kept going to the investigation. Why had the police not found the killer? Even though I know people get away with murder, even the high profile ones like the Zodiac, it seemed as though there should be enough evidence. Luke had occasionally updated me from what he knew, but there was never any real lead. There were too many suspects with motive, and the TWF legal wall erected to protect TWF was likely also helping to protect a killer. The chaos around therapists, staff leaving, transferring didn't make it any easier for the police. They never caught the killer of the therapist up north, and it was looking as if this was going to be repeated here.

James was still on disability and I heard he planned not to return to the west coast, least of all return to TWF. That seemed healthy to me. While business at the clinic was surprisingly "normal" now. That did not seem healthy to me.

I was headed out the door when my cell rang. It was Luke's number.

"Mik. I have news. David Bowman has been arrested in the murder of Burke."

"No."

"I'm afraid so. The police picked him up. He's at the station."

"Based on what?"

"There was a threat to Burke from David on Burke's computer a few days before the murder and the search of his place yielded evidence that linked him aspects of the unusual nature of the murder weapon."

"You mean Barbie?"

"I mean there was evidence that a man David's age would not normally have in his home. And he had purchased a one way ticket to Barcelona."

"But his grandparents have an estate in Barcelona."

"Regardless, there is enough to hold him at this point."

"No, that's not right. He didn't do it."

"How do you know?"

"I don't have any evidence but I know David's not a killer. A pretty boy narcissist, but not a killer. What was the other evidence?"

"David had purchased Barbies and clothes a month before the murder and there were doll clothes and accessories in his place. Tara said she saw David and Burke arguing a couple of days before the murder." Luke continued. "The steel band around the lower part of Barbie's waist with the surgical steel blades were not a significant piece of craftsmanship. Anyone with tools from a hardware store and internet access to information could have easily created it. It increases the pool of suspects. And David had no alibi for the time frame of the murder and he would have known Burkes password and how to circumvent the system."

"What else have the police done to investigate alternate suspects?"

"They started checking on sites for aberrant behavior associated with Barbie and with Burke. There were too many bizarre Barbie sites to even begin to narrow them down and none associated with TWF or with Burke. The profile indicates it was personal, the person smart, well organized, familiar with TWF. Most likely a male but a female is not excluded. Particularly with the Barbie angle. The problem is the one you mentioned. Too many people with motive and opportunity. Not enough information. But at this point, I think the political pressure to make an arrest was enough to bring in David, even if it doesn't hold up over time."

"For the record, I don't believe David did it. Is what you told me public knowledge?"

"There is no press release yet but only the arrest is public knowledge. I'm certain a blogger has posted it already, which means someone is reporting it as 'breaking news'. I wanted you to know."

"So I don't have to pretend I don't know."

"No, you don't. Not about the arrest, but you do have to keep the details quiet. That's one of the reasons I called you. You and James are the only civilians in this case who know about the details and it needs to stay that way."

"Got it."

"Another thing. Unfortunately, you may get your way for now in not seeing me, because I'll be busy working with the police on the community aspect of this, since it is a TWF therapist who is in custody. More involved than I would be if it was some random person. But I do plan to call you when this calms down. Have to go. Take care, Mik."

"You, too."

CHAPTER THIRTY-SEVEN

I was still thinking about David the next day. He didn't kill Burke. The evidence was circumstantial – even I knew that. I also knew people had been convicted on circumstantial evidence. The real killer was still free somewhere. I couldn't catch him. Him. I assumed it was a him, but I was not completely convinced. My mind wouldn't let go of trying to figure it out. I was to meet Rachel in 30 minutes for a drink. Our longstanding every couple of weeks get together so we could talk about things neither would discuss with our other friends. We each knew the other could keep secrets. She was already there when I arrived. Staring out the floor to ceiling windows that looked out over the Bay at the few fisherman and the seagulls circling above them. It was a peaceful place. I touched her shoulder.

"Hi, Mik. Good to see you." She stood up to give me a hug as if I hadn't just seen her yesterday. But that was Rachel. And it was genuine. Her eyes were calm. She seemed relaxed.

"You look peaceful."

"It is soothing here. The waves and the ships in the distance."

"Far from the madding crowd."

We both smiled.

"How are you holding up with everything, Rach?

"Not too bad. I suppose you already know David was arrested."

"I heard."

"Mik, I don't believe it. I don't believe David is a murderer."

"I agree with you. I think the police have the wrong man. They were desperate to arrest someone to reduce the community political pressure and outrage that the killer was walking free so they arrested David."

"I told him that if he quit he would appear guilty."

"He talked with you?" For some reason, I was surprised that David would confide in Rachel, although many of the staff did.

"He did. This is confidential but I know I can trust you. He told me he was afraid his conflicts with Burke would make him look like he had something to do with the murder and he told me details that I swore I would not tell anyone."

This was sounding disturbingly familiar.

"But I can tell you that Burke was hurtful to him and he had felt betrayed. He was planning to leave anyway. He told me he discussed it with Tara as an administrator and she supported him in leaving TWF. But it turned out to be the exact wrong thing to do. I bet Tara feels terrible now."

"I'm sure she must." I wasn't sure about that at all. Tara was showing up in places I never expected her to be. Talking with David. In the Escalade. I thought about talking with Rachel about seeing Tara in the car but dismissed it. I knew it would not be helpful. There was not a chance Rachel would be willing to explore possible dark hidden agendas. Everyone had their own strengths. That was not one of Rachel's.

CHAPTER THIRTY-EIGHT

The new gun range recommended by Erik was exclusive, gated. By invitation only. It had a sleek, seductive, futuristic feel to it. My usual black on black clothing fit in here. The staff and members all appeared in shades of grey and black, reflected in the light angled off the steel columns. The front area had transparent tables with an impressive computerized check-in system. Membership had to cost a fortune. The range master could have been Neo out of the Matrix. He motioned us to a private section for two. Erik obviously had the clout to obtain the shooting range equivalent of box seats.

I set up and starting shooting. I tried to focus but Rachel's disclosure about Tara and David, and Lizzie's hypothesis about Burke were distracting me. Maybe Lizzie was right about Burke and his young female patients. He ran rogue experiments. He played God. Maybe he viewed these girls as his right. Speculation about the direction and type of Burke's sexual proclivities was a topic that emerged periodically. Usually by a new staff member trying to figure it out. My belief was that Burke was straight and into some sort of sadomasochism. No one knew for certain. He usually attended TWF social functions alone or brought his stepmother. Occasionally, he would show up with a beautiful perfectly sculpted exotic woman no one had ever seen before. Tara and Burke – that relationship fit the sadomasochism theory. Although unclear if he was using her or she was using him. It was hard to know.

Jackman and Burke were the classic frat brothers to the end. Both predatory in their professional ambitions and their sexual practices. I could imagine them hunting together in college. Jackman was also similar to Burke in his seeking female mannequins as arm candy. Perfect, doll like creatures. William had not mentioned if Jackman was involved in Burke's experiments. But he had to have been. They were too close to not share that type of secret. This was making more sense. Target shooting was having its effect of clearing away the haze. Meditation, my ass.

"Anything new at the gulag?" Erik's first words since our initial greeting. I was feeling better at this point. Erik could usually sense when I needed to shoot and when I was ready to talk.

"You heard about the arrest?"

"Of course. It was all over the news."

"David didn't do it. He's not a killer."

"I believe that's what the neighbors of Jeffrey Dahmer said. And John Wayne Gacy."

"He wanted to kill Burke. But he didn't. He doesn't have the killer core."

"If it isn't David Bowman, then who do you think did it?"

"Too many possible suspects who had motive."

"So did you look at those job sites I sent you?"

"I did, but I'm not leaving at this point."

"Murder, illegal experiments, cover ups and corruption aren't enough to make you consider another job? Why is that Mik?"

It was a good point. I loved treating patients and many of my colleagues were also close friends. That might not be enough anymore.

"You're right. I'll think about it."

"I hope you do."

"How's work?"

"Going well. I talked with Luke the other day."

"And?"

"He mentioned he ran into you at the gun range."

"Did he say anything else?"

"About what?"

"Don't be a jerk, Erik. Anytime I ask about Luke you act as if we were back in high school."

Erik nodded. "Point taken. Did he say something about you? Is that what you mean? Let me see, I can't exactly remember but I understand there is a mutual attraction. Luke is a good guy. I figured you two would hit it off."

"It's not going anywhere because I can't be tangled up in another relationship with boundary problems; there is that little incident, you may recall, of murder where I found the body and Luke's working with the police on the investigation."

"I know, Mik. Just busting your chops. It has to be tough for you. I want you to know that if you ever want to talk more," he paused to replace the clip, "find one of your friends because I hate emotional catharsis discussions."

We both resumed shooting.

"There is a blues festival coming up next month. If I'm in town, do you want to go?" Erik and I had a few of the same music interests.

"I would love to. Thanks. Let me know."

"See you."

We both drove away. No hugs. We adhered to the beliefs from our father that hugs for a family member were for major events – someone going off to war would qualify, or a death. I felt energized after the range. Enough to face whatever was new on the latest TWF blogs. I logged on. Lots of sites. As many lauding Burke as demonizing him. But nothing new. Nothing about Barbie. I checked my email. Updates from my acquaintances – jokes, articles forwarded. No more e-mails to me re TWF. My previous e-mail had been traced to a free Wi-Fi 30 miles away. In other words, not traceable. Probably I had been on a list of TWF therapists a disgruntled psychiatric patient had decided to jerk around.

I had checked the Barbie sites shortly after the murder. Even though I knew the police would have done the same. My experience of the sites was the same as Luke had said. Too many. Lots of aberrant types who identified with Barbie. Sites that predated Burke's death but were not related in any way. Barbie was an icon. More accurately, Barbie is an icon. Not something that was expected to change for the foreseeable future. It was also clear that there was meaning attached to that choice of murder weapon, but no one could figure it out. Not that there weren't the obvious implications related to Burke being the sexist pig that he was. But hardly a motive for murder.

Tara was no longer the clinical adult team lead, now that she had taken the role of acting Chief. She had been cleared of any wrong doing in Jessica's suicide, which made her Burke's natural replacement. But TWF administration was always slow in assigning permanent replacements, and there was that rumor about Jackman taking the Chief position.

The clinic work was limping along but there were too many changes in the aftermath of Burke's death. Burke of course. And

Charles' transfer, David's resignation and arrest, and James on disability. The rest of us were being stretched to cover all the patients. It was impossible. I had little contact with Tara anymore. Less with William. It wasn't the same place anymore.

CHAPTER THIRTY-NINE

It was Monday again. I knew there would be an onslaught of "I can't believe David killed Burke" freak outs by staff and patients. It was one of the reasons I had arrived earlier than usual in the hope of organizing my day and returning patient calls before the first scheduled patient visit. The workload was becoming too heavy for me to finish at the end of the day even staying hours past the paid end of my day. That used to be enough. But that was pre Burke's death.

TWF was already in spin mode with the media. David had inadvertently helped them out by resigning. It made them look less culpable. Although there was still the inevitable question of how TWF could hire a killer to treat patients. The answer was obvious. It was someone else's fault. The State Board of Psychology licensed him. Didn't that make them at fault?

"Did you hear about David?" Tara had her TWF logoed cup of espresso in her hand.

I turned back to my computer, "He didn't do it."

Tara said nothing but continued to stand there.

I looked at Tara. "What are you thinking, Tara? That he killed Burke?"

She shrugged. "How do you know he didn't? We don't know what he's capable of. Or what Burke may have done to provoke him. And why he resigned"

"Why did he resign, Tara?"

"How would I know?"

"You said you and David 'bonded' after Burke humiliated him in the meeting."

"Bonding about Burke wasn't a basis for intimacy or even friendship. I told you that because I could finally empathize with David as a person. But perhaps you're right, Mik. It will be up to the legal system to sort it out. I want the person caught so everyone can feel safe and this clinic can return to normal. The clinic is my responsibility now. I know you're busy so I will head back to my office."

"Bye Tara."

I waited for a few seconds before I got up and closed the door. I realized I couldn't tolerate any more discussions about David or Burke. My patient arrival light was now on, and I chose to start the visit early. Seeing patients was a way for me to shift focus. The requirement of being present emotionally shut out the rest of the clinic "noise."

I saw patient after patient with no break in the day. No one else in the clinic had talked to me about David. I was grateful. I had also made certain my door was always closed. Even at my brief time for lunch. It worked better that way. Unfortunately, I had at the same time cut myself off from any new information. I needed to find out what was going on in the clinic without having to address someone's emotional melt down. I checked my home and cell phone messages. No news there. I entered Luke's number but it went to voicemail, and I didn't want to leave message. I took it as a sign that I should let this go for now. I finished up and drove home. As I parked my car in the garage, my phone rang. A private number. Maybe Luke? I answered.

"Mik, It's David."

"David. Hi. Where are you?"

"Did you tell the police about our conversation?"

"That's what you called about?"

"Did you tell them?"

"No one asked. So no, I didn't."

"I want to know who sold me out."

"Didn't the police tell you why you were brought in?"

"You can't trust what they say. You know that."

"You're right, David. Are you all right?"

He gave a short laugh. "As much as anyone who is considered a suspect in a murder investigation can be. My father hired Eldrige Fineman to handle my situation."

"He's one of the top defense attorneys in the country."

"Exactly. Protecting the family reputation generates surprising family loyalty."

"David. I am sorry this has happened. I know you didn't do it."

There was silence on the phone. "David?"

"I'm relieved to hear you say that. I wasn't certain if you were on my side."

"It's not about sides. I don't believe you are capable of that kind of murder."

"That's right, Mik. You know more than any of us. You found him."

"And you know I can't tell you anything about that."

"I know. I have to go but I'm glad I talked with you. I doubt we will talk again anytime soon. With all the legal complications."

"Take care, David."

"You too."

In a way I wasn't surprised David called. In another I was. I hoped he was cleared soon. For his sake and because there was a killer out there. I was also tired of keeping the secret of how Burke died. It was not becoming easier with time. I realized I had expected it would.

CHAPTER FORTY

Rapid fire images of Burke's body, David's face, even Billy Sanders. I had slept only an hour and I was using every sleep strategy I could think of. No success. It was now 5:00am. There was no point in trying to sleep, especially since I had to get up in two hours. I decided to take a short run before preparing for another TWF day. I needed a break. Or time off. But that would not be permitted with TWF in turmoil and short staffed. Maybe I should consider Erik's job options. A permanent break from TWF. Maybe. But it wouldn't be today.

I was able to sneak into TWF without making contact with anyone. No colleagues "checked in" with me this morning. Small favors. I was grateful for that. The TWF burning bush e-mails were fewer. A lull before the storm? I had mostly return patients today. They took less energy than assessing an unknown.

My next patient was new to me but had already been seen in the clinic by Tara. Patient was requesting a new therapist. It wasn't like private practice where the rejected therapist might be interested in what happened or if the relationship could be salvaged. In TWF, it was viewed as a gift. One less patient on your panel. Everyone occasionally had a patient who didn't feel understood or didn't like the therapist they saw. Then there were those therapists who frequently had new patients who didn't want to return to them. Tara had not been one of those until she became Assistant Chief.

Kristen Evans, age 18, depression past 4 months. No psych contact or previous history of depression. College sophomore, bright, social, acting in the local theater, and on the tennis team. She had seen Burke one time shortly before his death and Jackman before that for sports injury. No family psychiatric history. Tara had seen her, prescribed an antidepressant and referred her to group therapy. In the past few months, Tara started referring almost every patient to group therapy. As the designated TWF cost effective intervention.

Why see only one person in a room, when you can see 12 for the same cost to TWF but several times the co-pay? She had developed selective amnesia for the research that said most people won't go to group therapy, and that it's only effective for specific types of problems. Given the group referral, the patient's request for another therapist was not that big a mystery. I finished reading her chart. Successful treatment by Jackman in sports medicine. She was now playing tennis with no problem. No abuse or trauma history. This was someone I could help fairly easily. She was already registered and early for her appointment. Another good sign.

"Kristen?" I glanced around our full waiting room. The young woman who stood up was tall, athletic, white blond hair in French braid with the end curled forward over her shoulder. Someone with natural symmetrical beauty but with no conscious awareness of it. She made eye contact with me as I introduced myself and she walked back with me to my office in silence. I gave my initial required introduction, confidentiality parameters and mandated reporting requirements. She started before I could ask the reason for her visit, "Cyntheya referred me."

Damn. Treating patients who are friends especially young adults was usually a disaster. I avoided it if at all possible. "I can't-"

"You can't say anything about her because of confidentiality. I know. If you can't continue to see me that's okay because I wanted at least this one appointment."

She had my attention. "What is it I can help you with, Kristen? "

"I told Dr. Tara what I will tell you, but she didn't do anything. Cyntheya said you would understand and maybe you could help me."

"Help you with what?"

For the first time she sat silent, hands holding tightly to the arms of the chair. "I'm not sure now. I'm afraid no one will believe me. Everyone will think I'm crazy."

"But your friend Cyntheya didn't, did she? She believed you."

"Yes, she believes me. That's why she sent me to you."

"What happened, Kristen?" My adrenaline had kicked in overriding the fatigue from lack of sleep. It was the sense that a patient was ready to reveal some sort of secret or trauma.

"I don't know where to start."

"Start anywhere and I'll follow you."

"I'll start at the beginning." She took a breath. "I'm from a happy family. Not like Cyntheya's. I always felt so lucky. I'm an only child and my parents made sure I had friends over and encouraged me in anything I wanted to do like playing tennis, acting in the local community theater, singing in the college chorus. I love school. My mother is friends with Jessica Brauer's mother – that girl who killed herself and the family sued TWF. I know you know about it. Jessica and I were never friends though. A couple of years ago my mom and Jessica's mom tried to have us be friends but neither of us was interested. No connection and she was too competitive in sports and seemed a lot younger than me, even though she was only a couple years younger. When Jessica killed herself I was shocked. It didn't seem like her, but then I figured it was because I didn't know her that well."

"Thought? What are you thinking now? What changed your mind?" I knew better than to ask multiple questions at one time – psych 101 tells you that. My anxiety was leaking. I sat back in my chair. Now was not the time to ask questions. She needed to tell the story in her own way.

"I'm getting to that. Right after she died her mom was at our house a lot. My mom's great at helping people. She's a family practice doctor. I heard Mrs. Brauer talk to my mom about Jessica and trying to figure out what had happened. Over and over again. I started to hide out in my room or go out whenever I knew she would be over. She was horrified when she learned that I had seen Dr. Tara. Even though they settled the suit, I think Jessica's mom felt it was partly Dr. Tara's fault. I did hear her say how compassionate you were to her. That was another reason I felt okay when Cyntheya told me to see you. Jessica's mom said something changed with Jessica. That she thought something happened. At school. Or with a one of the guys she dated. Anyway, when Cyntheya and I were talking a couple weeks ago I told her about my nightmares and she told me about hers. They were so much the same."

"In what way?"

For the first time, Kristen looked away and started tapping her foot. She shook her head and I watched her neck and cheeks gradually redden. Anxiety? Embarrassment? Shame?

"You can tell me. Whatever it is."

She continued to look away from me. "We both had dreams of having to watch some guy touching himself until he came. We both heard a woman's voice in the background telling us to relax, imagine a white sandy beach, and hear the sound of the waves."

Cyntheya had not told me about the woman's voice. But I couldn't say that to Kristen.

"After you asked Cyntheya about Burke's experiments she asked me if I had been, and I told her I, like her, had been screened but excluded. And we thought maybe there was a connection somehow. Maybe Burke did something to us we didn't know about."

"Did the man in your dreams look like Burke?"

"No. That was one of the problems. Neither of us could describe him well but he was shorter and heavier that Burke. I know that doesn't make sense. But I still wanted to tell you that I think there is some connection, because when I told Dr. Tara, she acted as if Cyntheya and I were some sort of drama queens."

"She said that?"

"Not exactly. But you could tell she thought we were making it up. That Cyntheya made it up after I told her about my dreams, but then Cyntheya told me you would believe me because she had told you way before I told her. Dr. Tara acted like I was crazy, prescribed me meds that I didn't take and she sent me to a group starting next month." She glanced down for a moment. "Do you believe me?"

She asked a tough question. But I did. And at this point, she wouldn't trust me anymore if I did the "what do you think?" therapist response.

"I believe you. It all sounds very scary for you and overwhelming. Did you tell your mother about this?"

"I tried, but the possibility is so bizarre, even to me, that she thought I was using my 'creative story telling style' to quote her. I have times where I don't know if something happened or not, and I don't know that even if it did really happen, maybe it was at a party and not in this clinic."

I spent the little time left of her visit and the next 10 minutes afterward to find out more of the details and to try to determine what had happened. She and Cyntheya had nothing in common except TWF. Not the same schools or other friends or parties. It was all I could get, without it appearing I was interrogating her. I felt I needed some sort of follow up with Kristen although I knew I could not treat her and Cyntheya. I scheduled one follow up visit for next week with the caveat that it would be further assessment and someone else would treat her following that.

I saw my next patients but kept thinking through Kristen's story. It was my own psychologist's form of Boolean operation. At each question juncture. It led me to the point that I was certain there was an abuser. But the story didn't fit what I knew of Burke's experiments or of the subjects. What fit Billy Sanders, Cyntheya, Kristen, Jessica? Who else? I felt a sudden nausea. Lizzie's patient, Zoe. The abuse and the woman's voice. No dreams the same but the rest was too similar to ignore. Same type of young woman. Maybe it was Burke. He could have distorted his image for the young women just in case. That would fit. He would be too smart not to. The woman's voice was easy enough to manufacture. Burke was dead. But if it wasn't Burke, it meant there was another freak still out there.

This was now beyond me. I wasn't certain who to trust at TWF. Even if this was someone at TWF, there was no evidence to provide to police. Neither Kristen or Cyntheya could identify their abuser. If it was Burke, he was dead. Luke or Erik seemed to be my only useful options to help figure this out. I flipped a coin. My reflexes were slowed by sleep deprivation. The coin slipped off my hand and rolled under the metal filing cabinet where I couldn't retrieve it. Message received. It was on me now. Luke was limited by, well, the law, and procedures he had to follow and I could hear Erik "Get out of that hellhole now." I was the only one who could access TWF and its files with little trouble or suspicion. I worked late and on weekends. No one would think twice about my being at TWF at odd hours. Burke had been the only other psychiatry practitioner who did that.

I needed to step back and look at the entire picture. What did I know? Burke was conducting unauthorized experiments. There were likely at least three female patients who were victims of sexual abuse, although it wasn't clear who, and there might be other experiments that Burke was conducting but William didn't know about. Billy Sanders may have been a victim or not. Who else would have been "assisting" Burke? Jackman was the obvious partner for the experiments. Arrogant, misogynistic. Part of the fraternity. Would Jackman risk his cushy position at TWF and his extravagant lifestyle for something like this? Maybe. Who else? Amanda could never pull any of this off, but she might know more than she thinks. And Tara. It was difficult for me to think about Tara being involved in something this sinister but her ambition was now overriding the part of her I thought I knew. Her recent behavior with Jackman and how she treated Kristen confirmed that.

There was no point in pursuing any of this if Burke was the sole perpetrator. TWF had sealed off any evidence related to him permanently. I was certain of that. I also had to acknowledge that I had helped seal that off by alerting the police, and consequently TWF, about what William had said. Any evidence that had been still available about these patients would have disappeared at that point. Those closest to Burke, other than his stepmother of course, were Jackman, Amanda, William and Tara. For a time, David. Who could tell me something even if they didn't intend to? William still wasn't talking to me. That left Amanda and Tara. Amanda was in love with Jackman, and I was certain Tara was currently doing Jackman. Amanda had a role in Burke and Jackman's legitimate experiments but what else I wasn't certain. Amanda was smart but never felt she had to fully cover her tracks because she was protected by Jackman.

As a start, I could check the drawer Amanda kept at the front reception desk. I knew the combination because I had watched her open it a number of times and for certain details my visual memory was almost photographic. It would be worth the risk to check the drawer, if there was any connection to Burke or Jackman's experiments. The more I thought about it the more I believed Burke and Jackman were working together for their own reasons. Less Lewis and Clarke in their effort at exploration of new psychological arenas, and more Hillside Strangler serial killer partners Bianchi and Buono. They both had the capacity to dehumanize their patients, their research participants and even the women they dated or married. Narcissism and sociopathy. Or was I trying too hard to make this fit? Tomorrow at the end of the day I would check it out. I felt better that I could take action. I had a plan.

CHAPTER FORTY-ONE

The next day went by quickly and there was always charting to be done so I stayed in my office appearing busy as usual. I waited for the clinic to clear out so I could begin my research. It was after 7pm. The clinic should be empty. I did a walk-through of all the halls, checked the bathrooms, the lounge. No one in the clinic, and no sounds of activity. The environmental services staff was not yet in the clinic since they spent time until at least 8pm "setting up" in the television lounge in the main building. I grabbed my gloves, placed them inside the folder I brought with me as if I needed to copy something, in case I ran into someone. The reception area was dimly lit and lights were off in the waiting room.

I set the file folder on the desk, put on my gloves and entered the code on Amanda's lock. It opened. Little boxes and more little boxes. Everything in containers. I would have to open and replace each box one by one so that it would appear undisturbed to Amanda. The first box was filled neon colored rubber bands. A box of patient TWF medical cards Amanda should have already sent to patients who had left them at the front desk. Coins. This was turning out to be a colossal waste of time.

Maybe I was looking in the wrong place. What was more important to Amanda than anything else at TWF? Her chair. No one, with the exception of the occasional passive aggressive antics of the night shift staff like Jimmy to annoy her, dared to sit in it. Her sign was always in place "DO NOT USE THIS CHAIR. ERGONOMICS SET FOR AMANDA." Making it the perfect on site hiding place. I replaced all items as I had found them and locked her drawer. I could always resume my search there if I was wrong. I looked at all parts of her chair. There were a number of fabric pockets as part of the chair's upholstery. There was even a pocket under the seat of the chair for the chair instruction manual. I pulled out the plastic folder and opened it. There was a sealed envelope in with the other materials. No name. The standard TWF stationery with the general medical center return address on it. Nothing else.

If I opened it I would need to seal it exactly as it was or simply use another TWF envelope and reseal that one. It was worth the risk. I opened it. A long list of typed first names. Smart move for Amanda, or for whoever might have given her the list. Plausible deniability. No one could link her to the envelope itself and the contents were generic as well.

I had no idea who these patients were. There were 20 of them. I slid the paper into my folder and made my way to the copier. The irritating two minute "warm-up" time on the machine delayed me. I stood quietly, staring at the second hand on my watch. Finally it was in ready mode. I made the copy, grabbed the original, and went back to Amanda's chair. I found another envelope, resealed the information, and carefully surveyed the room to make certain it was as I found it.

The only way to find out if these were patients related to Burke and or Jackman would be to access their medical records. For all I knew, it might be Amanda's customer list for another new project. I couldn't find the charts without the medical record numbers. There was a way to search the electronic record by first name, but too many patient charts to open if I did that. But the list meant something. The names of Billy, Jessica, and Cyntheya were not on the list. The only patient first name that matched potential victims was Kristen. There were several names with handwritten checks by them. The checks must mean Amanda had already completed them, and Kristen's name was one of those.

I had done all I could for now. The next best potential source of information was Tara. I was certain she knew more than she was telling. I didn't believe I could trust her but I had known her a long time. When we had been friends, we would go out together for drinks and to meet men, but that had stopped when she was promoted. I hoped I could use our history to my advantage. It was too late for a call. I entered Tara's number and texted. I was almost home when I heard the tone of an incoming text. At the next red light I took a look. It was Tara. Meet me tomorrow at six at The Shadow. I had never been there.

CHAPTER FORTY-TWO

Tara was in the bar when I arrived. Leaning back in one of the chairs covered in tapestry retrieved from another century. A luxurious, decadent century. Alcoves for two to three people surrounded the edges of the bar. She had chosen one for two in the back – the next best form of confidential space outside an office.

"Hi Tara."

"Hi Mik." She raised her full martini glass but her glassy eyes and unsteady hand indicated this wasn't her first or even second drink of the evening. "Grab a seat. I'm so happy you called. We never have time to sit and talk anymore like we use to. With me being the new Chief. Where's Stanley?" We both scanned the bar.

"There's Stanley." Tara pointed across the room at a Marlon Brando in his youth look alike. The servers and bartenders were all male.

"They're all men, Tara."

"Of course they are."

"What is this place?"

"A bar."

"Yes, Tara, it appears to be a bar. Did you finally locate the Mustang Ranch for women?"

"I wish. This is a pay per view bar."

"As in pay for overpriced drinks to view the studs in too tight pants and snug shirts that accentuate every bulging muscle?"

Tara nodded. "I love how you get things. Everything does not have to be explained. Thank God."

Tara, Lizzie and I had spoken a number of times about the lack of equality for women. That included the lack of opportunity to be equal in ladies' man or stud status to men, without being labeled with the pejorative term whore or slut. Terms with inherent inequity. Who would want to be a whore or slut? But who wouldn't want to be a ladies' man or stud?

Tara waited until I had placed my order from Stanley who even had the Stanley Kowalski voice down perfectly.

"Is Stanley really playing the character from A Streetcar Named Desire?"

"Of course. My second favorite is Atticus over there on the right side of the bar."

Atticus did resemble Gregory Peck as Atticus Finch in To Kill a Mockingbird.

"Brilliant bar owners. They created literary porn with iconic movie actors. I love this place." Tara turned back to me, "So what's going on Mik?"

"I wanted to get together. I also heard a rumor I wanted to check out with you."

"The TWF air is saturated with rumors these days."

I thought about following up with Tara about Kristen, but my instincts stopped me. I chose the route that matched our surroundings.

"I heard you're doing Jackman."

"That's the rumor?"

"Is it true?"

"So I'm doing Jackman. Who cares? Certainly not his wife. All it means to her is that she gets another expensive 'grant me absolution for my sins' present."

"But why? He's a sexist pig. He collects women like trophies, with a wall of female heads on display."

"Don't be so dramatic. I don't plan on running off with him. He was entertaining and, in the beginning of the sexual relationship he was so desperate to demonstrate his sexual prowess that he was quite willing to do whatever I wanted him to. But don't worry, it was a fling. Not anything else. I'm done with him."

"What happened?"

"Nothing. We both knew it was a moment of insanity. The crisis breeding connection sort of sexual frenzy. We were the two in TWF who knew Burke the best and most directly affected by his death and we were dealing with it with sex. One of those flash fires. You know what I mean." It was a statement not a question.

"And…"Tara stopped.

"And what?"

"Jackman has some odd sexual proclivities."

"There's a surprise."

Tara shot me a shut up if you want me to continue look. I did.

"He's more into the whole Playboy plastic surgery perfect women than I thought. And no interest in men. I thought he might be bisexual but he's not. I admit I enjoy an occasional sexual role play but he has an entire closet of coordinated costumes, with shoes, purses, hair accessories for women. He also loves to watch himself – he has a room with what looks like flat screen TVs on the walls and ceiling but they are specially constructed high tech mirrors. He loves and I do mean 'loves' to watch himself."

"None of that surprises me, Tara. If the relationship is no longer sexual, is Jackman trying to replace Burke with you as his best buddy?"

"Maybe. It's weird. Jackman, even now, maintains a kind of disdain for Burke. As if they're still in competition and Jackman resents the attention Burke's getting even in death."

I couldn't get a sense of why Tara was telling me this. Maybe she needed to unburden herself or maybe it was the fourth dirty martini talking. We sat in silence for a moment.

"Mik, why don't I feel more traumatized?"

"You were traumatized, Tara. You were a wreck right afterward."

"I guess I was. You're right. I got through it because my daughter Brittany was so good to me. She finally forgave me for her father abusing her. But I've been thinking. Burke was one more abusive relationship for me, wasn't he?"

She had a point. There were tears forming and deep sadness on her face. "Even though that's true Tara, you didn't continue with another abusive relationship. You ended the one with Jackman. You are stopping the pattern."

"You're right. Burke is dead. Whatever it was with Jackman is over, and since he's not technically in our department, it's no big deal to TWF that we had sex. Although I don't want you to tell anyone. Let people keep it a rumor."

"Of course."

"But since we are talking about rumors and Jackman, Mik, you know who has been acting more strangely than usual?"

"No one more than anyone else."

"Amanda. There's something up with her and Jackman."

"Something other than the usual Amanda adoration?"

"She has been skulking around the clinic at odd hours with Jackman. I think she may be accessing charts for Jackman, but I'm not certain. I know she has to open lots of charts because of her dual roles with psychiatry and chronic pain, and things have not been business as usual since Edward's death, but I wondered if she has started another one of her projects and using patients she meets in the clinic. The auditor now sends me the unusual occurrence patterns of patient chart access when they show up on his radar because I'm acting Chief."

"And Amanda did?"

"Yes."

Interesting that Tara was confirming part of my suspicion, but Amanda did not have medical record numbers on that list. It didn't fit.

"I don't know what she's doing, Tara. But you're right that she seems to be more devoted to Jackman and his research than ever before."

"I'm not planning to confront her because there isn't any point. She wouldn't tell me the truth anyway and I have enough problems with the reactions of clinic staff to Edward's murder." Tara was staring off in the distance.

"What are you thinking?"

"I never told you, Mik, because I couldn't at the time, what was on the papers Billy Sanders had on him. I probably shouldn't now but that's all settled, and Burke is dead."

And you're drunk, I thought. "You know you can trust me." I wanted to hear this.

"The list had five TWF names on it. Burke, me, an ER doc, Jackman and Amanda."

"Why would Jackman and Amanda be on it? What contact did they have with him?"

"Good question. Not one that was ever able to be answered by them or the family. Since Billy was in paranoid decompensation at the end, their names were dismissed as part of his delusion. The paper also had one line that read: 'I'm not the only one.' There were hand drawn figures at the bottom of the page; a line of stick figures, male and female, and below each was a gravestone that had a skull and crossbones on it."

"Did anyone ever find out who they were supposed to be?"

"No."

"You think there is a connection between what Amanda's doing with the charts and Billy's death?"

"I think there's something going on at TWF and Jackman and Amanda may be involved in some way. I have been thinking about what a patient referred for a medication consult said to me recently, that I dismissed at the time but now I'm not so certain. I saw this young woman." Tara looked around the bar to make certain no one was in earshot and I leaned forward. "She told me she thought she might have been molested by someone at TWF. She said she couldn't identify the man, but her friends thought it could be Burke. She was one of those very blonde doll- like dramatic young women we see at times these days who are looking for their 15 minutes of fame, even if it's in some victim stance."

My thoughts were jumping inside my head – linking the information she was telling me. She had to be talking about Kristen. Was this real or was Tara playing me? Or maybe I wasn't the only one beginning to think there was something sinister, besides Burke's death, going on at TWF.

"Did she give any specifics?"

"No she said it all in a way too vague for me to do anything about it. But I started to wonder if something had happened and Jackman and Amanda were covering for Burke in some way. Trying to do damage control after his death."

"Or maybe, Tara, they knew something about whatever it was and are trying to cover for themselves." I shivered. "I assume you know I saw the same patient."

"What? Are you sure it's the same one?" Tara got out a pen and wrote on her drink napkin and handed it to me. I glanced at the name. It said Zoe, not Kristen. "Is it the same person?" I shredded the napkin and shook my head. There's another one.

"Wait. Tara, is that the same patient Lizzie presented – the young woman with the lucid dreaming, and the relaxation scene?"

"Yes. That's what made me think she might be telling the truth."

"And Jessica" I added. "She also fits the pattern. And I have another patient I think could fit as well."

I thought to myself, Cyntheya would have fit the pattern, too. What did William call her? Quite the little hottie.

"Holy shit, Mik. You may be right."

"What do we do now? Even if Burke was a pervert and Amanda and Jackman were somehow involved, how do we find out?"

"I don't know. I needed to tell someone and you are the only person I felt as though I could trust to deal with this rationally and not freak out."

"We need to find something that could help the investigators. This has to be linked to Burke's death. It can't be a coincidence. Maybe one of his victims or a family member suspected and killed him."

"Do you think that's likely?"

I did now. Because Barbie killed him. The perfect revenge. Even though the iconic Barbie image was everywhere in society, killer Barbie had to be related to this. I was certain of it. But that wasn't a piece of information I could trust giving Tara.

"I can't imagine another motive more powerful than that kind of revenge. Can you?"

"No."

We were both silent staring at our empty glasses. The medicinal intervention had reached its maximum impact. "I have an idea. Let's go." She took out the keys to her Mercedes.

"Your blood alcohol level is above the legal limit Tara."

"Then you can drive, and pick up your car tomorrow." She tossed me the keys and walked over to Stanley, stuffed a couple of bills in his shirt pocket next to his pack of Marlboros. She was rewarded with Stanley's well practiced but sexy grin.

Tara talked all the way to her house. Even drunk she was an effective strategist. We would need Luke's help at some point, but there was no legal way to introduce him into our plan without more evidence.

CHAPTER FORTY-THREE

"Amanda's the weak link," Erik agreed. I was proceeding with my plan but wanted to review it with Erik. He was willing to talk with me in a hypothetical scenario way about Tara and my theories, with attorney-client privilege in place. "If what you are suggesting is true, she can lead you to more information. I also don't know if you can trust Tara, Mik."

"I know I can't. I will have to be careful how I approach her but I'm guessing that she has information incriminating to Burke and she wants to punish him for what he did to her."

"She does know he's dead, right."

"Yes, Erik, even though he's dead. He was sadistic to her and she wants to be the one to mete out the consequences."

"I hate that psychological crap, Mik."

"Indulge me this time and we may be able to dispense justice to TWF and help patients."

"Then I'm all in. Tell me more."

I spent the next two hours going over what I knew that might be linked to Burke or Jackman. I omitted the Barbie part of the murder scene. That information I revealed to no one, not even Erik.

"If I can get the files from Amanda, which I believe she has, then that may lead to Burke or Jackman or both. The easiest way would be to involve the patients who led us to suspect something but there is no way around the legal and ethical problems with that, let alone the potential negative psychological impact of making their therapy into a search for a TWF pervert."

"Are you certain you want to be this involved in investigating a murder that took place at your work, when the killer is still free? You're not invincible."

"Can you think of any other alternatives to find out more information? To get behind the TWF wall?"

"Are you certain you can't use Luke to help?"

"You know the answer to that. Introducing the police at this point would only warn TWF and we both know that theories and vague memories of patients are not adequate for search warrants, particularly when patient confidentiality is involved. And Jackman's weird sexual obsessions don't even compete with half the perversions playing on cable or what can be downloaded from the internet."

"I agree. There isn't a good alternative. Do you really think Amanda tried to cover up sexual abuse by Burke?"

"I believe it was unintentional. Amanda adores Jackman and she had been tenacious in her pursuit of Burke's computer research files because wanted to help Jackman. She's greedy and ambitious but not cut from the same sadistic weave as Burke or Jackman. Thanks for your help, Erik. I'll let you know what happens."

As soon I as I left Erik's, I entered Tara's number. "Tara, it's me. Let's go ahead with the plan. I will talk to Amanda first to see what I can find out, and if that doesn't work we will go to Plan B. I'll call you as soon as I know anything."

I was unable to sleep. I was energized in a way I had not been since this all began. I didn't have to sit back and wait for something to happen. I could act. First step, I had to catch Amanda at lunch for a chat. I arrived to the clinic early, and I made it through my morning patients. I was on my way back to my office when Amanda came out from Tara's office. I assumed or rather hoped that their meeting was related to their roles as acting Chief and administrative assistant, and I tried not to start seeing conspiracies everywhere.

"Amanda! I haven't really talked to you since all that has happened here. I wanted to see how you are doing. Are you free for lunch?"

"That would be super. I'll get my purse and be right back."

So far, so good. We went to a little café across from the clinic. Clean, quick, inexpensive. Amanda's favorite. We both knew the menu by heart and ordered immediately. "How are you holding up, Amanda?"

"It's so hard. If it weren't for Bruce - Dr. Jackman – taking extra time with me and allowing me to be involved with continuing to help him with what Dr. Burke started, I would feel very lost." Tears were forming.

"I know it's been overwhelming and painful. I also know how hard you work to help the patients feel comfortable after all of this. You're the front line for all of us."

Amanda looked pleased. "Thank you for recognizing that. I can tell you that Dr. Jackman told me personally how much Dr. Burke had appreciated the work I had done to help out with their research."

"I'm certain he did. Was there something in particular?"

"Well, I can tell you because you've always been on my side, and this was perfectly legit. Dr. Burke and Dr, Jackman paid me to record CDs for their research patients so that they wouldn't have to pay a fee for one of the copyrighted ones. They said the money was less than they would have to pay otherwise, and it was good money for me. I also helped them with finding possible subjects and doing some data entry work."

"I know your contribution has been of great value, Amanda. What kind of CDs?"

"You know, those relaxation types. I read a script they had describing the calming scene. They would give me a list of patient first names so I could use their names in the recordings – to make them personal. That was why they asked me, because even just first names of patients meant it was confidential work. It takes some time so they gave me a list every month or so."

"When did you start doing that?"

"I don't know. Over a year ago. Why?"

"Interested. That's all. You've done a lot for the clinic. Did you get Burke's files back from Jackman?"

"Dr. Jackman found a way to get the information he wanted. I guess what the police had wasn't what he thought. TWF Legal has really pushed for the police to release the information Dr. Burke had."

We continued to talk, but I was only half listening; mostly I was thinking about what Amanda had told me. My instincts were right. She wasn't knowingly involved, but if my theory was correct about Burke then that had to be her voice that the victims heard. And that was why she had the list of names hidden. Burke could use the recordings with a woman's voice in the victim's drugged haze to make it appear as if a woman had been the perpetrator. When it was actually Amanda's voice. He and Jackman requested 20 at a time which is why Kristen was the only one on this list. I needed to follow up on this. I also didn't want to spook Amanda by asking too many questions. This was enough to confirm that I was moving in the right direction. I paid for her lunch as I usually did but the information was more than worth the money.

I almost ran back to my office and called Tara. No answer. I left a message for her confirming we were right without giving details and for her to call me as soon as possible. I could have gone to her office but I didn't want Amanda to start putting two and two together. I left a message for Erik as well. I could barely pay attention to my afternoon patients. I kept going back to what might have happened. I realized I was more interested in finding the abuser of these young women than the killer of Burke. I was even more convinced that Burke may have deserved what he got. I also knew the perils of vigilante justice. I went to the staff lounge for a quick break.

"Hi, Mik."

It was Lizzie. "What's going on? I haven't seen you much lately. You've been holed up in here all the time, more than usual. I told Rachel I would check in on you. She was concerned too, but she didn't want to interrupt you. Is there something wrong?"

"No, Lizzie. Sorry I've been sequestered away. I have a lot of tough cases. Still dealing with the Burke aftermath."

Lizzie looked as if she didn't quite believe me and was planning to park herself in my office for a while.

"Why don't we get together Sunday afternoon and go for a walk?" I asked.

"That sounds good. We can figure out the details later."

"Thanks. And thank Rachel for her concern, too."

"I will." Lizzie closed my door behind her.

If my behavior was starting to look odd to my friends, I needed to move faster on this thing or figure out an alternative plan. No message from Tara. Maybe the best thing was to go home for now.

CHAPTER FORTY-FOUR

Tonight, again, I couldn't sleep. Tara had left a message saying she thought we were on the right track. The information kept pointing in the same direction but there was no clear proof. The police must not have found anything in Burke's place when they searched it after his death. Or at least nothing I knew about. Would he have kept a record or mementos of his victims as serial killers often do? I needed to redirect my energy. Time to check my e-mail.

Sixty-seven new e-mails. That would keep me busy for a bit. I scanned the subject lines to see which ones I could delete first. There were quite a few. I was making progress. Toward the end was a subject line that only had the initials BJ. I always checked the size of the email before opening it and this was 2MB. I opened it.

Picture after picture of Jackman sitting nude in a large chair with his erect cock in his hand, eyes closed. A young woman who couldn't have been more than 16 was sitting in the chair across from him. She was partially clothed and looked unconscious. The pictures were like stills from a porn movie. First masturbation scenes, then pictures of him, still nude, collecting his semen, pipetting a substance into a vial, with a final picture of him placing the vial inside the door to a small refrigerator or freezer. There was nothing other than the pictures. Was this real? Jackman had been the perpetrator? Not Burke? He was the one who had used the tapes Amanda had made and molested those girls? I called Luke. If I didn't reach him, I would call the police. Thank God he picked up.

"Sustern."

"Luke it's Mik. I opened my e-mail and I was sent a series of pictures of Jackman masturbating and a young girl is there. She looks unconscious. I'm going to call the police but I wanted to call you first."

"Leave everything as it is. I will notify the detectives and the crime lab, and I will be right there. Don't try to do anything with the e-mail until we get there. And don't let anybody else know."

"I won't. Thanks, Luke."

Luke, the detectives, and the crime lab team arrived at the same time. They reviewed all my e-mails and requested permission to take my computer. They could keep it. It was as if it was a crime scene itself, a contaminated, defiled entity that I could never imagine using again. Not after those images. I answered all the questions from the detectives. Luke remained behind. "You don't need to stay Luke."

"I can't stay too long but I wanted to make certain you were handling all this. Or at least as best as anyone could."

"This feels familiar, doesn't it? You talking to me after I found Burke. Now this?"

We were both silent. "What's going to happen to Jackman?"

"This, with some other information we have, will allow us to get a search warrant. It's important you don't speak to anyone from TWF about this right now. You may want to call Erik, but no one else. For your safety as well as for the investigation."

"Don't worry, I won't. I don't suppose you can tell me the other information."

"I can't, but I can tell you we received an anonymous tip that paid off."

"The same person who sent this e-mail?"

"I don't know. Our technology experts will be doing everything possible to locate the e-mail sender. I have to leave but I am available anytime. You have my phone number."

"Thanks, Luke."

After everyone left, I called Erik and it went to voicemail. I left him a message with the basic information. I didn't know what to feel. But I did something I never do. I unlocked my 357 from my gun safe and loaded it. I had always adhered to the laws of the state to have your handgun in a gun safe separate from your ammunition. But I had never before felt the need to violate them. I drank a couple glasses of wine and started to feel sleepy. All those people who say firearms and alcohol don't mix had not been through what I had just been through. This was the most relaxed I had felt in days.

There was a pounding at my door. I must not have heard the doorbell. "Mik, it's Erik. Open up." It was 7:00am.

"I'm coming, Erik." I got off the bed and noticed I was still wearing the clothes I wore yesterday. I opened the door. Erik looked at me and then looked around the rest of the apartment. He picked up my 357 and the almost empty glass of wine that I had placed on my nightstand.

"Nice, Mik. Excellent judgment. Good thing I didn't use the key you gave me or you would have killed me."

"I wouldn't have killed you. Shot you maybe, but not killed you."

"How are you doing? For real?"

"I'm managing."

'Did you hear what happened this morning?"

"No."

He found my remote and flipped through the local news channels. Under "breaking news" there was footage of Jackman in handcuffs being led away by police.

"They arrested him for the sexual abuse?"

"That's not the whole story. They arrested him for the murder of Burke."

"What are you talking about?"

"I don't know all the details but they found evidence linking him to Burke's murder, and to the sexual abuse of several girls and young women."

"But why would Jackman kill Burke?"

"I don't know but I heard the search of Jackman's home yielded evidence of his sexual acts with women, including his victims, and other items were found that connected him to Burke's murder. Tara and that woman Amanda you work with were apparently instrumental in leading them to the evidence."

"They were?"

"And there were indications that there was something about a Barbie doll related to the murder."

I didn't respond.

"That was part of what you knew, wasn't it?" Erik stepped across the room and gave me a long hug. "Whatever you need me to do Mik, let me know. If you don't let me know, I will start doing whatever I think would be good for you, so I suggest you tell me. And unload your gun."

"Okay, Erik. Thanks."

CHAPTER FORTY-FIVE

Weeks of almost daily interviews and depositions were over. TWF was in chaos, but I chose not to be the rescuer this time. The patients Jackman had abused were receiving treatment paid by TWF but provided by private therapists in the community.

Jackman was in prison. No bail. He was charged for his sex crimes and for first degree murder. The prosecution was asking for the death penalty. The news indicated that with the amount of evidence against him, Jackman would take a plea. Life in prison without parole rather than risk lethal injection. That meant no trial.

TWF positioned themselves as another victim of Jackman, with a media blitz of management's shock and horror as they repeatedly distanced themselves from any responsibility for him.

I took a month's personal time, and Alexandra came out from New York to stay for a week. Erik stopped by regularly. He was the one to tell me, with anger in his voice, that Ryan had taken Jackman's case as defense attorney. It did not surprise me. Ryan chose the biggest spotlight and opportunity for financial gain for his first step into his new law career. It made me wonder if he had helped provide the pharmaceuticals for Burke, but I knew even if that was true it would never come to light.

I had very limited contact with TWF, except for my closest friends. Lizzie and Rachel had taken over my patient caseload. Tara made no attempt to contact me. William had taken retirement to Utah with his family. Rachel was the only one I talked to regularly. One day she stopped by and brought a bouquet of flowers that had been left at the reception desk for me, with a note attached from Cyntheya: "To Dr. Pearson, who connected the dots, and taught me to believe. Thank you for everything. Cyntheya." It had been Cyntheya who had sent the e-mail poem. Cyntheya had suspected something about TWF but did not know what was happening, or what had possibly happened to her and the others. It made sense to me now. And it also meant she could start the deeper process of healing by knowing the complete truth.

TWF management left me alone, after wisely sending me a supportive message that I should take as much time off as I needed. I was double knotting the laces on my running shoes when my phone rang.

"Hi Mik. It's Luke. Do you have a minute?" Luke had called regularly in the past month.

"Sorry, Luke. I'm on my way out. I can call you later."

"This will only take a minute or two, but I would like to talk to you in person."

"I could meet you on 24th Street by the bench outside Marshall Park. But I can only stay a few minutes."

"See you there in 15."

"Sounds good."

Luke was standing by the bench. He had a broad smile on his face as he saw me approach. "I won't keep you long, but I wanted you to know that you were right about a connection between Jackman and Burke, but not the one you thought. We suspect they were both involved in those rogue PTSD experiments that you reported and TWF denied existed. I am sorry to say I believe Billy Sanders was a subject, which I know you already suspected. However, since there is no usable evidence of the experiments, Burke remains viewed as the victim of Jackman. Or, more accurately, now one of his victims. We think there were at least 10 girls who were abused by Jackman."

I realized some part of me already knew and had accepted that Billy had been a victim. The only solace for me was that his prayer had been answered. Vengeance had been enacted.

"And those special muscle relaxant/pain control heat gels – the high end Ben-Gay that Jackman touted as something only he could create. He was correct. One of the ingredients was his semen. As was part of the coating for his special traction devices. He assumed no one would ever check them and he was right. Why would anyone suspect a highly respected award winning doctor of such depravity?"

I shook my head in disbelief. "So the pictures were accurate. He would drug his young female patients when he did his pain treatments, then jerk off and use the semen in his special creations."

"That's correct. He would give the coated devices only to the perfect young women who met his Barbie standard."

"That explains a couple things for me," I said. It explained why he traded Cyntheya's device in for another when she gained weight. She no longer qualified. Even at this point I couldn't say that to Luke.

"A couple things that fall under doctor-patient privilege?" "You read my mind, Luke. Yes. I didn't realize before this whole disaster how that confidentiality protection for patients could bind me from taking more direct action, and that it could be used for legal cover to allow a killer and sociopathic degenerate like Jackman to do whatever he wanted."

"But you found a way a way to do everything you could, Mik. Jackman is the killer and molester. He was smart enough not to rape the girls. Although it's possible he couldn't perform even with his implant; the psychiatric work-up may answer that. He knew not to leave any marks or usual signs of abuse. His need to keep the pictures of his victims as trophies was his downfall."

"What about Burke?"

"The irony is that it appears Burke didn't know what Jackman was doing; Burke never intended to harm anyone. He ran his experiments because he thought his mission of finding a cure for PTSD meant that the usual ethics didn't apply to him. He was above the law because he was working for a higher cause. Although he destroyed patients for that cause. When Burke found out what Jackman was doing with the girls, he was enraged. He intended to report him. I think Jackman assumed Burke would support their long term brotherhood, no matter what he did. When Burke didn't, he chose to retaliate in a way that would both humiliate and silence Burke."

"How were you able to find evidence linking Jackman to Burke's murder?"

"Evidence came from different sources. A deleted encrypted e-mail that the crime lab retrieved from Burke's hard drive on his home computer. It was written to Jackman from Burke stating he would 'no longer tolerate Jackman's Barbie doll fixation.' We believe that may have been what set Jackman off. He had access to materials, the mechanical know how to create the weapon, Burke's computer, and had 'treated' all the victims. The smoking gun was a Ken doll version of the same type of Barbie murder weapon Jackman had killed Burke with; it was in Jackman's home safe. Jackman wouldn't say why he created both of them. He had a closet filled with adult size Barbie costumes, shoes, the whole works."

A closet full. An adult Barbie collector. Validation of Tara's story of Jackman.

"It was another twisted dimension of Jackman's sexual fantasy life. His current wife says she never wore any of them for him so…" Luke shrugged. "Jackman has refused to say anything more than he absolutely had to."

"His need to control whatever he could to the very end."

Luke nodded. "I doubt we'll ever know the complete story. Gotta give it to Jackman, though. The Barbie doll murder weapon was poetic, creative and the perfect misdirection for the investigation. You should know that David helped us in finding the e-mail that ultimately connected Burke and Jackman. Your instincts were right about David, but there was so much I couldn't tell you without compromising the investigation. I wish I could have."

"Did you ever find out who sent the Jackman pictures to me or that other anonymous tip you mentioned?"

"No we didn't. We will probably never know who the 'Deep Throat' of this series of crimes was."

"Why do you think those pictures of Jackman were sent to me?"

"You may not realize it but your involvement was essential to solving these crimes; you were the center for information critical to us catching Jackman. You were on the right track following up with Amanda and Tara, and trusting your gut about Jackman and Burke. I think you were chosen for the e-mails because it was clear you were one of the very few, maybe the only one at TWF who would do what was right even if it meant going up against TWF. That you could tolerate receiving the pictures and you wouldn't emotionally disintegrate with the knowledge of what Jackman did."

"Disintegrate. Good word choice." I knew Luke was also thinking of James who remained destroyed by finding Burke's body.

"And you were the right person to choose."

There was another part of this that continued to nag at me. I had to ask. "Was Tara directly involved?"

"There is no evidence of that, but I don't think it's a coincidence that you were sent those pictures so soon after you talked with Tara about suspecting both Burke and Jackman. She may have figured out that Jackman would keep pictures or DVDs as trophies if he was guilty. And because of her sexual involvement with him, she also knew where he might keep them, including that he might have her on film as well. But there is nothing to indicate she was aware at the time that he was sexually abusing those girls and there was no evidence linking any of it to her. The only red flag is that she was unusually cooperative in providing information that led us to Jackman and Burke. Both Amanda and Tara were."

The better part of me wanted to believe Tara had found a way to take action this time when she suspected the truth about Jackman. She could try to make right what she wasn't able to do for her own daughter, and at the same time protect her career from being destroyed. She was not going to let herself become collateral damage of Jackman. There were other, darker explanations for what she did, but for now, that was the interpretation I chose.

Luke continued, "I assume you know that Tara is the new Associate Chief Physician Officer of the Medical Center. Quite a promotion."

"Yes, it is. I also heard that Amanda was promoted to the position of her executive assistant."

"What are you going to do Mik? Think you'll stay with TWF after all this? Or perhaps you're considering being a private investigator. You've got great instincts."

"Thanks, Luke. I haven't decided what I'll do with TWF or my career. Treating patients was always what was most important to me. I won't abandon the patients who were in treatment with me so I'll return to TWF to follow up with them. But whether or not I'll stay, I don't know yet."

"I get it. But now that the murder investigation is over, other possibilities may open for you as well." He stepped closer to me.

I held out my hand. He took it, leaned forward, and gave me a gentle kiss, his lips lingering on mine. I felt a sharp tug on my other arm.

"Sorry Luke, first things first. Let's go, Riley." My newly adopted golden retriever, patiently waiting, took less than a second to bound forward, dragging me with him down the street toward the dog path.

"See you later, Luke."

"Count on it."

Made in the USA
Monee, IL
23 August 2021